I0634656

# The Other Side of the Trench
# The Spirit of War

By

# Garry. S. Willmott

*War would end if the dead could return.*

*Stanley Baldwin*

## Copyright

First published 2013 by G.S. Willmott
Revised and updated 2015

All rights reserved.
No part of this publication may be reproduced, stored in a retrieval system, or transmitted in any form or any means electronic, mechanical, photocopying, recording or otherwise without the prior permission of the publisher.

Copyright © G.S. Willmott 2015

ISBN: 9781925280814 (paperback)
ISBN: 9781925280821 (eBook)

The Other Side of the Trench is a work of fiction. Any resemblance to real persons, living or dead, is purely coincidental.

Garry Willmott has released a revised edition of *The Other Side of the Trench*: this second edition streamlines and refines the events of the first edition, without losing any of the essence of the earlier version.

This is a more tightly woven, more precise narrative that intertwines historical fact with imagined characters. Structurally it is a tour de force; Willmott skilfully creates a contemporary drama among the 'pilgrims' travelling to various battle sites of World War 1 to honour their ancestors, which he parallels with a re-enactment of the emotions and challenges experienced many years earlier among the young soldiers facing battle.

It is a novel that works on many levels and it is impossible to locate it within any single genre; it is all the more impressive as it blends a considerable amount of informative research with elements of magic realism and realistic human drama. It manages to work on a spiritual level as well, thanks to the creation of an ingenious narrator. The incidents he selectively recounts are accumulated for maximum impact.

It is an important book. Not only does it remind us of the courage and sacrifice of all the young Australians who lost their lives on the Western Front but it reminds us of the significance of those battles that are often overlooked in favour of Gallipoli.

There are some unforgettable moments in this book; the characters of the dead and missing soldiers stay with us. It's a haunting reminder that bodies and bones are still being uncovered in foreign fields but they've not yet had appropriate burials and they remain largely unidentified and unclaimed. Through writing this story, the author seeks peace for these lost souls. By showing the waste and futility of war, he also seeks a more general lasting peace for mankind.

# Acknowledgments

Thank you to my wife Anna, for putting up with me disappearing into my study at all hours to write this novel.

Thank you to my daughters Emma and Sophie for giving their opinions and suggestions.

Thank you Andy Causon for your advice and encouragement.

Thank you Janet Upcher for completing a great edit.

Thank you Paul Daley for inspiring me to write it.

# Table of Contents

# Introduction

When I was a young boy living in Melbourne, Victoria, my introduction to the Great War was when my father, Sam, showed me the spurs and leather leggings that my Grand father wore as part of his uniform when he was in the 4th Australian Light Horse.

I attempted to wear them around the back yard pretending I was in the Light Horse myself – a very romantic notion. The fact that they kept falling off my skinny little eight year-old legs was irrelevant.

My next experience with the Great War was when my mother, Vida, told me about her brother, Harry, who had died in the war four years before she was born. It was she who told me her mother's hair turned white overnight when she learnt of Harry's death. My mother knew that Harry died somewhere in France but was unsure exactly where.

Harry had lied about his age; he was only sixteen when he got shipped off to Egypt, Gallipoli and then France only to die at the Battle of Fromelles.

The term "Missing" is not a very confronting term; it can apply to your dog or cat, to your favourite piece of jewellery or even when a footballer has a bad game, he is mentioned as "Missing in Action".

In war terms, 'missing' means a soldier has been buried alive from a shell explosion or ripped in half by an enemy machine gun or bayoneted to death and left to die in the most slow and agonising way. The following soldiers have never been found and their photos may sit in an old frame on the mantle-piece in a living room of a house far away from where he now lies.

Young Harry Daniel
Born 1899
Died 1916

Harry Daniel Senior
Born 1882
Died 1918

Charles Wooley
Born 1898
Died 1918

Jack Abbey
Born 1893
Died 1916

Fred Vardy
Born 1894
Died 1917

Antoine Bellepoire
Born 1895
Died 1917

Athol McKenzie
Born 1996
Died 1918

William Hansen
Born 1898
Died 1918

David Abbott
Born 1895
Died 1916

Archie Shearer
Born 1895
Died 1915

Albert Shearer
Born 1897
Died 1916

These are the men and boys we follow throughout this story. All had parents, some had sweethearts, none had a future.

I also had a great uncle, Harry Daniel, who died in the war in 1918 at Amiens. He was a hero; he received the King George Military Medal for Bravery (M.M.) in the Field for going out into No-Man's Land at Menin Road near Ypres and retrieving wounded comrades under heavy enemy shell-fire.

So my interest in the Great War stemmed from having my Grandfather and two uncles serve in the war.

Both Harry Daniels have no known grave.

My mother gave me a framed collection of World War One medals in 1980 along with my father's World War Two medals and they have always taken a pride of place in our house since. Amongst those medals is Uncle Harry's Military Medal for Bravery in the Field. Also, young Harry's Gallipoli Medal is a prized possession.

I have never served in the military not even the cadets. I have always detested the fact that Governments can make the choice to send our young men and women to fight in wars that are usually fought for greed and gain. There are exceptions such as the Pacific War against the Japanese, where Australia was under real threat.

So why write a book about the First World War, my first book?

I have authored six others as of November 2014.

In April last year I read an article by Ian McPhedran. The article was based on the experiences of his friend and fellow author, Paul Daley, and well known photographer, Mike Bowers' experiences while on a research trip to the Western front for their new book. Their French guide, Dominique Zanardi, discovered the remains of a Digger in an excavation trench:

'Now, on Saturday, we find ourselves standing in the bitter wind, the mud sucking at our boots, beside a one-meter newly excavated drainage ditch outside Mouquet Farm near Pozières - the scene of a bitter three-week battle in August 1916 that claimed 11,000 Australian casualties - as Mr Zanardi gingerly passes us bones that we, in turn, place in a hessian sack.

He uncovers the soldier's boots, still holding the bones of his feet, and places them on the side of the ditch. As we carefully carry the rest of the man's remains from the ditch to the bag containing his skull and his jawbone, his arms and his legs, one thought dominates: dignity and glory do not belong to the battlefield.

As with the many thousands of others who lost their lives in the terrible fighting on the Somme during World War I, the battlefield has claimed this soldier's identity. And were it not for Mr. Zanardi he would probably have stayed anonymously beneath the sticky mud of the Somme for an eternity.'

Paul Daley, The Age, January 2011

This story really moved me yet angered me. Paul and Mike tried to notify the Commonwealth War Graves Commission but, being a weekend, the Commission was closed. The Mayor of Pozières , Bernard Delattre, was planning to remove the body from the site on the day to prevent it from being reinterred by the bulldozer. He called the Australian Embassy in Paris to inform them an Australian Digger had been uncovered but had no response.

I decided to try to do something about this situation and subsequently formed Let Them RIP: I created a web site www.letthemrip.com to make the public aware something very wrong was happening to our 'missing' soldiers. I also wrote many emails to a number of politicians, including the Prime Minister, to try to implement procedures that would minimize our soldiers and the soldiers from all the participating nations in the Great War being simply covered over when unearthed by ploughing and excavation work.

I have over four hundred emails in my sent file and have not received any real support from the Australian Government or the New Zealand Government. Only one independent MP, Andrew Wilkie, has demonstrated support by addressing a question to the Prime Minister in Federal Parliament. The question was asked; the answer was given and now they think the issue is buried, never to be raised again.

After six months of trying to get some action, I decided to write this book with the encouragement from Ian McPhedran and Paul Daley.

The fact is over 300,000 are still missing on the Western Front: 18,000 are Australian.

If you bring the casualty rates of the war into today's terms, the world's population is currently over 7 Billion, the population in 1918 was 1.8 Billion.

| 1918 | 2012 |
|---|---|
| Killed 20 million Soldiers | Killed 100 million Soldiers |
| Killed 12 million civilians | Killed 60 million civilians |
| Total 32 million | Total 160 Million |

Can you imagine 160 million slaughtered over four years in our world today?

Missing 1.5 million in 2012 terms.

That's why I wrote this book.

I hope you enjoy and learn from the experience.

# War

## "War is mainly a catalogue of blunders"

**Winston Churchill**

## Chapter One

Oxford Dictionary Definition
war/wôr/
Noun:
A state of armed conflict between different nations or states
or different groups within a nation or state.

Verb:
Engage in a war.

Synonyms:
noun. warfare - battle - fight - struggle - combat - strife
verb. fight - combat - battle - make war

The Australian Digger lying in a pool of vile sludge in the middle of
what was once a beautiful meadow was listening to the sound of

11

shellfire and machine guns pouring out their deadly poison with the intensity that defied comprehension; it was deafening, it was frightening.

Harry had no real understanding of the art of war. All he knew was that war was horrible, destructive and took most of his mates, to where he did not know. He didn't really believe in God anymore. If there was a God how could he let this Armageddon happen? Hundreds of thousands of soldiers killed fighting for their King and country?

How could he allow women and children to be killed and be mutilated by the foul weapons of war?

Yet, he sort of hoped there was a God; if there was, it might give him some hope that if he did die in this war, he may go to a better place.

Harry heard the command from his platoon leader to go forward. Go forward to what? Another stretch of foul smelling mud with the corpses of soldiers or limbs of soldiers spread all over the place they call no-man's land? To fight for every inch of ground against the enemy, the Krauts and the bloated rats that fed off the fruits of battle?

Not that there was much choice: if he was ordered to go forward, that's where he must go.

He looked at his cobber beside him.

'Come on, Paddy, let's see if we can get to Passchendaele or what's bloody left of it!'

They started to crawl out through the slime, there was no thought of walking, as their boots got stuck in the mud; besides, the foul-smelling whale oil they were forced to rub over their feet to minimise trench feet made their boots extremely uncomfortable. They made little progress and had gone about ten yards when they heard someone scream – 'GAS'!

Gas Clouds

All the remaining attacking troops scrambled to put on their gas masks and by now, visibility was almost non-existent.

'This is all we fucking need, mate', said Harry.

'Strange though, I don't see or smell any gas. What the hell is going on?' said Paddy.

What was 'going on' was the Germans were using mustard gas for the first time. Shells were used to deliver it and it was odourless.

'This isn't the usual stuff the Huns use. This is something entirely different!' yelled Harry.

The two Diggers continued their treacherous journey across no-man's land, however the officers in charge knew it was pointless so they gave the order to retreat back to their own line.

Harry and Paddy made it back to the trench having passed countless mates in various states of dismemberment.

The tried to get some sleep after eating their meagre rations of beef jerky, biscuits, jam and a little tea.

In the middle of the night Harry was woken by the cries of his mate, Paddy.

'What's the matter, cobber?'

'I'm burning… my eyes, my face, even my balls. You've got to help me, mate!'

'OK, Paddy, I'll go and fetch a medic! You'll be OK, mate, don't you worry!'

Harry ran as fast as he could along the partially flooded trench, dodging Diggers trying to sleep in the pouring rain as well as rats and overflowing bogs and other obstructions. When he reached the dressing station he was horrified to find there were Diggers everywhere moaning and screaming. The medics were having real trouble applying the bandages: the poor bastards screamed when they were touched. Harry had seen plenty of wounded since he arrived at the front, some with atrocious injuries but he had not seen anything like this before.These blokes had been burned down to the bone, a yellow festering mess.

Harry caught the attention of one of the medics, asking him if he could come and see Paddy. The Medic just looked at him in disbelief.

'Take a look around you, soldier. There's no way in the world I can leave the Dressing Station. If you want your cobber to be seen to, you'll have to get him here.'

Harry raced back to his mate and lifted him up over his shoulder. Paddy screamed.

'Put me down! I can't stand the pain'.

Harry tried to work out how to get him back, when another mate, Bluey, offered to help.

They lifted him up by the arms and legs despite Paddy's cursing and screaming and made their way along the obstacle course until they reached the Station.

The medic looked around and instructed Harry and Bluey to place Paddy on a stretcher.

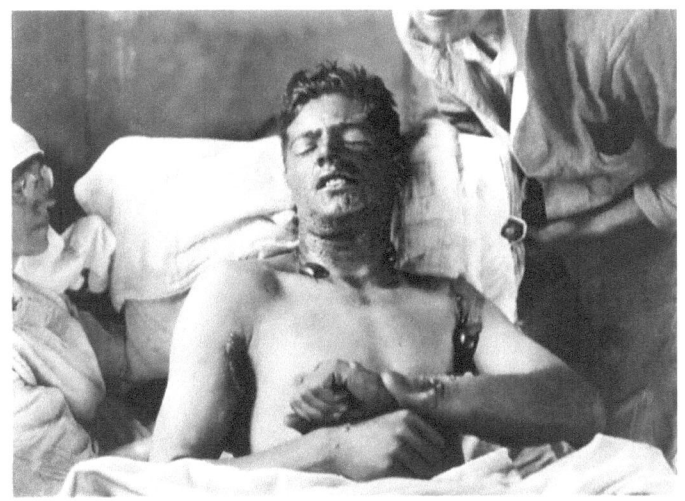
Paddy Being Treated in Hospital

The two Diggers left him in the hands of the medics and returned to their posts. The Medics told Harry that mustard gas was like no other; the victim did not feel the effects until hours after the attack. That's why Paddy felt fine when they got back to their trench.

Paddy had received medium to severe mustard gas burns and as a result was transferred to The Australian Auxiliary Hospital at Harefield, Middlesex, England.

He received magnificent care from the medical staff but because of the nature of the burns, he was required to stay in hospital for five months. He was shipped back to Australia and took no part in the war again.

The incessant rain made the trenches almost uninhabitable if indeed they ever were habitable in the first place.

These disgusting conditions made it almost impossible to get any rest before the British Tommies and the ANZACs would go out again and try to regain the territory they gained the day before.

Shell holes were always handy to jump into and take cover from the German machine guns but now they had turned into murky fetid pools with the odd corpse floating and the ubiquitous rats swimming at a frantic pace and devouring these unfortunate young soldiers. This is what the lads called ANZAC soup.

No-Man's Land Passchendaele

Harry was woken by Lieutenant Simmonds; he was told they were going over the top again at 5am. Harry checked his 303 Enfield rifle, which had been his constant companion since he joined this awful conflict. He fixed his bayonet and made sure he had his full allocation of grenades and bullets. He was ready to face hell again.

The five-minute whistle sounded, which alerted Harry and the rest of the troops that the time was near. It also alerted the Germans and they were well and truly ready for the attack.

The Senior Officer, Captain Blainey, looked at his watch and blew the whistle three times.

Harry climbed up the ladder and started to run but became hopelessly bogged down. He managed to make some headway by crawling through the mud and slime. He saw sickening sights, limbless men screaming in pain, dead men on either side with atrocious wounds however Harry didn't react; any feelings or emotion were long gone. This horrible situation had become a natural sequence of events not only for Harry but all the Australian troops.

# You Never Know Who You Might Meet in No-Man's Land

## Chapter Two

It was Passchendaele where three significant events happened to Harry. He and his good cobber, Bluey Cooper, volunteered to creep into no-man's land and try to retrieve the wounded. The Krauts were shelling their defences relentlessly and it was not going to be easy. They crawled out with shells raining down all around them; the smoke haze made it difficult to see but they persevered.

Harry was crawling in the mud so thick that he crawled over a Digger without even seeing him until the soldier screamed when Harry put his knee into the young soldier's chest. Harry was startled. He looked down only to see one of his cobbers from the platoon lying on his back with a severe chest wound.

'No wonder he screamed,' Bluey thought.

'Georgie, mate, are you OK?'

'No I'm not, you bastard. You nearly finished me off,' the young soldier whispered; his chest was making a strange gurgling sound.

'I am sorry, mate, I just didn't see you. Can you move at all?'

'No I don't think so.'

'I am going to find a stretcher-bearer team, so don't go anywhere, alright?'

George just looked at Harry through glazed eyes.

Harry crawled off under constant shellfire. He cast his eyes around to see if he could see any medical teams but it was almost impossible through the dense smoke.

He was lucky to stumble across a stretcher-bearer team, which had just decided the Digger they were going to take was too far gone and they would have to leave him. The priority was for casualties who could be saved.

'I have a soldier who I think can be saved, fellas. Would you have a look at him for me? He's a cobber.' There was urgency in Harry's voice.

'Every one of them is somebody's cobber, mate, but OK, where is he?'

'Follow me.'

Harry crawled to where he left George, with the six-man team following in close pursuit.

'Georgie, mate, I have got the boys here to load you up and take you back to the dressing station. They will fix you up. George, can you hear me?'

George Phillips

It was too late. George Arthur Phillips aged 22 from Ballarat, Victoria, had died. Left in No-Man's Land, he was to be collected later when the battle finished. Chances are he would never be found.

Harry and Bluey rested in the trench for twenty minutes and then went out again. There were many more wounded to find and bring back.

Harry and Bluey Resting in the Trench

'Come on, mate, I can still hear the poor bastards moaning; let's try one more time'.

As they crawled out they came across a digger who was hurt very badly. It took both of them to carry him. They began to make their way when they noticed a German soldier whom they assumed was dead; they were wrong. He raised his rifle and aimed it at them. Harry reacted instantly, thrusting his bayonet into the German's chest. He died instantly as the blade penetrated his heart. Harry pulled off his dog tag and stuffed it in his pocket to hand in to the Red Cross for identification. He also took his wallet. He had just killed someone's son; surely his family deserved the dog tag and personal papers. They got the soldier back to their trench and the medics took him.

Both Paddy and Harry were recommended for the Military Medal for bravery and gallantry in the field. They had rescued eight Diggers.

Harry sat down in the trench, utterly exhausted; he pulled out the dog tag and the dead soldier's identification papers contained in a battered leather wallet. He was shocked when he read the name: "Helmut Iffinger." That was his Grandfather's family name, a very unusual German name from the village of Neckargemünd, near Heidelberg. He could have just killed a relative, one of his own kin. *'Oh My God!'*

19

The following day Harry and the 5th Battalion were ordered to attack the German defences again. They were all exhausted, having been in battle for weeks, contending with the constant rain, the mud, the rats and the shelling as well as the German bullets and shells. Their officers informed them that this was the last attack before the Canadians came to relieve them.

Harry decided he should write a quick letter to Emma:

My darling Emma,

I am about to go out there again but this time I know it will be the last time for a while; they are going to relieve us and give the Canadians a go.

I am well and looking forward to some R&R especially a bath and wash my uniform. I don't think you would like the look of me right now.

I really hope this war ends soon and we can all come home. I cannot wait to see you and hold you close again my darling.

I have to go as they have given us the five-minute notice call.

I love you with all my heart.

Love

Harry

Harry, Bluey and the other Diggers heard the whistle and clambered over the top. It was hard going in the mud and the ground was pock-marked with shell craters. As usual the noise was deafening; just when Harry was looking for some cover, a German shell exploded and he was thrown into a crater. He lay there feeling the warm blood oozing from his wounds and then nothing. Harry awoke to Paddy slapping his face and yelling at him. Harry was still alive. Bluey carried him back to the Trench and the Medics took him immediately.

# Victoria Dock to Prince's Park

## Chapter 3

**1899**

As Harry lay there on the stretcher his life passed before him. Would this field hospital at Ypres be where he would die? Harry's unconscious mind took him back to Melbourne, Australia.

**Melbourne 1901**

The day was dull with the promise of rain; Harry hated playing in the rain especially at his home ground, Prince's Park, the home of Carlton. It held the water and made playing conditions very unpleasant.

This was to be his last game with Carlton; he had played all year with them but now he was heading back to his beloved Port Melbourne and all his mates. It wasn't that he did not like playing with Carlton, despite their recent form slump; it was more to do with enjoyment and the comradeship.

He felt at home back at Port.

It was going to be a tough match against the old foe, Collingwood.

Little did he know that his opponent from Collingwood playing at half forward flank, Paddy Rowan, would end up being his "brother in arms" and a great mate.

Harry's last game ended with a loss and Collingwood went on to win the premiership that year.

Harry's parents lived in Ballarat for the first part of their marriage. Gold was discovered, ironically, at Poverty Point, in 1851 by John Dunlop and James Regan who found a few ounces while panning in Canadian Creek. By the following year there were around

20,000 miners searching for gold in the Ballarat Goldfields. Due to this population explosion, Ballarat was proclaimed a town in 1852. By 1855, Ballarat was a municipality, a borough by 1863 and a city in 1870.

Harry's father, James, was a carpenter however he decided the way to make some real money was to join the thousands of 'hopefuls' on the goldfields. He laboured for twelve hours a day, six days a week and after two years of gold digging, he decided to move back to Melbourne. He earned about forty per cent of what he would have earned as a carpenter in Melbourne if he had stayed and far less than he would have made using his trade, building Ballarat's four hundred odd pubs and many other buildings in and around Ballarat.

He and his wife, Annie, moved into a three-bedroom cottage in Northcote located about seven kilometres from the city of Melbourne, where Jim got a job as a carpenter working for Carlton United Breweries.

Things went pretty well from there on and they started to build their family and, when finished, they had six children. Harry was born in 1879, the last child born.

Harry was not an exceptional child academically but showed strong traits of determination and will power, which would serve him well in his later years.

He left Northcote Primary when he completed year six and went to work as a labourer at the Victoria Docks at the age of fourteen, a tough learning experience for such a young boy.

Harry was given the address where he was to report on his first day at the docks. It was a small office, which was located on the pier. He gingerly knocked and a gruff voice commanded him to 'enter.'

He opened the office door and looked inside.

'Don't just stand there, lad! Get your skinny arse inside and let me take a look at you.'

Harry did as he was commanded . Behind a desk was a very large man with a huge beard; Harry had never seen a beard like it, and it made the man look very intimidating to young Harry.

'Well what's your name, son?' he bellowed.

'Harry Daniel, Sir'

'Sounds like you have two first names. That's bloody stupid. I have you on my list to start as labourer, is that right?'

'Yes, Sir'

'Have you done any hard work before, son?'

'Well, Sir, I had a paper round for a couple of years.'

'A bloody paper round! Sitting on your skinny arse riding a bicycle around, delivering papers is not my view of hard work. Do you know what I consider hard work, Daniel, Harry or whatever your bloody name is?'

'No, Sir.' Harry was really starting to regret turning up for this job.

'Arriving at the Dock at 6am, unloading a bloody great big ship, stacking the boxes so a heavy wagon can take them and deliver them to all sorts of places. Your hands are sore, you are exhausted and at the end of the day, you ride home on your paper-delivering bicycle where your Mum is cooking Brussels sprouts, cabbage and cauliflower with a pissy little piece of meat, all of which you hate. That's hard work, son!'

'Well, Sir, I am keen and I will work very hard for you. By the way, I quite like Brussels sprouts.'

Bushy Beard frowned at Harry.

'Do you? Well I hate the bloody things and that is all that matters.

Mr Bushy Beard rose from his chair and strode out of his office.

'All right, come with me and I will introduce to your new boss. He hates Brussels sprouts too, so don't mention your love of them.'

Harry followed the bearded giant. He did not tell Harry his name but he figured he would find out soon enough. They walked along the pier; well, Mr Bushy Beard walked; Harry had to half run to keep up. They walked, or half ran, into a large shed with windows on the top of the highest roof Harry had ever seen. There were men everywhere pushing trolleys loaded up to the tops of their heads and there seemed to be a lot of yelling going on. Mr Bushy Beard, who Harry would discover was called Mr Worthington, introduced him to his boss, Mr Creighton. Mr Creighton was the opposite of Mr Worthington: he was quite short and very burly, and there would not have been an ounce of fat on his body.

'This skinny little lad is called Daniel Harry or something... doesn't really matter because I don't think he will last more than today. However, he might surprise us all.'

'All right, Daniel, let's put you to work and see if you can prove us all wrong,' said Mr Creighton, whose nickname was 'Chook'.

'Thank you, Mr Creighton, but my name is Harry Daniel.

'Is it? OK, Daniel, I want you to take these orange boxes and load them all on this platform ready to be picked up. Do you have any questions?'

'Where do I get a trolley, Sir?'

'Sorry, lad, no trolleys left. You will have to carry them. You OK with that?'

'Yes, Sir,' Harry said with as much conviction as he could muster, eyeing the one hundred odd crates of oranges he had to move to the loading dock by 4 o'clock.

Harry went about carrying each box weighing sixty pounds out to the truck loading dock. By the time 3.45pm arrived, he realised he was not going to make it. Chook came over and checked his progress.

'Well, Daniel, you are not going to make it, are you?'

'No Sir, I don't think I am, but I haven't stopped.'

'Stand aside.'

Chook grabbed a trolley loaded three boxes on to it and finished the remaining twenty boxes in ten minutes just as the truck pulled up to load them for market.

Daniel walked two kilometres to the tram stop and arrived home in Bent Street, Northcote at 5.30pm. His mum told him to clean up for dinner, which was always on the table at 6.00 pm, come rain or shine. Harry did as he was told and by the time dinner was served he could not keep his eyes open. He barely could answer the few questions his dad asked about his first day on the job, when he fell asleep at the kitchen table. He was absolutely exhausted.

He did not even touch his beloved Brussels sprouts.

The next day was easier as they allocated him a trolley. The first day was a test and Chook gave him a low pass. This meant he could stay and have his own trolley. Harry started to enjoy the work and the pay, albeit puny, was better now than in 1890 when the great strikes hit the Melbourne docks.

He worked on the docks as a labourer until his twenty-first year. He was then given an opportunity to become a paviour laying blue stone pavers initially in the dock area and then all over Melbourne. Although the work was hard, just as hard as labouring on the dock, it paid well and he enjoyed the work. The men he worked with were generally good blokes and he quickly made some great cobbers.

Harry was only five foot six but he was strong, stocky and fast. These attributes made it easy for him to become a champion Australian Rules footballer for Port Melbourne before he was recruited to play for Carlton in the 1901 season.

It was at Carlton that he learnt the art of war; these were tough individuals who took no prisoners.

Harry Daniel, Carlton 1901

Harry drank at the pub he had always frequented in Port Melbourne since his eighteenth birthday when the boys from the dock took him down to the "Exchange" and got him drunk for the first time. He came into the public bar at 5pm and, with only an hour to go before the pub closed, he ordered his first pot of beer. He knew all his Port mates would be there after the game.

'G'day, Bluey, how did ya play, mate?' Harry yelled across the bar.

'Fucking hopeless. Three kicks all day… bloody useless.'

'Never mind, cobber, there's always next week. Harry attempted to console his old mate.

'Hey, Bluey, I am back playing for the old Port next week…together we'll kill the bastards! By the way, who ARE the bastards we are going to kill next week?

'Williamstown.'

'Bloody hell, they are number one.'

'Don't worry, Bluey, we'll kill em!'

Next week came and went and Port got thrashed 16.10 to 4.2. Harry played well on the back line but nothing was going to stop the Williamstown forwards. Port ended the season in sixth place and did not play in the finals.

# Love and War

## Chapter 4

Harry continued to play for Port Melbourne until he turned thirty, one of the oldest players in the league. Nothing really eventful took place over the next few years. Harry continued also to live at home with his parents while all his old mates had married and had kids. It wasn't that Harry would not have liked to follow the same path as his mates, it was just that he hadn't met any young lady who really took his fancy. Until he met Emma. She was ten years Harry's junior with a pretty face, a little bit chubby and with a great sense of humour. Emma made Harry's life fulfilled in many ways. The year was 1914 and the European war had just been declared. Harry did not quite understand what it was all about; some Duke got shot by a Serb and all hell broke loose. All Harry knew was that the Germans and the Austrians and Turks were at war with Britain and therefore Australia.

Harry's grandfather, a bloke called Conrad Iffinger, was German-born and raised in a little village called Neckargemund, just ten kilometres from Heidelberg.

When he was just sixteen he stowed away on a ship going "goodness knows where", to avoid National Service in the German army. The "goodness knows where" turned out to be Melbourne, Australia.

The other side of his ancestry, the Daniel side, was English so he had all sides covered.

As 1914 progressed into 1915, more and more of his football mates were enlisting for the *'great adventure.'* Harry was now thirty-six and deeply in love with Emma. He dreaded the thought of leaving her behind. He also felt a great compulsion to fight for his country and for Mother England so he really faced a conundrum( a dilemma?).

Harry walked the two blocks to Emma's house to pick her up to go dancing at the Palais in St Kilda. When he knocked on her door, her elder brother, Tom, opened it.

'G'Day, Harry. Where you taking my young sis tonight?'

'To the Palais, mate, she loves dancing and she can even make me look alright on the dance floor.'

'Well there should be plenty of space for you two to dance,as most of the blokes I know have enlisted, in fact I enlisted today. What about you, Harry?'

Harry leaned forward.

'Tom, don't tell your sister. I want to break it to her tonight but I've enlisted too, I'm leaving for training camp in two weeks.'

'Bloody Hell, I won't say a word,' Tom said in a hushed tone.

Emma came to the door, Harry looked at her beautiful face, and his heart sank. How was he going to tell her about his imminent departure to join the great force half way around the world?

'You look beautiful, Emma'

'Thank you, Harry, and you look very handsome'. They left to catch the tram, which, after two changes, would deliver them to the famous Palais.

All night Harry was trying to build up the courage to tell Emma his news but every time he tried, he would just clam up. It was not until they were at Emma's front gate that Harry finally blurted it out, but not at all how he had rehearsed it:

'Emma, I've enlisted in the army. I will be going to basic training at Broadmeadows in two weeks' time.'

'Harry, my love; I have been expecting this news for some time now. I'm very proud of you.

'I am going to miss you, Emma, very much and I would be honoured if you would marry me on my return.' Harry had a tear in his eye.

Emma moved toward Harry and hugged him tight and would not let go for what seemed an eternity.

'Harry I would be honoured to be your wife. There is only one condition, Harry, my love.'

'Oh,' said Harry surprised, 'and what would that be darling?' This was the first time he had called her 'darling'.

'We get engaged before you go off to war.'

'But what if I don't come back?'

'You will, my darling, you must.'


The couple became engaged the next Saturday night, witnessed by a few friends and Emma and Harry's families. Everybody was very happy for the couple but also worried for Emma What if Harry did not return?


On the following Wednesday 14th of July, 1915, Harry entered the new Broadmeadows training camp. It was a huge tent city with muddy roads and very basic facilities. So basic were the facilities that many of the new recruits became ill and were hospitalised – not a great start to what they thought would be a great adventure.

# Family Reunion

## Chapter 5

### 1915 Egypt

Harry endured four months of training and waiting around before he got notice he was to embark on to the troop ship, the SS Ceramic, the largest troop ship in the fleet. It used to be a cruise liner but this was to be no bloody cruise. After two months of rough weather and high seas and countless games of 'two up', they disembarked at a place Harry had never heard of before: Serapeum in Alexandria, Egypt. Harry had always wanted to see the pyramids however he would have to wait until they were stationed in Cairo. There were many ancient ruins which Harry and his cobbers did find intriguing but it was bloody hot and the hawkers would not leave them alone.

After about a week of heat and sand storms they were moved to a new camp at Mena near Cairo. Now Harry and the boys could see the pyramids and the sphinx.

Mena Camp, Cairo, Egypt

They became tourists climbing the Great Pyramid and taking camel rides. There were other benefits also; they could go into Cairo, a city like nothing they had ever seen.

To be honest, Harry and his mates had only seen Melbourne so Cairo with its people and nightlife was something to behold. They were pretty well behaved but did have a few run-ins with some toffy British officers.

'Hey, Harry!' yelled his good mate, Dave. 'Come and have a look at this'.

Harry came over and looked inside the small café.

'Have you ever?'

There were several men smoking large water pipes and watching a belly dancer going through her motions, so to speak.

'Do you wanna go in and give it a burl, mate?'

'Why not?

Both Dave and Harry took a spot on some big fluffy cushions; the Arab who ran the show introduced himself as Ammon.

'Would you like some coffee and a Shisha?'

'What the bloody hell is a Shisha, mate?' Dave asked.

'It is a water pipe. See, everyone has one. You will like it… very relaxing.'

'Bloody hell, mate, I could do with a bit of relaxing with what we have been through lately. 'It's not going to cost us an arm and a leg is it, Ammon?'

'Excuse me, Sir?' Ammon was confused. 'I don't want your arm or leg, just a pound each'

They both laughed.

'It's just an expression we use in Australia, meaning expensive'

'Oh I see', said Ammon starting to become impatient 'Well, would you like a coffee and Shisha?'

'Yeah, why not? You only live once don't you?'

Ammon departed and came back fifteen minutes later with two very exotic Shishas.

'I have selected a very fragrant tobacco for you,' said Ammon 'it is mixed with strawberries, apple and grapes. I am sure you will enjoy it. I will bring your coffee shortly so relax and enjoy the dancer and your Shisha.'

'If the boys down at the footy club could see us now!'

Dave broke up laughing and agreed.

As they smoked their special blend and sipped the coffee that Ammon had brought them, they really did feel relaxed. The belly dancer was quite pretty but quite chubby; she danced in front of them, shaking all the flesh she could, smiling the whole time.

Harry's thoughts went back to Emma in Melbourne and how he missed her and could not wait to get back and marry her, have a family and live a happy life. At the same time he was looking forward to the great adventure that lay in front of him.

After about an hour, Harry and Dave decided to move on and find somewhere they could have a drink. They found a very rowdy bar full of ANZACs and Tommies.

They ordered a couple of beers and started to chat with the other Diggers and a couple of Poms. Things were going very nicely until a pompous Pommy Captain walked in with a couple of Military Police and closed down the bar for the night.

Dave couldn't help himself and started shouting.

'You Pommy bastards are always trying to ruin our fun! You can't play cricket and you can't play football and you can't fight either!'

Dave then turned on his heels and bolted out of the bar, running down laneways and ducking under awnings with the two policemen giving chase. He finally lost them in the night market. He then tried to find his way back to Mena without being sprung. He sneaked in around midnight and lay down on his stretcher. Harry had been back for nearly two hours.

'Geez, mate, you were lucky they didn't throw you in the clink.'

'They would have had to catch me first, but they were too bloody slow.'

The next day while Harry was resting in his tent after the big night out in Cairo, another mate, Bill Hawkins, called out to him.

'Harry, you have a young bloke who says he knows you. Will I send him in?'

'Who is it?'

'Well, that's the funny thing... he says his name is Harry Daniel.'

Harry sat up on his stretcher.

'There is only one other Harry Daniel I know of, and he's me nephew. It can't be him! He's too young to enlist.'

'Well what do I do with him, Harry?'

'Hold on, I'll come out.'

Harry gingerly got up and walked out to see who the impostor was.

'Hello, Uncle Harry,' said the slightly built young man.

'Bloody hell! What are you doing here?'

'Same reason you're here, Uncle Harry, to fight for King and country.'

'But you're only a kid. How old are you now?'

'Well, my enrolment papers say I am eighteen.'

'Bullshit, you're about fifteen from memory.'

'Uncle Harry, please, an officer might hear you.'

Young Harry spoke in a hushed voice.

'I am seventeen but was sixteen when I enlisted. Dad signed my papers, so I am O.K. Don't worry.'

33

'Don't bloody worry!'

'I have just got back from that hellhole, Gallipoli. Four months of hell, so if I can survive that, and I can tell you lots of me mates didn't, I can survive anything.'

Harry ushered young Harry into his tent.

'What battalion are you in, kid?'

'I was in the 10th but just got transferred to the 59th. How about you?'

'The 5th,' grunted Harry Senior.

'Have you got any idea where they are sending you next and when?'

'Not a bloody clue, I did hear a rumour that we're moving out soon.'

'Alright, you keep me posted'. 'I will write to your Mum and Dad and let them know we caught up and you are safe and well.'

'I did write a few letters from Gallipoli and I sent them a couple of post cards of the pyramids and the sphinx with a few words.'

Post Card From Egypt

34

# Gallipoli

## Chapter 6

**1915**

'Tell me what Gallipoli was really like, Harry; I have heard a few stories and it sounds pretty rough.

'Well Uncle Harry it really was hell on earth. I suppose I should start when we landed at the wrong beach...'

'You're kidding me! Who fucked up?'

'Don't know, but most of us believe it was the Pommy Generals although they blamed it on the currents.'

'So it was pretty rough?'

'Bloody oath, first they brought us in on war ships which were meant to give us protection. They then told us in hushed tones to climb down the ladders and into the wooden landing boats. That was a bloody trick in itself climbing down a rope ladder with a full pack, including a spade and your rifle slung over your shoulder. Anyway I made it to the boat and squeezed in next to me good mate, Frankie Lowe. We were just about to push off when I heard one of the officers say.'

'Oh my God they have taken us to the wrong beach. They'll be slaughtered.'

'I bloody hope not,' Frankie muttered.

'It was still dark when they started towing us to the beach; it was bloody freezing but they told us we weren't allowed to wear our great coats; we had to carry them in our packs.

The trip to the beach felt like hours but in fact was only forty minutes. The officers told us that Abdul's bullets would sound like little birds as they whizzed past us.

It was starting to lighten up and the sea shimmered in the half-light. I heard what I thought was a shot, then another one

'I think they have spotted us, Frankie.'

'Yeah, it all starts now, Harry.'

'Just then, the few angry shots turned into mayhem; the sky was alight with a huge fireworks display except this wasn't Guy Fawkes day. These bastards were serious. Most of the blokes didn't show any fear and thumbed their noses at Abdul until a few of them slumped in the boat with blood oozing from their wounds.

I said to Frankie, 'If this is what little birds sound like, I'll be fucked.' He didn't answer I turned to look at him and half his head had gone.'

'Fucking hell, Frankie, why didn't you have your stupid head down? Bloody hell!'

The officer on board told us:

'Make a landing where you can, lads, and hold on!'

'They were using leather megaphones attached to their wrists because nobody could hear them over the sound of firing. The tows cast off and we were on our own.

Those blokes at the oars rowed like demons. Some were shot so others took their place at once and not a word was said. Finally we grounded and, in an instant, we were in the water up to our waists and wading ashore with bullets flying all around us.

My landing was a bit awkward. I was responding to an officer's call:

'Hop out and after 'em, lads,' but I bloody lost my footing on the slippery stones of the seabed, then fell a second time as I stepped ashore because of the weight of my saturated uniform. Meanwhile, Abdul's bullets were killing and maiming so many blokes and of course the rest of us were pretty bloody upset. A medical officer recalled a calm midshipman handing him his satchel, 'as if he were landing a pleasure party' when he fell back into the boat, shot through the head.

The water became red with the blood and the corpses of our mates were floating everywhere. I am telling you Uncle Harry, it was bloody horrible.'

'But you made it to the beach, Harry?'

'Well, yeah, but that wasn't any picnic either. We were running and we looked up at these bloody big cliffs. Abdul was gunning us down with their fucking machine guns and starting to send their shells down on us. The noise was shocking and my cobbers were falling all around me. All I could do was fire back, but we had little chance of hitting one of the bastards.

They tried to organise us so we could start climbing the cliffs and dig some trenches for some sort of protection, however a lot of the blokes were running in different directions to avoid Abdul's bullets, so it was a bit difficult. We were crawling along the cliff face, which was falling away from under our feet. Every time we seemed to make some progress, the Turks would spot us and open fire, killing more than fifty of my group that first night. Our officer was Lieutenant Jack Paul; he was a good bloke and cared about his men. He received orders from General Birdwood to dig in and establish a trench line against the Turks. That was easier said than done but we gave it a bloody good go.

The next day it was obvious that we were not going to hold our ground and we needed to piss off to the beach and consolidate our forces. We were crossing a place called Lone Pine when the Turks let loose and nearly killed the bloody lot of us. It was a slaughterhouse.

### Gallipoli 6th of August, 1915

Young Harry Daniel had survived the first three months or so in Gallipoli.

He had survived numerous clashes with the Turks and, despite them trying to kill him and his mates, they had earned his respect as a fighting force.

He had survived the meagre rations that tended to be stale biscuits and jam.

He had survived dysentery, which everybody seemed to suffer and which made the race for the bog a critical win. The only two things he had real difficulty coping with were the fucking flies and the smell of rotting corpses.

Harry was waiting in the trench, waiting for the whistle to go over the top.

He was checking out his sewing skills: the soldiers had been ordered to sew a strip of white calico on each arm and the back of their uniforms so that the artillery boys didn't blast the living daylights out of them when they were charging the Turks.

Australian Trench at Lone Pine

'Harry, you all right, mate?' said Alfie Whitecross, one of Harry's few mates left alive from the troop ship that brought them to Gallipoli.

'Yeah just checking out my sewing. Mum would be proud of me. I will be knitting a scarf next.'

'I must admit I'm just a little nervous,' whispered Harry.

'We are all fucking nervous, mate, no doubt about that.'

'She'll be right, mate. I reckon this bombardment will be giving Johnny Turk a bit of a shake up. With any luck there won't be any of the bastards left.'

'I wouldn't bet on it, Alfie'.

'They're giving back as good as they're getting.'

The smell of cordite was suffocating and the noise coming from the artillery of both sides was deafening.

'I forgot to write Mum and Dad a letter so I better make it back or they will be really disappointed,' said Harry half joking.

'Well, we don't have far to run before we are on top of them, Harry. Must be only a hundred yards.'

The Lieutenant was moving amongst his men, reassuring them and ensuring all bayonets were fixed and they were ready to go over the top.

At 5pm, Lieutenant Paul was present with his fob watch in his hand calling 'three minutes to go, two minutes to go, one minute to go, half a minute to go'. Then he shut the cover of the watch and blew three shrill blasts of a whistle.

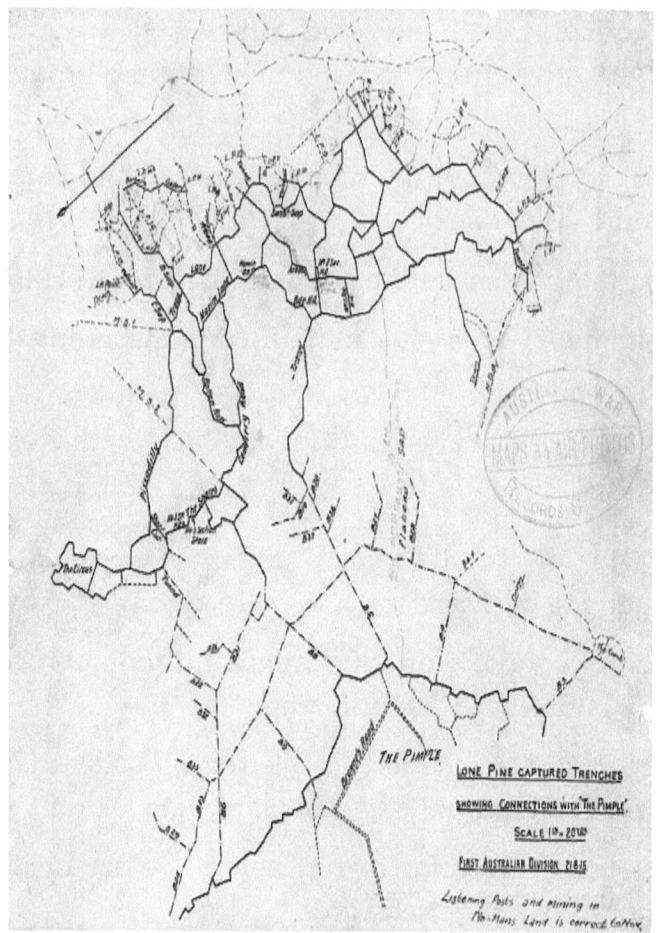

Trench Lines at Gallipoli

Out scrambled the Diggers.

Harry and Alfie were running like mad; there was no nervousness now. The shrapnel was falling like hail and they were both firing their rifles as they ran. Harry saw Alfie fall; he didn't get back up; he had been ripped apart by a Turkish machine gun.

Harry kept running and was one of the first ANZACs to reach the Turk's trenches.

The trench was completely covered over with logs and branches and dirt. It was impossible to penetrate it.

'Come on, men, we'll take the next trench!' shouted the Lieutenant, who started running again with his pistol at the ready and with his men following in hot pursuit.

Harry jumped into the next trench and found several Turks; they were ready for a fight.

Harry recounted to his Uncle Harry the fight.

'I shot one and stuck another with my bayonet. I looked around and saw the Lieutenant shooting Turks with his pistol. I reckon he must have shot three or four.

I saw the Turks running down the end of the trench and disappearing; it must have been a cave or a dug-out.

The Lieutenant called for Jackie Wilson, the bomber, to throw in a few bombs.

He started to light the fuses and throw them. You could hear the Turks yelling and moaning. It wasn't a pleasant sound but it had to be done.

Lieutenant Paul sent me and another bloke around to the other side of the dug-out to see if we could flush them out. The other bloke…I didn't even know his name… was in the lead and got a bullet in the eye. He dropped like a stone.

I fired my rifle through the opening of the cave and although I couldn't see, I heard a scream so I figured I'd got one.

Meanwhile at the other side of the trench the bombs had done their job so we experienced no more resistance.

We occupied the Turk's trenches for the next three days; they kept counter-attacking but by the end of the fourth day, we could claim victory.'

Lone Pine was a significant victory for the ANZACs but at what price?

There were ten thousand casualties comprising seven thousand Turks and three thousand Australians. Nine thousand were fatalities.

Harry Daniel, along with his remaining Battalion, was shipped out to Egypt before moving on to the Western Front, leaving their comrades to fight on but not for long.

Anzacs Landing at Gallipoli

# From Desert to the Green Hills of France

## Chapter 7

**Cairo, Egypt, July 1916**

Harry senior was playing a game of desert cricket with his cobbers from the Battalion on a balmy Egyptian Sunday afternoon when young Harry wandered up and started cheering on his Uncle's team. Harry senior was a bloody good sportsman all round. After the game they got together for a chat.

'Are you alright, mate?' asked Harry Senior.

'Well, we just got our orders to pack up and be ready to move out tomorrow morning.'

'Bloody hell,' scowled Harry, 'we have been waiting around for what seems eternity and you bastards are on the move again.'

Young Harry embarked on the troop ship with his mates, steaming off to France. They landed in Marseilles and were then transported by train to a place called Fromelles in Northern France.

They were allowed to rest for all of one day, then they were ordered to start digging their defensive trenches. This was no easy task as the water table was very close to the surface which meant the Diggers were constantly standing in water. They couldn't go as deep as they had planned, as the water level prohibited them. Consequently sand bags were placed as high as possible without hindering them from going "over the top" when the order was given to attack the Germans.

The Germans had been developing their bunker system for two years; from their vantage point they could observe the Australians hard at work. Once the trenches were finally dug, it became a waiting game. On 16th of July 1916, the Australian and British troops were informed that the attack would be taking place in a few days. The officers also assured them that the aerial bombardment's duration would be three days. The theory was the German defences would be destroyed enabling a significant victory.

The worst day in Australia's wartime history was about to begin.

## Chapter 8

### July 1916, Fromelles, France

Harry was in the trench with his mates from the 59th Battalion. They had been enduring the bombardment of the German positions for hours.

'Geez I hope Pompey and the other officers were right; this bombardment should knock the shit out of Fritz. Just a quick sprint and we take the German trenches.'

'You're bloody mad, Harry, it's not going be that easy.' said Frankie, 'no bloody way.'

'Just joking, Frankie. Are you a bit scared, Frank?'

'Fucking oath, mate, I really don't want to die here, I was rather hoping I would die in my sleep when I'm about fucking ninety.'

'Yeah, me too,' said Harry.

'Did you hear what happened to Bruce Cook?'

'No, what happened?'

'He copped a fucking shell in the trench.'

'How do you know?'

'The runner told me. You were having a bit of a kip… fucked if I know how with all this bloody noise.'

The officers and NCO's started to move along the trenches, informing the Diggers that they were due to go over the top in thirty minutes. They instructed them to check their equipment, most importantly their rifles, bayonets and grenades. It had been reported that inexperienced troops were forgetting to pull the pin on their grenades before hurling them, silly bastards.

Harry took the time to write a quick note to his Mum and Dad back home in Melbourne.

*"Dear Mum and Dad,*

*I have been told we are going over the top very soon. I know what that is like from my time at Gallipoli and it's hell on earth. I survived Gallipoli and I have no doubt I will survive here with the help of God.*

*I will put this letter in my pocket and if anything does happen to me, my cobbers will find it and send it on to you.*

*I want you to know that I love you both.*

*Well I said a quick note and there's the five-minute whistle so I better sign off.*

*Love*

*Harry*

Harry's parents never received his letter.

'Well mate, this it, I'll see you in Jerry's trenches soon.'

'See you there, cobber,' responded Frankie.

They heard the whistle. The officer close to them yelled,

'Give them hell boys! Over you go!'

Harry and Frankie clambered over the top and started to run. Sugar Loaf, a massive German gun emplacement, was directly in front of the running soldiers.

Machine Guns were firing from all directions and Harry could hear the bullets tearing through the flesh of the Diggers running beside him. He jumped into a shell crater only to find three mutilated Australians lying in the water at the bottom.

'So this is what they call ANZAC soup,' he thought.

He knew he had to keep going; he clambered up the slope and headed for the German line. He hadn't fired a shot yet, a waste of ammunition from this far away.

He could feel his heart pumping; the adrenalin rushing through his veins was like a river torrent: the noise of the guns and shellfire was deafening. Then silence.

Harry had received a mortal wound. He would not be going home. His body would never be found. The Last Post would not be played as they lowered him down. He would be one of the missing, an unknown soldier.

Sugar Loaf

The 59th Battalion was ordered to take Sugar Loaf. This was a near impossible mission. It was from this fortification that Harry received his mortal blow.

Back home in Northcote, Melbourne, Harry's mother was bathing the youngest of her three children, James, when there was a knock at the front door. She took James from the bath and covered him with a towel. Slowly she opened the door. She didn't get many visitors. Standing there was Robert Hayes, the Minister from their church, looking grim; he had a yellow envelope in his hand.

'No, NO it can't be! Not Harry... NO!' she screamed.

'I am so sorry, Jane. Can I come in?'

'Sorry, Father, not now.'

'If there is anything I can do, please let me know.'

Jane closed the door and leaned against the wall, she let out a primal scream and began to wail uncontrollably. James began to cry and the whole Daniel house was encompassed in grief.

Sam Daniel came home from work about 4.30 pm only to find Jane in the kitchen, sitting quietly.

'What's wrong, love? You look like you have seen a ghost.'

Jane stared at him and pointed to the telegram on the kitchen table. He picked it up and read it: "*It is my painful duty to inform you…*" That is all he read. He slumped down on the chair and wept.

Jane and Sam did not sleep much that night, managing only a couple of hours. Sam got up first and made a cup of tea. He went into the bedroom to wake Jane and was astounded. Jane's hair had turned completely white overnight.


## Melbourne, Australia, 2012

Lois Kennedy was Harry's niece; she often wondered about her uncle Harry; he had died well before she'd been born. She had seen a news report only that week about Australian and British soldiers being discovered in mass graves in a place called Pheasant's Wood at Fromelles. Apparently they were seeking relatives of soldiers who died in the Battle of Fromelles to give a DNA sample to try to identify the unknown soldiers who had been unearthed. Lois contacted the Department of Defence and requested a DNA kit.

The kit arrived a few weeks later; she was required to swab the inside of her mouth and place the swab in a plastic bag, posting it back to The Department of Veteran Affairs in Canberra.

She hoped that Harry would be identified and be properly buried in the newly created cemetery in the Fromelles village in Northern France.

**January, 2011**

Lois was sitting in the sun on her back veranda reading 'The Age'

She saw an advertisement, which took her interest.

WWI Battlefield Weekend 2013

YPRES SALIENT, THE SOMME, VILLERS-BRETONNEUX, FROMELLES & VIMY RIDGE – 'This three day introductory tour allows visitors to see the major areas of British and Commonwealth involvement across the Western Front. All the major Commonwealth countries, Canada, Australia, New Zealand, South Africa and India, as well as Britain, played major roles in ensuring ultimate victory and the tour is flexible enough to ensure that visitors from all countries will see the memorials to their countries' fallen, as well as gaining a greater understanding of the overall conduct and strategy of the war.'

She'd always wanted to visit The Western Front battlefields as not only had her Uncle Harry died there but her Great Uncle, also named Harry, died in 1918 in Amiens.

She had recently retired from her position as an administrator with the Catholic Church and was therefore free to go.

She decided to email for the information pack and it arrived four days later.

Lois read the brochure; it really did look like a wonderful trip. She had travelled to Europe with her daughter years before and fell in love with Paris so she did not need any prompting to return. The tour went to both Fromelles and Ypres close to where young Harry died in that horrendous battle and where Harry Senior endured horrible machine gun wounds. Harry Senior had died at Amiens and she hoped to travel there also. Neither of the Harry's had "no known grave" and therefore she would see their memorials. Young Harry was at V.C. Corner and Harry Senior at Villers – Bretonneux.

Nephew and Uncle
The Daniels

Lois put the brochure away for a few days although she did dwell on it; should she join the tour? Eventually she made her mind up; she was going.

She emailed Back-Roads Touring Co. and requested a registration form, which Mandy, the sales and marketing person, promptly sent via return email. The cost, including airfares, accommodation and the tour was $3500. She would be away for two weeks unless she decided to extend and do some more travelling. That decision could wait.

Lois completed the registration form that night and transferred the funds from her bank account. *'There, I am committed,'* she thought.

Lois then rang all four of her children and told them what she was doing. They were all delighted, although her youngest son, Terry, was concerned that his Mother at seventy-two would be travelling alone. He spoke to his wife, Claire, the next day and they both decided that Terry should travel to France with his mother. He had not been to Europe before so he was quite excited by the prospect of seeing Paris and some of France.

He went around to Lois's house the next day and told his mother the news. She was absolutely delighted. The only downside of the trip had been the prospect of travelling alone and now her son, whom she loved dearly, was going to accompany her.

'I'm excited too, Mum. I have always had a strong interest in what happened to my ancestors in the First World War. The fact that I get to see Paris and some of the French country- side is an added bonus.'

Archie Shearer

On the other side of the globe in Edinburgh, Scotland, Stewart McDonald read the same advertisement in the Edinburgh Herald and Post. He too was keen to see where both his Great Grand Father and Great Uncle had fought and died. Stewart was a barrister, practising in Edinburgh.

His Great Grand Father, Archie Shearer, had been with the 15th Scottish Division.

He was sent to the Western Front in June 1915.

He fought in the Battle of Loos, 25 September – 14 October 1915.

He died on the 26th of September 1915.

Albert Shearer

His other Great Grand Uncle was Albert Shearer. He had been in the 9th Infantry Division.

He was sent to the Western Front in May 1916.

He participated in the Battle of the Somme, 1 July - 18 November, 1916.

He died on the 1st of July, 1916.

Archie and Albert had a younger sister, Jane, who was only fourteen when the war broke out; Jane was Stewart's Great Grandmother.

The children grew up in Leith, a suburb of Edinburgh.

Both Archie and Albert were shipwrights as was their father and his father before him. In fact the Shearers had been shipwrights since the 1700's.

When the war broke out, the need for shipwrights became critical; Britain needed to build more and more ships for battle and troop carrying.

Both the Shearer brothers wanted to join their mates and go to war, not stay home and build ships. They both decided to enlist, their occupation was recorded as Labourer. Archie enlisted at the age of twenty, Albert was eighteen.

Albert and Archie undertook six weeks intensive training at Redford Barracks. Archie shipped out to France in June 1915 with the 15th Scottish division. Albert followed two weeks later with the 9th.

Archie's first taste of battle was in The Battle of Loos; it was also to be his last.

During the battle the British suffered 50,000 casualties. German casualties were estimated much lower, at approximately half the British total. The British failure at Loos contributed to General Haig's replacement of General French as Commander-in-Chief at the close of 1915.

### Edinburgh, Scotland, 2012

Stewart made the decision to go on the battlefield tour.

The tour, being in April, made it more difficult for Stewart to extricate himself from his practice. It was a very busy time of the year.

His Father often spoke about the sacrifices his grandfather made, along with the other 700,000 British who died for their King and country.

He requested the registration form, which Mandy duly emailed to him. He transferred the funds and emailed back the completed form. Stewart started to plan his weeklong absence from his practice. At least he didn't have to travel all the way from Australia like Lois and Terry.

## Grove, Huon Valley, Tasmania, Australia 2012

Ian Wooley lived in a beautiful region of Tasmania, although it would seem Tasmania was pretty much beautiful throughout. He lived in the little town of Grove, the gateway to the Huon Valley, in the southernmost part of Australia. His family had been apple orchardists for generations. Ian had continued the family tradition but was finding it more and more difficult to make a reasonable living. Competition from overseas had reduced margins down to the point when Ian had to make the decision on whether to continue growing apples or bulldoze the trees and burn the lot. Fortunately he had seen this coming and had gradually converted to growing cherries. Cherries were much more profitable; the only reason he had hesitated in getting out of growing apples altogether was the family history. He considered family history and tradition an important part of his life.

That belief system led him to register for the battlefield tour, which he discovered on the Internet. It was something he had wanted to do for a long time and he felt the time was right.

## Ranelagh, Huon Valley, Tasmania, Australia 1916

Charles Wooley

Ian's Great Uncle was Charles Wooley, an apple orchardist from the Huon Valley in a little community called Ranelagh. Charles was twenty-four when he enlisted, having heard a rousing call to arms at a meeting in the Ranelagh Community Hall. He went home full of patriotic fervour and announced his enlistment to his wife and little boy, John. His wife, Sophie, was devastated.

'What happens to John and me if you get yourself killed over there?' she cried, 'Why didn't you discuss it with me before you signed up?'

Charlie started to feel guilty about leaving his family but this was war and the King and his country must be defended from the German menace, at all costs.

After a very restless night, Sophie got out of bed and prepared John's breakfast before waking him; he was only four but he had a voracious appetite. She knew plenty of other wives in the valley were losing their husbands to this war and, in retrospect, felt that Charlie was doing the right thing.

Charlie started basic training at Broadmeadows in Victoria two weeks later. After two months of marching and learning the correct method to make a bed, he embarked on the troop ship, *SS Ceramic*, landing in Egypt two months later on 14th of July, 1916. He was assigned to the 47th Battalion.

He was able to do a few tourist things such as climb the great Pyramid as well as march in blistering heat on the sand for miles with a full pack. He was not sure how this would help in France, which he was told was green and quite cold and wet in winter, although mild in summer.

He was shipped out to France and saw action almost immediately.

The apple orchardist fought in a number of battles including Passchendaele and Pozières and, apart from a leg wound, survived some of the most ferocious fighting in the war.

His final battle was Dernancourt.

The five divisions of the AIF, now consolidated into the Australian Corps, had spent the winter of 1917–18 in Belgium. As the crisis developed on the Somme, Australian units were hurried south to help hold back the German advance. On 27th March 1918, elements of the Fourth Division took up positions around Dernancourt. This village on the River Ancre is on the southwest outskirts of Albert, which had been occupied by the Germans. On the 28th of March, the Germans attempted to resume their advance. In the morning mist, the Germans emerged from Albert along the railway line.

On that day, fighting spread along the whole front between Dernancourt and Albert. The 48th Battalion (South Australia and Western Australia) and the 12th Machine Gun Company, supporting a British unit, were attacked, however all attacks were repelled. British and Australian artillery interfered with German attempts to rally troops and to bring forward support troops for further assaults. One German attempt to mount an attack was ruined by what Charles Bean, the Australian official historian, called 'a rather strange occurrence'. As the Germans were massing for the attack, a chance shell caused an old British ammunition dump to explode. The noise was deafening and the Germans scattered. By this time the Australians, who had had three days and three nights of moving, marching, digging, fighting and little sleep, were nearly exhausted. However, rain, which began with a drizzle in late afternoon, became heavier during the night and made further German attacks unlikely. The Australians were soon withdrawn from the line for a rest. The rest did not last for long.

Charlie died from massive bullet wounds on the 5th of April, 1918.

He has no known grave. His memorial grave is at Villers-Bretonneux Memorial, France.

## Melbourne, Australia, 2012

George Abbey is a retired banker; he had been with The Commonwealth Bank for forty-five years. He has four adult children and a wife, Anna, to whom he has been married for forty-two years. George is regarded as a model citizen and a keen Rotarian, however, a bit boring and has not done anything mildly adventurous in his life.

George's uncle was John Abbey, 'Jack' to his mates. He was born in Yorkshire, England, in a beautiful and ancient village called Bolton Percy in North Yorkshire. The village was established under William the Conquer.

Jack, unlike George, was an adventurer; he left home at seventeen and spent his life's savings on a one-way fare to Melbourne, Australia, where he thought his prospects would be better.

He enlisted in the Australian Imperial Forces on the 18th of December, 1914 in Melbourne, Victoria. His unit was 8th Battalion, 2nd Reinforcement.

On the 2nd of February, he boarded the HMAT Clan Macgillivray to England and then went on to Gallipoli.

He survived the carnage of Gallipoli.

He then went to Egypt and joined the 60th Battalion and then shipped to France.

The first and only action in France for Jack was the disastrous battle of Fromelles.

He died on the 19th of July, 1916.

Jack has "No Known Grave".

George made the decision. He and Anna would travel to Europe and as part of their European adventure, they would take part in the "Back-Roads Touring Co" battlefields tour. He hoped this would give him a greater appreciation of his Uncle Jack's short life.

Jack Abbey

## Sydney, Australia, 2012

Christine Abbot is a medical doctor practising in Bondi Junction in Sydney, NSW; her husband, Tony Hailes, is also a doctor practising as a cardiologist out of the Royal Prince Alfred Hospital. Both are dedicated and very good at what they do. They have two boys, Ben, 16 and Adam, 13. Both attend Sydney Grammar.

They live in Belleview Hill in a multi million-dollar villa with swimming pool and tennis court. Things are pretty good for the family.

Things were not so easy for Christine's Great Uncle, David Abbott, who was a boot salesman who lived in Surrey Hills, which was, in the early part of the twentieth century, a working class suburb.

At the age of twenty-one he enlisted in the AIF at Holsworthy Army Base, where he completed his basic training and embarked from Sydney on board HMAT, Star of England, on a sunny balmy day on the 8th of March, 1916, heading for England, then France.

He arrived in England at the end of May, 1916 and was immediately shipped to Marseilles, France and then moved out to Fromelles to help with the trench digging prior to the Battle, a battle which would take his life.

Christine had never really taken any interest in the First World War, or any war for that matter. She was more interested in saving lives rather than reading about the carnage of war.

She never really had any interest in her family history either… that was until she saw a documentary on the Battle of Fromelles and how a mass grave had been discovered at a place called Pheasant Wood. She knew that she had a relative who had died in France but didn't know where or how. Her father never talked about it and apart from ANZAC day and Remembrance Day, she never really thought about the war or the millions of lives lost.

She turned to her husband who was still watching the documentary: 'Tony, did you know I had a relative, a great uncle I think, who died in the First World War?'

'No, darling, you've never mentioned it to me before. Where did he die?'

'I don't know, but I intend to find out.'

'Well,' said Tony, ' let's look it up on the Net.'


After a little research they found the Commonwealth War Graves Commission web site.

There he was:

*David Roylestone Leslie Abbott*

*Sydney NSW*

*Single*

*Five feet seven inches*

The key piece of data was: *killed in action, 19th July, 1916*

They knew from watching the documentary that was the date of the Battle of Fromelles.

It was decided then and there that they would all go to France and visit Fromelles and learn more about the battle in which her Great Uncle fought and died.

Christine searched the web and discovered "Battlefield Tours of France and Belgium" led by Back-Roads Touring Co. She requested the registration forms, completed them and paid the $13,000.

David Abbott

The following morning over breakfast, Christine and Tony made the announcement to their two sons, that they would all be travelling to France and Belgium and would take the battlefield tour.

Adam was very excited and could hardly wait to tell his mates at school.

'Hold on, Mum and Dad, you didn't consult me first. I have pre-season football training to attend and it's not a good idea to take time off in my final year. You guys and Adam go and I can stay home and look after the house.'

'You are certainly not staying home alone, Ben, end of discussion. You are coming with us. You might just learn that there are more things in the world other than you and only you,' said Tony in a stern fatherly voice.

Ben asked to be excused from the table and went to his bedroom to listen to his IPod and sulk.

'He'll come around, Darling, don't worry,' said Christine.

'I really do hope that this experience will enlighten him. Kids his age were fighting on the frontlines of Gallipoli and the Western Front and here he is being all petulant because it interrupts his diary. I think leaving his new girlfriend has something to do with it as well.'

Ben's behaviour did not improve, including when they boarded the plane for Paris. They had all checked in their luggage and gone through security when Ben could not be found.

'I've looked everywhere. He doesn't seem to be in the terminal,' Tony said in a frustrated tone.

The announcement came over the PA that fight AF1267 was boarding.

Tony raced to the men's toilet again to see if Ben was there and he noticed the cubicle with the door closed twenty minutes ago was still closed. His suspicions aroused, he got down on his knees and looked underneath. There were no tell-tale pants around the ankles. He knocked on the door and surprisingly Ben answered.

'What do you want?'

'You get the hell out of there right now, you little bastard, or I will break the door down and lead you through the terminal and onto the plane by the ear.'

Ben reluctantly opened the door and walked out looking very sheepish.

'I don't have time to talk to you about this now. Just get your skates on and rest assured we will talk about it later.'

The family boarded the 747 last and were shown their seats.

The plane took off on time.

Ben, having been reprimanded severely by his parents, spent most of the flight listening to his music and reading magazines.

## Brisbane, Australia 2012

Steve Vardy has lived in Brisbane for all of his fifty-nine years and has worked in the Information Technology industry for the past thirty years. He loves his family and his golf and apart from a divorce twenty years ago, nothing dramatic has happened in his life. Steve decided to research his family history as many people are now doing and paid his subscription to Ancestory.com. He enjoyed doing the research and was having some success in tracing his ancestry back to England and in particular the Nottingham area where the Vardys seemed to inhabit. It was while he was researching, that he found he had a Great Uncle, Frederick Vardy, who was a soldier with the Sherwood Foresters and had fought and died in the First World War.

Frederick Vardy
Born 1896
Died 1917

Fred Vardy came from an adventurous background; his father, Henry, came from a small village called Hucknall-under-Huthwaite in Nottinghamshire. At the age of fifteen, Henry joined the army. He lied about his age and was dispatched to Australia via the Crimean war and the Maori Wars in New Zealand. He eventually returned to

England, married and had several children. One of those children was Frederick Vardy.

Fred was just twenty when he enlisted and was sent to France in September 1916. He had been a framework knitter, as was the Vardy tradition but life in the army was a world away from his life in Nottingham where he used to drink a pint or two, or sometimes three, with his mates at his favourite pub, the oldest pub in England, in fact, "Ye Old Trip to Jerusalem".

Fred died on the seventh of June, 1917 at the Battle of Messines.

It has been argued that the Battle of Messines was the most successful allied battle of the war, certainly of the Western Front. Managed by General Herbert Plummer, Second Army, it was launched on 7 June, 1917 with the detonation of nineteen underground mines underneath the German mines.

There were sixteen thousand British killed in the Battle of Messines; one of them was Fred Vardy. He has no known grave.

Steve discussed it with his wife, Brenda, and his daughter, Sarah; they all agreed it would be a great sixtieth birthday present. Steve was going on a battlefield tour to learn more about his Great Uncle and the Great War.

## Massachusetts U.S.A. 2012

Mike Hansen lives in Sudbury, Massachusetts, about twenty miles outside Boston. It is a beautiful leafy suburb with many historic homes similar to where Mike and his wife lived at Widow's Rites Lane.

He has his own recruitment company which has operated very successfully for many years. He had been considering a very lucrative offer to sell to a competitor and retire and do a bit of travelling, play golf and do some fishing.

A keen amateur historian, he has spent many an hour researching the American Civil War and the American War of Independence. Recently, he has become interested in World War One and the USA's late involvement.

Mike's great uncle had fought in the war but he wasn't sure what battles he had fought in. He decided to do some research and found that William Hansen had been conscripted in 1917 and had been sent to France, taking part in the battle of Belleau Wood which was critical to the Aisne Offensive. Mike also discovered that William had died fighting in that battle, along with nearly two thousand of his compatriots.

The decision taken, he would register for Back-Roads Tour.

He e-mailed the company and requested a registration form, which was duly sent to him. Mike's wife, Loretta, decided that she would stay at home and look after their cats. She didn't really like flying so it suited her. Mike completed the form and transferred the money.

## Christchurch, New Zealand 2012

The penultimate person to register for the tour was Grant McKenzie, a New Zealander from the South Island. Grant owns an Apple computer store in Christchurch. It is a very successful business and sales have been strong. Grant is a very patriotic New Zealander who reveres the ANZAC spirit, the 'All Blacks' rugby team and any country who beats Australia in any sport.

Grant, thrice married but now single, didn't need to consult anybody before he decided to register for the tour.

Athol McKenzie

Grant's Grandfather, Athol McKenzie, was raised in Canterbury on the South Island, on his parent's dairy farm. They ran a sizable herd of one hundred Friesians. This was above average for the Canterbury area in the early 1900's. They were one of the first dairies in New Zealand to adopt vacuum-based milking. Life was hard on the farm but very satisfying. Young Athol helped with the milking in the morning, having risen at 5am; he would then have breakfast and head off for school. After school he had an hour to play, before it was time to round up the herd and milk the cows. After dinner it was homework and then off to bed.

Athol had two sisters, Susan and Claire, who also helped around the farm and had a similar regime to Athol.

Athol took a keen interest in what was happening in Europe although by the time the news reached Canterbury, it was pretty old. There had been recruitment drives all over New Zealand. On 21st of

February, 1916, they came to Ashburton, having recruited five hundred lads in Christchurch.

Athol enlisted; he then returned to the farm to break the news to his family. Needless to say, they were upset. After all, their only son was marching off to war. They also had concerns about being short-handed running the dairy.

Athol sailed to England on 30th of May, 1916.

He had learned a lot about England when he was at school and it intrigued him. The thought of spending some time in the mother country excited the young man. He was hoping to visit London and see all its sights, however this was not to be the case. He was dispatched to a training facility called Sling Camp in Wiltshire. Athol completed training in six weeks as a rifleman and was assigned to the 4th Battalion. In May 1917 he was sent to France where he joined his Kiwi and Australian comrades in arms; little did he know that he would take part in one of the most horrific battles on the Western Front.

Athol fought in The Battle of the Somme and Passchendaele, two major battles with great loss of life, including 15000 New Zealand casualties; these included 5000 killed at Passchendaele plus 6000 casualties. The Kiwis suffered 8000 casualties including 2000 killed at the Somme. New Zealand was second only to Serbia in the percentage of soldiers killed and missing in action. Athol survived both these horrendous battles, only to die seven days before the war ended at the attack on Le Quesnoy.

## Whistler, British Columbia, Canada, 2012

The final person to register for the tour was Philippe Bellepoire; he owned ski shops in Whistler and Blackcomb and a restaurant in Vancouver. He was a wealthy bachelor who competed in the slalom at the winter Olympics in 2002 at Salt Lake City where he came fourth.

He lived at Whistler in the winter and Vancouver in the summer. Life was good for Philippe.

He had never been married but always had a beautiful girl friend on his arm. Whenever the relationship reached the stage where marriage was mentioned or intimated, Philippe quickly ended it and went looking for the next one. He certainly didn't have to look far as he was in demand.

Philippe was very proud of his French heritage; his Great Grandfather immigrated to Quebec in 1875. His name was Henri Bellepoire, a wine maker from the region of Bordeaux. He decided that France was losing its way and better opportunities were "out there" somewhere. He chose Canada because Quebec was French-speaking and the way of life would better suit him, rather than the other options of America or Australia.

He established a small vineyard, growing cool climate wines from grapes such as Labrusca and V. Riparia. He worked hard and after ten years started to turn a healthy profit. He expanded the vineyard and introduced other grape varieties. By 1900, he had built a beautiful home on the property he called Chateau Bellepoire where he had a work force of more than fifteen.

In 1901 the temperance movement won their battle and prohibition was introduced to Canada. That was the end of Henri's business, as he knew it. Rather than roll over and die, Henri continued to press grapes for grape juice and to supply grapes for dried fruit production. He also started to press apples for apple juice and by 1920, his business, although not as profitable as wine production, was making a reasonable profit. He was able to keep the property and the big house on the hill.

Henri married his sweetheart, Antoinette, in 1890 and they had three children, two boys and a girl. The first-born was Nicholas, the second was Antoine and the third child was Anne.

The children worked on the property part-time while they were at school, Nicholas was keen to take over the business when his father retired: young Antoine was always the rebel and had no interest in the business. His sister, Anne, had always wanted to be a schoolteacher and that was the direction she was taking. She married another schoolteacher, Jacques, who subsequently enlisted in November 1916 and was sent to France to fight Britain's war. He never discovered that he had become a father, as his daughter, Marie, was born after he died.

Philippe invited a cousin to come and stay for a week of skiing. She had been researching the family history and showed Philippe the family tree she had developed using Ancestry.com Her name was Marie and her father had also enlisted and gone to war at the same time as Antoine, his brother in-law. Philippe was vaguely aware that he had a great uncle who had served in the First World War, but did not know the details. He learned that Antoine was ostracised from the family for daring to fight for Britain and its King and that he had been killed.

Philippe had no idea where or how. He decided to find out. He found the Back-Roads Touring Co's website and decided he would take the tour.

Antoine Bellepoire

In 1916 Antoine was twenty- one and looking for adventure. The war in Europe had been going for two years and Canada had been involved from the start. The war was unpopular in French Canada as most of the French Canadians didn't support Britain and were not too keen about supporting France either. As a result not many volunteers came from Antoine's neck of the woods.

This didn't stop him from enlisting despite his family's protests and on the 21st of March, 1916, he became Private Bellepoire. Antoine started his basic training immediately, at Val Cartier, Quebec and endured the hard slog for six weeks. He then boarded the *Andania* and sailed off to England.

After an initial four-week training period at Sling Camp, Britain, he, along with his Canadian brothers in arms, set foot on French soil for the first time.

He took part in and died in the Third Battle of Ypres along with four thousand of his countrymen. He died at Passchendaele, a hero.

# Not so Gay Paris - 1914

## Chapter 9

**by Edith Wharton**
**from her book Fighting France 1915**

Paris at the beginning of the Great War was not the Paris of fun and gaiety that it was prior to 1914. Edith Wharton captured the mood of Paris. As a highly successful author of considerable wealth, she decided to revisit her beloved Paris, knowing there was a war imminent. This is her account of life in Paris in 1914.

**Paris 1914**

It was sunset when we reached the gates of Paris. Under the heights of St. Cloud and Suresnes the reaches of the Seine trembled with the blue-pink lustre of an early Monet. The Bois lay about us in the stillness of a holiday evening, and the lawns of Bagatelle were as fresh as June. Below the Arc de Triomphe, the Champs Elysees sloped downward in a sun-powdered haze to the mist of fountains and the ethereal obelisk; and the currents of summer life ebbed and flowed with a normal beat under the trees of the radiating avenues. The great city, so made for peace and art and all humanist graces, seemed to lie by her river-side like a princess guarded by the watchful giant of the Eiffel Tower.

The next day the air was thundery with rumours. Nobody believed them, everybody repeated them. War ? Of course there couldn't be war! The Cabinets, like naughty children, were again dangling their feet over the edge; but the whole incalculable weight of things–as–they–were, of the daily necessary business of living, continued calmly and convincingly to assert itself against the bandying of diplomatic words. Paris went on steadily about her midsummer business of feeding, dressing, and amusing the great army of tourists who were the only invaders she had seen for nearly half a century.

All the while, every one knew that other work was going on also. The whole fabric of the country's seemingly undisturbed routine was threaded with noiseless invisible currents of preparation, the sense of them was in the calm air as the sense of changing weather is in the balminess of a perfect afternoon. Paris counted the minutes till the evening papers came.

They said little or nothing except what every one was already declaring all over the country. "We don't want war—mais il faut que cela finisse!" "This kind of thing has got to stop"; that was the only phrase one heard. If diplomacy could still arrest the war, so much the better: no one in France wanted it. All who spent the first days of August in Paris will testify to the agreement of feeling on that point. But if war had to come, then the country, and every heart in it, was ready.

At the dressmaker's, the next morning, the tired fitters were preparing to leave for their usual holiday. They looked pale and anxious — decidedly, there was a new weight of apprehension in the air. And in the rue Royale, at the corner of the Place de la Concorde, a few people had stopped to look at a little strip of white paper against the wall of the Ministere de la Marine. "General mobilization" they read—and an armed nation knows what that means. But the group about the paper was small and quiet. Passers-by read the notice and went on. There were no cheers, no gesticulations: the dramatic sense of the race had already told them that the event was too great to be dramatized. Like a monstrous landslide it had fallen across the path of an orderly laborious nation, disrupting its routine, annihilating its industries, rending families apart, and burying under a heap of senseless ruin the patiently and painfully wrought machinery of civilization...

That evening, in a restaurant of the rue Royale, we sat at a table in one of the open windows, abreast with the street, and saw the strange new crowds stream by. In an instant we were being shown what mobilization was — a huge break in the normal flow of traffic, like the sudden rupture of a dyke. The street was flooded by the torrent of people sweeping past us to the various railway stations. All were on foot, and carrying their luggage; for since dawn every cab and taxi and motor-omnibus had disappeared. The War Office had thrown out its drag-net and caught them all in. The crowd that passed our window was chiefly composed of conscripts, the mobilisables of the first day, who were on the way to the station accompanied by their families and friends; but among them were little clusters of bewildered tourists, labouring along with bags and bundles, and watching their luggage pushed before them on hand-carts — puzzled inarticulate waifs caught in the cross-tides racing to a maelstrom.

In the restaurant, the befrogged and red-coated band poured out patriotic music, and the intervals between the courses that so few waiters were left to serve were broken by the ever-recurring obligation to stand up for the Marseillaise, to stand up for God Save the King, to stand up for the Russian National Anthem, to stand up again for the Marseillaise. .

As the evening wore on and the crowd about our window thickened, the loiterers outside began to join in the war-songs.

'Allons, debout!"—and the loyal round begins again. "La chanson du depart!" is a frequent demand; and the chorus of spectators chimes in roundly. A sort of quiet humour was the note of the street. Down the rue Royale, toward the Madeleine, the bands of other restaurants were attracting other throngs, and martial refrains were strung along the Boulevard like its garlands of arc-lights. It was a night of singing and acclamations, not boisterous, but gallant and determined. It was Paris badauderie at its best.

Meanwhile, beyond the fringe of idlers the steady stream of conscripts still poured along. Wives and families trudged beside them, carrying all kinds of odd improvised bags and bundles. The impression disengaging itself from all this superficial confusion was that of a cheerful steadiness of spirit. The faces ceaselessly streaming by were serious but not sad; nor was there any air of bewilderment— the stare of driven cattle. All these lads and young men seemed to know what they were about and why they were about it. The youngest of them looked suddenly grown up and responsible: they understood their stake in the job, and accepted it.

The next day the army of midsummer travel was immobilized to let the other army move. No more wild rushes to the station, no more bribing of concierges, vain quests for invisible cabs, haggard hours of waiting in the queue at Cook's. No train stirred except to carry soldiers, and the civilians who had not bribed and jammed their way into a cranny of the thronged carriages leaving the first night could only creep back through the hot streets to their hotels and wait. Back they went, disappointed yet half-relieved, to the resounding emptiness of porterless halls, waiterless restaurants, motionless lifts: to the queer disjointed life of fashionable hotels suddenly reduced to the intimacies and make-shift of a Latin Quarter pension. Meanwhile it was strange to watch the gradual paralysis of the city. As the motors, taxis, cabs and vans had vanished from the streets, so the lively little steamers had left the Seine. The canal-boats too were gone, or lay motionless: loading and unloading had ceased. Every great architectural opening framed an emptiness; all the endless avenues stretched away to desert distances. In the parks and gardens no one raked the paths or trimmed the borders. The fountains slept in their basins, the worried sparrows fluttered unfed, and vague dogs, shaken out of their daily habits, roamed unquietly, looking for familiar eyes. Paris, so intensely conscious yet so strangely entranced, seemed to have had curare injected into all her veins.

The next day—the 2nd of August— from the terrace of the Hotel de Crillon one looked down on a first faint stir of returning life. Now and then a taxi-cab or a private motor crossed the Place de la Concorde, carrying soldiers to the stations. Other conscripts, in detachments, tramped by on foot with bags and banners. One detachment stopped before the black-veiled statue of Strasbourg and laid a garland at her feet. In ordinary times this demonstration would at once have attracted a crowd; but at the very moment when it might have been expected to provoke a patriotic outburst it excited no more attention than if one of the soldiers had turned aside to give a penny to a beggar. The people crossing the square did not even stop to look.

The meaning of this apparent indifference was obvious. When an armed nation mobilizes, everybody is busy, and busy in a definite and pressing way. It is not only the fighters that mobilize: those who stay behind must do the same. For each French household, for each individual man or woman in France, war means a complete reorganization of life.

The detachment of conscripts, unnoticed, paid their tribute to the Cause and passed on.

All wheeled traffic had ceased, except that of the rare taxi-cabs impressed to carry conscripts to the stations; and the middle of the Boulevards was as thronged with foot-passengers as an Italian market-place on a Sunday morning. The vast tide swayed up and down at a slow pace, breaking now and then to make room for one of the volunteer "legions" which were forming at every corner: Italian, Roumanian, South American, North American, each headed by its national flag and hailed with cheering as it passed. But even the cheers were sober: Paris was not to be shaken out of her self- imposed serenity. One felt something nobly conscious and voluntary in the mood of this quiet multitude. Yet it was a mixed throng, made up of every class, from the scum of the Exterior Boulevards to the cream of the fashionable restaurants. These people, only two days ago, had been leading a thousand different lives, in indifference or in antagonism to each other, as alien as enemies across a frontier: now workers and idlers, thieves, beggars, saints, poets, drabs and sharpers, genuine people and showy shams, were all bumping up against each other in an instinctive community of emotion. The "people," luckily, predominated; the faces of workers look best in such a crowd, and there were thousands of them, each illuminated and singled out by its magnesium-flash of passion.

I remember especially the steady-browed faces of the women; and also the small but significant fact that every one of them had remembered to bring her dog. The biggest of these amiable companions had to take their chance of seeing what they could through the forest of human legs; but every one that was portable was snugly lodged in the bend of an elbow, and from this safe perch scores and scores of small serious muzzles, blunt or sharp, smooth or woolly, brown or grey or white or black or brindled, looked out on the scene with the quiet awareness of the Paris dog. It was certainly a good sign that they had not been forgotten that night.

DES PATROUILLES DE SOLDATS CIRCULENT DANS PARIS POUR MAINTENIR L'ORDRE

Pendant la guerre, les Parisiens seront bien gardés et l'ordre régnera dans la capitale. Depuis le lundi 3 août l'état de siège a été déclaré; des patrouilles d'infanterie et de gardes républicains circulent dans les rues, empêchant désormais toute manifestation de quel-que côté qu'elle vienne. Les rares tramways et le métro qui assurent encore le transport des voyageurs s'arrêtent à huit heures du soir et les cafés doivent être fermés à la même heure. Les soldats restent maîtres des rues; les Parisiens peuvent dormir tranquilles.

From the French magazine 'Le Miroir' – French soldiers in the streets of Paris

We had been shown, impressively, what it was to live through a mobilization; now we were to learn that mobilization is only one of the concomitants of martial law, and that martial law is not comfortable to live under—at least till one gets used to it.

At first its main purpose, to the neutral civilian, seemed certainly to be the wayward pleasure of complicating his life; and in that line it excelled in the last refinements of ingenuity. Instructions began to shower on us after the lull of the first days' instructions as to what to do, and what not to do, in order to make our presence tolerable and our persons secure. In the first place, foreigners could not remain in France without satisfying the authorities as to their nationality and antecedents; and to do this necessitated repeated ineffective visits to chanceries, consulates and police stations, each too densely thronged with flustered applicants to permit the entrance of one more. Between these vain pilgrimages, the traveller impatient to leave had to toil on foot to distant railway stations, from which he returned baffled by vague answers and disheartened by the declaration that tickets, when achievable, must also be vises by the police. There was a moment when it seemed that one's inmost thoughts had to have that unobtainable visa — to obtain which, more fruitless hours must be lived on grimy stairways between perspiring layers of fellow-aliens.

Meanwhile one's money was probably running short, and one must cable or telegraph for more. Ah — but cables and telegrams must be vises too—and even when they were, one got no guarantee that they would be sent! Then one could not use code addresses, and the ridiculous number of words contained in a New York address seemed to multiply as the francs in one's pockets diminished. And when the cable was finally despatched it was either lost on the way, or reached its destination only to call forth, after anxious days, the disheartening response: "Impossible at present. Making every effort." It is fair to add that, tedious and even irritating as many of these transactions were, they were greatly eased by the sudden uniform good nature of the French functionary, who, for the first time, probably, in the long tradition of his line, broke through its fundamental rule and was kind.

Luckily, too, these incessant comings and goings involved much walking of the beautiful idle summer streets, which grew idler and more beautiful each day. Never had such blue-grey softness of afternoon brooded over Paris, such sunsets turned the heights of the Trocadero into Dido's Carthage, never, above all, so rich a moon ripened through such perfect evenings. The Seine itself had no small share in this mysterious increase of the city's beauty. Released from all traffic, its hurried ripples smoothed themselves into long silken reaches in which quays and monuments at last saw their unbroken images.

So, gradually, we fell into the habit of living under martial law. After the first days of flustered adjustment the personal inconveniences were so few that one felt almost ashamed of their not being more, of not being called on to contribute some greater sacrifice of comfort to the Cause. Within the first week over two thirds of the shops had closed — the greater number bearing on their shuttered windows the notice "Pour cause de mobilisation," which showed that the "patron" and staff were at the front. But enough remained open to satisfy every ordinary want, and the closing of the others served to prove how much one could do without. Provisions were as cheap and plentiful as ever, though for a while it was easier to buy food than to have it cooked. The restaurants were closing rapidly, and one often had to wander a long way for a meal, and wait a longer time to get it. A few hotels still carried on a halting life, galvanized by an occasional inrush of travel from Belgium and Germany; but most of them had closed or were being hastily transformed into hospitals.

The signs over these hotel doors first disturbed the dreaming harmony of Paris. In a night, as it seemed, the whole city was hung with Red Crosses. Every other building showed the red and white band across its front, with "Ouvroir" or "Hopital" beneath; there was something sinister in these preparations for horrors in which one could not yet believe, in the making of bandages for limbs yet sound and whole, the spreading of pillows for heads yet carried high. But insist as they would on the woe to come, these warning signs did not deeply stir the trance of Paris. The first days of the war were full of a kind of unrealising confidence, not boastful or fatuous, yet as different as possible from the clear-headed tenacity of purpose that the experience of the next few months was to develop. It is hard to evoke, without seeming to exaggerate it, that mood of early August: the assurance, the balance, the kind of smiling fatalism with which Paris moved to her task. It is not impossible that the beauty of the season and the silence of the city may have helped to produce this mood. War, the shrieking fury, had announced herself by a great wave of stillness. Never was desert hush more complete: the silence of a street is always so much deeper than the silence of wood or field.

The heaviness of the August air intensified this impression of suspended life. The days were dumb enough; but at night the hush became acute. In the quarter I inhabit, always deserted in summer, the shuttered streets were mute as catacombs, and the faintest pin-prick of noise seemed to tear a rent in a black pall of silence. I could hear the tired tap of a lame hoof half a mile away, and the tread of the policeman guarding the Embassy across the street beat against the pavement like a series of detonations. Even the variegated noises of the city's waking-up had ceased. If any sweepers, scavengers or rag-pickers still plied their trades they did it as secretly as ghosts. I remember one morning being roused out of a deep sleep by a sudden explosion of noise in my room. I sat up with a start, and found I had been waked by a low-voiced exchange of "Bonjours" in the street. . .

Another fact that kept the reality of war from Paris was the curious absence of troops in the streets. After the first rush of conscripts hurrying to their military bases it might have been imagined that the reign of peace had set in. While smaller cities were swarming with soldiers no glitter of arms was reflected in the empty avenues of the capital, no military music sounded through them. Paris scorned all show of war, and fed the patriotism of her children on the mere sight of her beauty. It was enough.

I remember the morning when our butcher's boy brought the news that the first German flag had been hung out on the balcony of the Ministry of War. Now, I thought, the Latin will boil over! And I wanted to be there to see. I hurried down the quiet rue de Martignac, turned the corner of the Place Sainte Clotilde, and came on an orderly crowd filling the street before the Ministry of War. The crowd was so orderly that the few pacific gestures of the police easily cleared a way for passing cabs, and for the military motors perpetually dashing up. It was composed of all classes, and there were many family groups, with little boys straddling their mothers' shoulders, or lifted up by the policemen when they were too heavy for their mothers. It is safe to say that there was hardly a man or woman of that crowd who had not a soldier at the front, and there before them hung the enemy's first flag—a splendid silk flag, white and black and crimson, and embroidered in gold. It was the flag of an Alsatian regiment — a regiment of Prussianized Alsace. It symbolized all they most abhorred in the whole abhorrent job that lay ahead of them; it symbolized also their finest ardour and their noblest hate, and the reason why, if every other reason failed, France could never lay down arms till the last of such flags was low.

That, in August, was the look of Paris.

UN AUTRE ASPECT DU DÉPART DEVANT LA GARE DE L'EST

Une musette à l'épaule, et dans un paquet le « jour de vivres » soigneusement préparé par la maman, l'épouse ou la sœur, les soldats de la réserve sont partis simplement, sans forfanterie, sans fanfaronnades, mais bravement, à la française. Beaucoup riaient et chantaient, d'autres s'attachaient seulement à dissimuler l'angoisse inévitable des séparations. Une foule immense les avait accompagnés pour leur témoigner sa sympathie et ses encouragements enthousiastes. Et cette multitude pleine de sang-froid était très belle.

From a French magazine 'Le Miroir' – conscripts leaving at the Gare de l'Est Train Station

## FEBRUARY 1915

February dusk on the Seine.

The boats are plying again, but they stop at nightfall, and the river is inky-smooth, with the same long weed-like reflections as in August. Only the reflections are fewer and paler: bright lights are muffled everywhere. The line of the quays is scarcely discernible, and the heights of the Trocadero are lost in the blur of night, which presently effaces even the firm tower-tops of Notre-Dame. Down the damp pavements only a few street lamps throw their watery zigzags. The shops are shut, and the windows above them thickly curtained. The faces of the houses are all blind.

Such, after six months of war, are the nights of Paris; the days are less remarkable and less romantic.

Almost all the early flush and shiver of romance is gone; or so at least it seems to those who have watched the gradual revival of life. It may appear otherwise to observers from other countries, even from those involved in the war. After London, with all her theatres open, and her machinery of amusement almost unimpaired, Paris no doubt seems like a city on whom great issues weigh. But to those who lived through that first sunlit silent month the streets to-day show an almost normal activity. The vanishing of all the motorbuses, and of the huge lumbering commercial vans, leaves many a forgotten perspective open and reveals many a lost grace of architecture; but the taxi-cabs and private motors are almost as abundant as in peace-time, and the peril of pedestrianism is kept at its normal pitch by the incessant dashing to and fro of those unrivalled engines of destruction, the hospital and War Office motors. Many shops have reopened, a few theatres are tentatively producing patriotic drama or mixed programmes seasoned with sentiment and mirth, and the cinema again unrolls its eventful kilometres.

For a while, in September and October, the streets were made picturesque by the coming and going of English soldiery, and the aggressive flourish of British military motors. Then the fresh faces and smart uniforms disappeared, and now the nearest approach to "militarism" which Paris offers to the casual sight-seer is the occasional drilling of a handful of piou-pious on the muddy reaches of the Place des Invalides. But there is another army in Paris, Its first detachments came months ago, in the dark September days — lamentable rear-guard of the Allies' retreat on Paris. Since then its numbers have grown and grown, its dingy streams have percolated through all the currents of Paris life, so that wherever one goes, in every quarter and at every hour, among the busy confident strongly-stepping Parisians one sees these other people, dazed and slowly moving — men and women with sordid bundles on their backs, shuffling along hesitatingly in their tattered shoes, children dragging at their hands and tired out babies pressed against their shoulders: the great army of the Refugees.

Their faces are unmistakable and unforgettable. No one who has ever caught that stare of dumb bewilderment — or that other look of concentrated horror, full of the reflection of flames and ruins — can shake off the obsession of the Refugees. The look in their eyes is part of the look of Paris. It is the dark shadow on the brightness of the face she turns to the enemy. These poor people cannot look across the borders to eventual triumph. They belong mostly to a class whose knowledge of the world's affairs is measured by the shadow of their village steeple. They are no more curious of the laws of causation than the thousands overwhelmed at Avezzano. They were ploughing and sowing, spinning and weaving and minding their business, when suddenly a great darkness full of fire and blood came down on them. And now they are here, in a strange country, among unfamiliar faces and new ways, with nothing left to them in the world but the memory of burning homes and massacred children and young men dragged to slavery, of infants torn from their mothers, old men trampled by drunken heels and priests slain while they prayed beside the dying. These are the people who stand in hundreds every day outside the doors of the shelters improvised to rescue them, and who receive, in return for the loss of everything that makes life sweet, or intelligible, or at least endurable, a cot in a dormitory, a meal-ticket — and perhaps, on lucky days, a pair of shoes.

At a moment when real wants are reduced to a minimum, how else account for the congestion of the department store?

Even allowing for the immense, the perpetual buying of supplies for hospitals and work-rooms, the incessant stoking-up of the innumerable centres of charitable production, there is no explanation of the crowding of the other departments except the fact that woman, however valiant, however tried, however suffering and however self-denying, must eventually, in the long run, and at whatever cost to her pocket and her ideals, begin to shop again. She has renounced the theatre, she denies herself the tea-rooms, she goes apologetically and furtively (and economically) to concerts — but the swinging doors of the department stores suck her irresistibly into their quicksand of remnants and reductions.

No one, in this respect, would wish the look of Paris to be changed. It is a good sign to see the crowds pouring into the shops again, even though the sight is less interesting than that of the other crowds streaming daily — and on Sundays in immensely augmented numbers — across the Pont Alexandre III to the great court of the Invalides where the German trophies are displayed.

It is still true of Paris that she has not the air of a capital in arms. There are as few troops to be seen as ever, and but for the coming and going of the orderlies attached to the War Office and the Military Government, and the sprinkling of uniforms about the doors of barracks, there would be no sign of war in the streets — no sign, that is, except the presence of the wounded. It is only lately that they have begun to appear, for in the early months of the war they were not sent to Paris, and the splendidly appointed hospitals of the capital stood almost empty, while others, all over the country, were overcrowded. The motives for this disposal of the wounded have been much speculated upon and variously explained: one of its results may have been the maintaining in Paris of the extraordinary moral health which has given its tone to the whole country, and which is now sound and strong enough to face the sight of any misery.

And miseries enough it has to face. Day by day the limping figures grow more numerous on the pavement, the pale bandaged heads more frequent in passing carriages. In the stalls at the theatres and concerts there are many uniforms; and their wearers usually have to wait till the hall is emptied before they hobble out on a supporting arm. Most of them are very young, and it is the expression of their faces which I should like to picture and interpret as being the very essence of what I have called the look of Paris. They are grave, these young faces: one hears a great deal of the gaiety in the trenches, but the wounded are not gay. Neither are they sad, however. They are calm, meditative, strangely purified and matured. It is as though their great experience had purged them of pettiness, meanness and frivolity, burning them down to the bare bones of character, the fundamental substance of the soul, and shaping that substance into something so strong and finely tempered that for a long time to come

Paris will not care to wear any look unworthy of the look on their faces.

A French palisade.

Edith Wharton on the French lines, 1915

# Gay Paris 2012

## Chapter 10

**Paris, France 2012**

Things had certainly changed from Edith Wharton's time in Paris by the time Lois and Terry arrived on 18th of April 2012.

It was Terry's first time in Paris and he had been looking forward to discovering this great city with all its icons and monuments.

Lois had visited once before but was just as excited as her son.

They checked into the Hotel de Buci in the Saint-Germain-des-Pres district, they had chosen this area because of its proximity to the Latin Quarter, as well as the Palais de Luxembourg, Notre Dame Cathedral and the Louvre.

The two travellers had planned to have breakfast at Le Mouffetard, which had been recommended to them by friends back in Melbourne. It was decided to take a walk down Rue Mouffetard and experience the small shops and the cobbled streets of the Latin Quarter.

They then strolled to the Pantheon, a magnificent building built by Louis XV in 1757. Everywhere they walked they observed magnificent architecture.

The next stop was the Sorbonne; Robert de Sorbonne founded the college in 1253AD for theology students without money. 'Nothing much has changed!'

Luxembourg Gardens was next on their list, described as a 60-acre park known for its extraordinary public amenities, including fountains, sculptures, ponds, flowerbeds, tennis courts, pony rides and open-air cafes. The foot weary discoverers took a rest before taking off again on their Paris exploration. It was lunch- time and they wandered down to Le Balzac a very well know café near the gardens.

'Well, Mum, Paris has certainly lived up to my expectations so far.'

Lois smiled, 'You have only experienced a very small part of what Paris has to offer.'

They finished their lunch and headed to Notre Dame Cathedral, a kilometre away.

As they approached the cathedral Terry looked up at the twin towers 'That has to be the quintessential structure in Paris: forget the Eifel Tower,' he thought.

Lois and Terry were overwhelmed with the beauty of the interior and exterior of the cathedral. Lois, being a devout Catholic, was more entranced by her second visit than the first some years ago.


Now he really knew he was in Paris. There were hundreds of people milling around, including the Gypsies whose reputation for scams and stealing was well known.

The sheer size and majesty of the cathedral lit by enormous, yet intricate, stained glass windows made for a Divine atmosphere.

The final attraction they intended to visit was the Eiffel Tower; they decided to hail a taxi, as it was too far to walk. The tower could be seen from kilometres away, the iconic symbol of French ingenuity and engineering.

The lift took them to the top where they marvelled at the view. Once down at street level they refrained from buying any of the trinkets from the street hawkers; instead, they caught a taxi back to the Hotel de Buci.

Once showered and changed, they were ready to embark on the much-anticipated night in Paris, the city of lights. The'Seine River Cruise' beckoned.

They were taken aback with the beauty of the city at night, with the buildings along the Seine illuminated, as were Paris's famous bridges. Notre Dame looked surreal, even more majestic at night.

After the tour, they were driven by bus to the Chez Clement restaurant, passing many of Paris's beautiful and historic buildings including The Louvre. They enjoyed their dinner while overlooking the Arc de Triomphe on the Champs-Elysees.

'Now this is what I call living,' said Terry.

The next day they had decided to take a one-day tour to Versailles. The bus picked them up at nine the next morning and drove to the magnificent Versailles. Terry and Lois were amazed at the beauty and the opulence of Versailles and how the French Royal families had lived. One could understand why the French Revolution occurred. As they walked through the beautifully sculpted gardens admiring the magnificent fountains, they both agreed that Paris, and all it offered, was unmatched. They returned to the Hotel de Buci and decided to cancel going out to dinner and the Moulin Rouge as they were absolutely exhausted. The fact that they needed to be at Gare Du Nord at 9am to catch the train helped determine their decision. They also wanted time in Lille to explore the old district of the city.

Gare Du Nord was the same station where the French soldiers had departed to meet their fate in 1914.

# Tour de France

## Chapter 11

**21st April 2012**

The twelve battlefield tourists were to meet Brad in the city of Lille on 21st of April 2012. Brad had organised rooms at a beautiful hotel called L'Hermitage Gantois Hotel located at 224 Rue de Paris.

Grant was the first to check in; the porter showed him his room; he was more than impressed. He dropped his small suitcase on the bed and opened it up. He was concerned that the baggage handlers on the train were a little rough and it contained his iPad and Nikon camera. He had purchased the D 700 the week before he'd left for France and the $5,000 price tag was at the very upper limit of his budget.

Once he reassured himself that all was O.K. and after taking various shots of the luxurious room, he decided to explore Lille. Grant walked from the hotel and headed for the old section of Lille. He had done some research before leaving Christchurch. He had discovered that Lille had been occupied in 2000 BC but the main occupation had been around 1066 AD. He also discovered that the name Lille came from "the Island" as the area was once very marshy. Grant wandered around the town taking photos of the various old buildings including the Opera House. He sat down and had a coffee in one of the many cafes dotted around the old town and reflected on why he'd made the trip and what he might discover about his Great Uncle Athol. The instructions received from the tour company stated that all participants were to meet in the hotel dining room at 7 pm on 21st April, which was a Saturday night. Grant decided to return to the hotel room and have a rest before dinner. It didn't take long before he was snoring; he woke and looked at the hotel clock beside the bed: it was 6.30 pm. He jumped out of bed, showered, shaved and entered the dining room at 7 pm precisely.

He looked around the lavish dining room for a large table reserved for the tour. He spotted what seemed to be the right table at the far end next to a large gothic window overlooking the illuminated Cathedral.

There was only one person sitting at the table, a grey balding gentleman who looked very distinguished. Grant guessed his age as middle sixties.

'Good Evening,' said Grant.

'Good Evening.'

'My name is Grant McKenzie. I take it that this is the Battlefield Tour table?'

'Yes, that is correct; my name is George, George Abbey.'

'Do you mind if I sit next to you, George? After all, it would be a bit silly sitting down the other end wouldn't it?'

'Yes I suppose it would, Grant. It is Grant isn't it? I am terrible with remembering names; it used to cause me all sorts of grief in the bank.'

'Oh, so you are a banker?' said Grant with some cynicism in his voice.

'Yes, I was with the CBA for forty five years.'

'I take it you are retired then?'

'Yes, I retired three months ago, hence being able to take this battlefield tour.

'How about you, Grant, what do you do?'

'I am an Apple store owner.'

'Are you? Do you only sell apples? Surely you sell other fruit as well?'

Grant laughed. 'George, I sell Apple computers'

'Oh! I feel pretty stupid, I thought New Zealand, apples, you know...'

'Don't worry, an easy mistake,' said Grant still with a hint of amusement in his voice.

'Are you doing the tour for interest's sake or did you have a relative who died over here during World War One?'

'My Grandfather died at Le Quesnoy,' Grant said with a much more serious tone in his voice.

'How about you, George?'

'My great Uncle died in the Battle of Fromelles not far from where we sit now.'

'Was he one of the Australian Diggers they identified in the mass grave at Pheasant's Wood, George?'

'I am afraid not; he's one of the many who have never been found. No grave, just a name etched in stone at VC Corner.'


They both looked up, as a very handsome couple sat down opposite them.

'Hello I am Christine Abbott and this is my husband, Tony Hailes.'

The two men introduced themselves.

Grant and George asked the same questions of Christine and Tony and discovered they were from Sydney. Both were doctors and they were on the tour because Christine's great uncle, David, had been killed in the Battle of Fromelles and was one of the missing. Christine and her cousin, Ian, had completed the DNA test to ascertain if he had been one of the Diggers identified at Pheasant Wood. Unfortunately he was not identified and remains missing under the fields of Fromelles.

Over the next twenty minutes all the tour participants arrived and introduced one another.

The only person who had not arrived was Brad Jones, the tour group leader; the group was starting to worry when it was 7.45pm and still no Brad.

Then a very good looking and debonair gentleman walked up to the group's table.

'Hello everybody. As you are no doubt aware from the photo in the brochure, I am not Brad Jones, I am Edwin Bean. Please call me 'Ed'. Brad sends his apologies but his mother died two days ago and as you can all imagine, he is not only deeply distressed but has to make all the funeral arrangements. Back-Roads Touring Co. has asked me to take his place. I am an Australian but have lived in France for many years therefore I speak fluent French. I am a military historian and specialise in the battles of the Western Front.

Does anybody have any questions?'

Christine was the first to speak:

'I take it that the itinerary we signed up for will remain the same, Ed?'

'Absolutely, there will be no changes to anything apart from your tour guide.'

Lois was the next person to speak:

'Ed, your last name, is it spelt the same way as the famous correspondent and military historian, Charles Bean?'

'It certainly is and for good reason. Charles Bean was my grand uncle.'

'Well you certainly have the right pedigree to lead this tour,' said Lois, obviously impressed.

'That's good. I would hate it if he had been related to the other Mr. Bean,' whispered Grant to George.

George chuckled into his napkin and whispered:

'Yes I was worried the tour guide's assistant was a little brown Teddy Bear.'

They were all asked to introduce themselves and state briefly why they had signed up for the tour and which battlefield, if any, was of particular interest.

They finished their meal chatting and laughing as any group of people would do in a good restaurant anywhere in the world. Ed then went over the next day's itinerary.

'As you know, our first day will be visiting Fromelles. The village is about an hour's bus trip from here and we are due  to leave Lille at 9am. We need to be down at reception by no    later than 8.45am.

Bring the information packs that you will find in your rooms and don't forget your cameras and video cameras.'

'How in hell could I forget the Nikon it cost me five grand,' Grant thought to himself.

'Just one other thing, in your information packs you will find a nametag. Could I ask you all to wear it tomorrow and every day of the tour? Makes it easier for you and me and ensures no body is left behind.'

They all left the table and made their way up to their rooms; it was going to be a big day tomorrow.


Lois and Terry went to their respective rooms and looked forward to a good night's sleep. About 3am, Terry woke to the sound of marching in the street below. He got out of bed and looked out the window and was astounded at what he saw. There were German soldiers matching in full uniform escorting Australian and British prisoners of war.

Quickly he dressed and took the hotel lift to the ground floor where he stepped outside onto the pavement. Looking both ways, he saw the street was deserted. There was a misty haze lingering over the cobblestone street.

'Where had they gone?' He couldn't just be seeing things; he saw the soldiers, he heard their boots on the cobbled street, he could see the faces of the Australian Diggers looking sad and defiant at the same time. Terry was totally mystified, and then he noticed a solitary figure, down the end of the street under an old street lamp. He walked towards the figure hoping that this person had also seen the marching troops. As Terry got closer, he realised he was dressed in the uniform of an Australian Digger, very young.

'Did you see the Germans march past here? Were you one of the Australian POWs?' Terry asked.

The soldier ignored the question, saying simply.

'I want you to find me.'

Terry looked at him bemused.

'What do you mean?'

'They found me once, but then they sent me back.'

'Who are you?'

'I am your Great Uncle Harry.'

Terry was gob-smacked.

'You can't be. My great uncle died at Fromelles in France over ninety-five years ago.'

He couldn't believe what he was seeing and hearing; he turned his head to look behind him to see if anybody else was there. He heard one more time:

'Just find me so I can be at peace.'

Terry turned back and no one was there. He ran down the street looking for the soldier but he'd completely vanished.

After some time pacing the street he went back to the hotel, caught the lift to his room on the third floor and tried to get back to sleep. He wasn't very successful but did manage to doze. When the alarm woke him at 6.30, he just lay there; he couldn't get out of his mind what had just happened to him.

*'Maybe it was a dream; of course it was a dream.*

*Best not mention it to Mum or anybody else in the group for now.*

'Why are you so grumpy?' Adam asked Ben. 'We're in France and are going to learn lots about the First World War.'

'I don't give a toss about the war. It was ages ago, nothing to do with me, mate. I don't fancy driving around in a mini bus with a whole lot of old people and some joker explaining the facts about a bloody war, for God's sake.'

'Well I think it is going to be interesting. I am sure it will be a great experience.'

'Bugger the experience, Adam, I just want to be home.'


Christine and Tony entered their two-bedroom apartment and greeted their boys who were watching an in-house movie, Avatar; they had both seen it before but had no problem seeing it again.

'Hi, guys, how's it going?'

'Good, Mum, how was the dinner?' Adam said cheerfully.

'It was good, nice food and interesting company.'

'That's good. What's Brad like?' asked Ben.

'Well, we didn't actually meet him,' said Tony.

'What do you mean, Dad?' asked Adam.

'Well, apparently Brad's mother died last week.'

'Oh, I am sorry to hear that,' said Adam.

'So who's taken his place?' asked Ben.

'A fellow called Edwin Bean,' replied Tony.

'I told you it would be some Joker. Mr Bean! Well that just about caps off this whole holiday,' snarled Ben.

'Mr Bean is taking us on the tour… that'll be fun' laughed Adam. 'I wonder if he has Teddy with him?'

Ben just looked at his younger brother and shook his head.

'Boys, Ed Bean is the grand nephew of Charles Bean. Have you ever heard of him?'

'No,' said Adam.

'Don't care,' said Ben.

'OK, let's look him up on Google,' said Christine, ignoring Ben's negativity.

Tony pulled out his laptop and connected to the hotel's WiFi.

He typed in Charles Bean and discovered over twenty pages of web sites.

'Wow', said Adam 'he must have been important.'

'He was, Adam, said Christine, 'let's pick the Australian War Memorial site.'

They all read the page devoted to Mr Charles Bean.

*Date of birth: 18 November 1879*

*Place of birth: Bathurst, NSW*

*Date of death: 30 August 1968*

*Place of death: Concord, NSW*

*Charles Bean is perhaps best remembered for the official histories of Australia in the First World War, of which he wrote six volumes and edited the remainder. Before this, however, he was Australia's official correspondent to the war. He was also the driving force behind the establishment of the Australian War Memorial. Bean was born on 18 November 1879 at Bathurst, New South Wales and his family moved to England when he was ten. He completed his education there, eventually studying classics and law at Oxford.*

*Bean returned to Australia in 1904 and was admitted to the New South Wales Bar. He travelled widely in New South Wales as a barrister's assistant and, struck by the outback way of life, wrote and illustrated a book, The impressions of a new chum. The book was never published but in mid-1907 much of its content appeared in a series of Sydney Morning Herald articles under the by-line 'CW'. In these articles Bean introduced a view of Australia, particularly its men, which foreshadowed much of what he would write about the AIF.*

*Having dabbled in journalism, Bean joined the Sydney Morning Herald as a junior reporter in January 1908. He published several books before being posted to London in 1910. In 1913 he returned to Sydney as the Herald's leader writer. When the First World War began, Bean won an Australian Journalists Association ballot and became official correspondent to the AIF. He accompanied the first convoy to Egypt, landed at Gallipoli on 25 April 1915 and began to make his name as a tireless, thorough and brave correspondent. He was wounded in August but remained on Gallipoli for most of the campaign, leaving just a few days before the last troops.*

*He then reported on the Australians on the Western Front where his admiration of the AIF crystallised into a desire to memorialise their sacrifice and achievements. In addition to his journalism, Bean filled hundreds of diaries and notebooks, all with a view to writing a history of the AIF when the war ended. In early 1919, he led a historical mission to Gallipoli before returning to Australia and beginning work on the official history series that would consume the next two decades of his life.*

*Along with his written work, Bean worked tirelessly on creating the Australian War Memorial in Canberra. He was present when the building opened on 11 November 1941 and became Chairman of the Memorial's board in 1952. He maintained a close association with the institution for the rest of his life.*

*During the Second World War, Bean liaised between the Chiefs of Staff and the press for the Department of Information. He became Chairman of the Commonwealth Archives Committee and was instrumental in creating the Commonwealth Archives. Between 1947 and 1958 he was Chairman of the Promotion Appeals Board of the Australian Broadcasting Commission and continued to write - a history of Australia's independent schools and finally a book on two senior AIF figures, Two men I knew.*

*Bean received a number of honorary degrees and declined a knighthood. He had married Ethel Young in 1921 and the couple adopted a daughter. Bean, one of the most admired Australians of his generation, died after a long illness in Concord Repatriation Hospital in 1968.*

Even Ben had to admit to himself that Bean's record was pretty impressive, for a dinosaur.

'Well as you can see, Ed has a wonderful family history,' said Christine.

'He said over dinner that he was a military historian with many years' experience and has lived in France for many years.'

'Why don't we Google him too?' said Adam.

'OK let's have a look,' said Tony. He typed in "Edwin Bean": nothing, not even one mention.

'That's strange,' said Christine, 'let's try Ed Bean.' Still nothing. They tried several variations, including Ed Bean, Military Historian and every search drew a blank.

'Well, I am sure there is a very logical explanation for his anonymity. I am just not sure what it could be,' said Tony.

'Maybe he doesn't exist at all. He might be a vampire.'

'Ben, shut up. If you don't want to be part of this conversation, go to bed… now!' his mother said.

Not long after Ben had slunk away, they all decided they should retire. It was going to be a big day ahead.

# From Here to Eternity

## Chapter 12

**22nd April 2012**

The next morning various people from the tour wandered down to the dining room to have breakfast. It was a Sunday and it was very busy with not only guests but the residents of Lille enjoying a Sunday breakfast at L'Hermitage.

Some tour participants enjoyed breakfast in their rooms.

Ed Bean was one of those who ate breakfast in his room thinking about the day ahead and going over his notes that he would reference when describing the Battle of Fromelles.

He went down to the foyer at 8.30 am to ensure he was there to greet his group on time. After being late the previous night, he didn't want to be late again.

At 8.45am the group had assembled, except for Stewart McDonald. When 9am had come and gone, Ed went to reception and asked the hotel receptionist to call his room. There was no answer. He decided he would wait until 9.15 a.m. and if Stewart hadn't turned up by then, they would have to leave without him. He asked the rest of the group to board the bus, a Mercedes Benz fourteen seater, and explained the situation to them.

Just as they were about to leave, a taxi pulled up and Stewart got out and ran to the bus.

'Stewart where have you been? We were just about to leave without you.' Ed had a certain amount of aggravation in his voice.

'I am so sorry, Ed, but I have been in hospital all night and I had real trouble convincing the doctor and nursing staff to let me check out early.'

'Well, board the bus and you can tell me what happened.'

Stewart boarded and apologised to all the other tour participants for holding them up. They noticed that Stewart had a bandage across his forehead.

'What happened to your head, mate?' asked Ian Wooley.

Stewart looked at Ed.

'I might as well tell everybody at once. Ed, can I use the microphone?'

'Sure, go ahead.' said Ed.

Stewart sat on the most forward seat as the Mercedes pulled away from the hotel car park and spoke into the microphone.

'I am sorry I kept you all waiting. It certainly wasn't my intention. I spent the night in the Lille General Hospital. Let me explain. After dinner last night I decided to go for a walk before going to bed. As I was walking; I felt a presence behind me, although I couldn't hear any footsteps. I looked around and before I knew it, I had been struck on the head, hence the bandage. The next thing I remember, I was lying in a hospital bed with a Doctor examining me. I had a whopping headache but after the appropriate medication, I could feel no pain. Anyway that is why I am late and in the same clothes I wore to dinner last night. They took my watch and my wallet so things will be a bit tight until I can get to a bank. At least they didn't take my mobile phone enabling me to cancel my credit cards etc.'

Ed thanked Stewart and offered any assistance the company could provide. They drove out of Lille and started to pass through some attractive countryside.

They arrived in the pretty town of Fromelles at 10.30 am. Lois and George commented on the number of village houses that were flying Australian, British and French flags; it was really quite moving.

Ed announced that they would first visit the Fromelles Cemetery.

The driver parked the Mercedes in a car park about one kilometre from the cemetery; they all disembarked and Ed addressed them.

'Welcome to Fromelles. As you are no doubt aware, not far from where you are all standing now, Australian troops had their first taste of battle on the Western Front along with their British Brothers in Arms.' Unfortunately it was a disaster for the Australian Diggers and the British Tommies. I will describe the battle and its prelude when we go to the actual battlefield.'

Fromelles Battle Field 1916

'We are going to walk through the village until we reach the Fromelles cemetery which was only established in 2010. I am going to give you the history of how this cemetery came to be. Some, or all of you, may know the story but I think it is worthwhile going over it again as it is in some ways the essence of the Battle of Fromelles'

A number of years ago I was made aware of research being carried out by an Australian of Greek descent, Lambis Englezos, into the possible location for a mass grave created by the Germans in the immediate aftermath of the Battle of Fromelles in July 1916.

The Divisional casualty return at the conclusion of the Battle of Fromelles at midday on the 20th of July 1916 totalled 5355 lost, of which 506 were known to be dead and a further 1700 missing

Lambis had already spent a number of years researching the matter and was convinced that not only could he place the mass grave but that it was almost certainly still there.

Both he and his research partner, Tim Whitford, visited the prospective area a number of times over the years and formed the opinion that a field to the side of what we know as Pheasant Wood was the place where up to 170 Australian Soldiers and perhaps twice as many British had been laid to rest in a number of pits.

The 6th Bavarian Reserve Division undertook the defence of Fromelles and their records confirmed that pits had been dug to take the hundreds of dead.

It has been a very long road for the group trying to motivate three governments to look into the matter but in early 2007, Dr Tony Pollard from Glasgow University came to Fromelles to carry out some preliminary probes.

Lambis had barriers thrown up by many Departments including Veteran Affairs, The Commonwealth War Graves Commission and the Defence Department. They all refused to believe there was a mass grave and therefore refused to investigate it.

The same Departments are throwing up the same barriers to 'Let Them RIP' to investigate those hundreds of thousands of soldiers missing in action of whom some are being uncovered by excavators, builders and farmers, then being buried again, once their discovery has been reported. Sorry, I digress.

Dr Pollard's initial findings, using a range of means but without actually digging into the field, revealed a lot of British and Australian battlefield debris plus enough evidence to suggest that, under the surface, the pits (which appear in period aerial photographs) were intact.

In May 2008 Dr Pollard and his team returned to Fromelles with the backing of the French, Australian and British governments to conduct an archaeological dig on the site.

After three weeks of searching, over thirty bodies had been discovered. The team worked on five of the eight pits and only a partial area of each. The discoveries would suggest that the remains of numerous more soldiers must lie here as well.

From an Australian perspective, the discovery of Australian Rising Sun collar badges in pit 4 was the first real proof that some of those bodies were indeed Australians.

A British matchbox and buttons were also found which tends to confirm the presence of British soldiers alongside the Australians.

Following a great deal of careful and intricate work, the recovery of the remains of 250 British and Australian soldiers has been completed at the original site in Fromelles.

The archaeological site has been levelled and grassed over.

Tests on the skeletons have shown that teeth, where available, seem to offer the best chances of gaining good specimens of DNA.

The old methods of identification — personal items etc were combined with the more modern methods but even with the enormous advances in our abilities to identify people, we are still capable of taking the trail only so far.

It has to be realised that to make an identification based on a DNA sample, it is necessary to have a living relative. Despite best efforts there are still going to be numerous graves marked simply — "A Soldier Of The Great War".

On 17th March 2010, the Australian and British governments announced the results of the first Fromelles Joint Identification Board. After analysing all of the available evidence: historical, anthropological, DNA and artefacts, 75 soldiers had been identified by name.

The 75 identified all served with the Australian Army, with a further 128 soldiers also identified as having served with the Australian Army. Three British soldiers were confirmed to be among the 250, leaving 44 soldiers currently unknown.

A second Joint Identification Board took place in May 2010 to consider samples that were not available for the March board. A further nineteen soldiers, all Australian, were identified. Further Boards will take place yearly from 2011 until 2014 to analyse any new evidence that may be presented.

The small plaque placed next to the original Pheasant Wood burial site has been moved. It is obviously still possible to walk down the pathway to visit the emplacement which we will do after we leave the cemetery.

At 1100 hours on 30 January 2010, the ceremony to re-bury the first of the two hundred and fifty Australian and British soldiers recovered from Pheasant Wood took place at this cemetery.

Steve whispered to Grant 'That's military talk.'

Re-burials continued until Friday the 19th February when the 249th soldier was laid to rest with full military honours.

The Joint Identification Board reconvened in London on 4th April 2011 as part of the continuing effort to identify some of the remaining one hundred and fifty four unknown soldiers. As a result, a further 14 Australian soldiers have been identified.

This means that not a single British soldier has been identified. I can't help but wonder if this is because Australians are more conscious of their family's involvement in the battle and have been quicker to come forward with DNA samples.'

Stewart grimaced; even though his Great Grandfather had died at Passchendaele in Belgium, he still felt embarrassed that his countrymen had been so apathetic to the Battle of Fromelles and not given DNA.

'The fourteen new headstones you can see on your left were dedicated at a special ceremony commemorating the 95th Anniversary of Fromelles on 19th July 2011.'

Ed had not read this account from notes as he knew the facts and related them to the group.

'Has anybody here got a relative buried in the cemetery?'

'Yes, Ed,' replied Lois, 'my uncle Harry may be here but he is one of the unidentified Diggers, although, from the research I have done, it is unlikely. Uncle Harry was in the 59th Battalion and this was one of the first Battalions to go over the top. This would indicate that Uncle Harry would have been killed in the first fifteen minutes of the battle'.

'Lois, did you give a DNA sample?'

'Yes I did, along with several other relatives but to no avail.'

Ed asked if anybody else had a relative who took part in the Battle.

'Yes,' replied George, 'but like Lois, my uncle Jack has not been identified.'

Finally Christine Abbott spoke.

'I have a Great Uncle David who also died at the age of twenty-two. He was in the 53rd Battalion. I have recently given a DNA sample, as have my mother and sister. I have not heard yet whether Uncle David is one of the identified, and I suppose I won't, until the Joint Identification Board meets again next year.'

Ed encouraged the group to walk amongst the head stones and show their respect.

George walked up and down the rows of tombstones, reading the names and their epitaphs; he passed a tombstone of an unknown soldier, one of the one hundred and thirty soldiers unidentified. He stopped in front of the grave and felt an amazing affinity with the soldier who was buried there. He walked on but after a little while felt compelled to return to the grave. He stood there for some time and said a prayer asking God to help identify this soldier. Eventually he moved on but the feeling of closeness did not leave him. George had actually found Jack, his uncle, but he would never know it.

Once they boarded the bus, they all seemed unusually quiet. Terry quietly asked Lois, 'Did you feel a little uneasy at the cemetery, Mum?'

'What do you mean, Terry?'

'I don't know... the atmosphere, or a feeling of spirits present. I'm not sure.'

'Well let's talk about it when we get back to the hotel and we can speak openly'

'OK Mum.'

Ed had noticed the mood of the group had changed but he was not surprised: he knew that the cemetery would have this effect.

'We are just going to travel a kilometre through the village and stop at Pheasant Wood to view the site where the mass graves were discovered.'

When they stopped and disembarked from the bus they were looking at a wheat field with a line of trees bordering the perimeter.

Ed addressed the group.

'You are looking at the hallowed ground where two hundred and fifty brave soldiers were buried by the German Army in July 1916. These soldiers were not given a military burial, the Last Post was not played and they had no loved ones to stand over their grave and weep. It is only now that some of these soldiers have been identified and their souls will be at peace.

How many lost souls are still buried under the fields of Fromelles is unknown but we must all ensure that they rest in peace and not be dug up or ploughed up and covered over again because it is too much trouble to report these finds to the authorities.'

George had a tear in his eye. He felt the aura of Pheasant Wood and looked out over the serene fields and wondered where his Uncle John was lying and prayed that he was at least safe and undisturbed for eternity.

Landscape of the band line 1916 · Photographer unknown

| Fromelles 2010 | Fromelles 1916 |

The same thoughts were going through Lois and Terry's minds, Christine's also; Tony and the boys were also talking amongst themselves about Uncle David. Christine had only recently discovered her Great Uncle was here, but she now felt like she was on a road to discovery. She was.

The Opening of the Fromelles Cemetery 2010

Ed approached every person in the group and asked them to board the bus when they were ready; he understood that they all were feeling very emotional and did not want to hurry them up although there was a timetable they needed to keep to and they were already thirty minutes behind because of the late start.

Ed took the microphone and announced that the next stop was VC Corner and then on to The Australian Memorial Park. This is where the Battle of Fromelles took place.

V.C. Corner is just a few kilometres from Fromelles village.

The cemetery has no headstones, however, recorded on the screen walls are the names of 1,299 Australians who died in the Battle of Fromelles in July 1916 and have no known grave. The unidentified bodies of 410 of them are buried under the lawn.

Ed knew this was going to be another emotional moment for Lois and Terry, George and Christine and her family. They were going to see their descendants' names etched in stone on the monument. The bus parked in the car park and they all disembarked. Ed spoke to them as a group.

'We have thirty minutes here to reflect on where you are. This point is where the German lines crossed the road. This is where so many men lost their lives. I will leave you with the words of my great-uncle:

"We found the old No-Man's-Land simply full of our dead," he recorded. "The skulls and bones and torn uniforms were lying about everywhere."

Shortly after the war, the remains were gathered to construct this Cemetery. I will see you back at the bus at 2.30pm. We will gather there before walking to the Australian Memorial Park.'

Ed was right: it was an emotional moment for the group who had lost their relatives at the Battle of Fromelles.

Lois in particular was upset that Harry, her mother's brother, a brother she had never met, had died at the tender age of seventeen and his name was now engraved on the wall in front of her. The likelihood of Harry ever getting a proper burial and a headstone was extremely remote.

George and Christine were also moved but not to the same extent as Lois. They collected their thoughts and went back to the meeting point in the car park. Ed was there to greet them.

'I hope all of you got something from VC Corner. It is a sad reminder of what happened here on the 19th of July 1916.'

They agreed and waited on Ed's instructions.

'OK we are going to walk down this path which will take us to The Australian Memorial Park.'

They started off on the walk; Ben and Adam were walking behind their parents.

Adam tapped his older brother on the shoulder.

'Yes, mate, what is it?'

'Both at Pheasant Wood and just now, I got a very strange feeling.'

'What do you mean?'

'Well I can't really explain it. I felt like someone was standing behind me but there was no one there. I think it was a ghost.'

'Mate, it's your imagination; there is no such thing as ghosts. This place is just the same as any other bloody cemetery, holes in the ground with blokes buried that died a very long time ago for no good reason.'

'Yeah, I suppose you're right,' admitted Adam

The group reached the park's entrance.

'The Battle of Fromelles was a black day in Australia's wartime history and the British did not fare much better,' explained Ed.

'General Haig and General Haking, the two British Generals, were determined that this attack should take place. Brigadier General Elliot (Pompey), Australian Imperial Force, was totally against it.'

# Attack or not to Attack, That is the Question

## Chapter 13

| General Haig | General Haking | General McCay |

**Northern France 1916**

General McCay was sitting at his desk in his beautiful office located in a villa far from the trenches of the Western Front. He had just finished lunch, prepared by his French chef and was feeling a little drowsy.

A knock on the door aroused him.

'Enter,' he said.

An officer, Lieutenant Irvine, entered the General's office and passed him an envelope, which came from the British High Command. It was stamped "Top Secret". He asked the Lieutenant to stand at ease while he read the orders.

From: General Richard Haking Commander British Forces

To: General McCay Australian Commander AIF 5th Division

The Australian 5th Division will be required to take part in an offensive against the German 6th Bavarian Reserve Division

108

at Fromelles.

The British 61st Division will also be taking part.

Your objective is to attack the German lines and occupy their trenches.

Briefing will be at General Headquarters on the 2nd of July 1916

Signed

General Richard Haking

McCay was delighted he had been ordered to provide the Australian 5th Division to take part in an offensive to prevent the Germans moving their reserve troops to the Somme battlefront. He knew his troops would be delighted. They had been restless and itching for a fight with "The Boche".

His orders also requested he go to the Chateau where General Haig and General Haking were located to discuss the plan and stay overnight.

'Lieutenant Irvine, are you aware of these orders?' asked McCay.

'No, Sir, I am only the messenger.'

'Alright, well can you return to General Haig and inform him I will be there as ordered and could you ask him if there is anything I should bring in preparation for the meeting.'

'Yes, Sir.'

As the young Lieutenant departed, McCay's telephone rang: it was his second-in- command, Brigadier Bunting.

'Brigadier, it is quite opportune that you have rung.'

'Why is that, Sir?'

'We have just received our orders and it's all good news.'

'Should I come around Sir? It certainly sounds exciting.'

'Yes, straight away, if you please.'

'I am on my way, Sir.'

Brigadier Bunting knocked on General McCay's door before entering.

'At ease, Michael, take a seat. I am pleased to inform you that we have been given the honour of leading a very significant battle against the Germans.'

'Really, Sir, where?'

'Apparently at Fromelles, not that far from here. We are to halt the Germans from taking their reserve troops away from Fromelles and deploying them on the Somme front. I am leaving in the morning to meet with General Haig and General Haking to get a full briefing.'

'Well, Sir, this is what we have been waiting for. I am sure the men will be delighted to have a go at old "Fritz"

'I am sure they will do us all proud, Michael. Well that's all for now, I will see you upon my return.'

The Brigadier saluted and left McCay's office.

The next morning a staff car pulled up outside the villa for General McCay. He asked the driver, a young British private, to proceed to GHQ.

When he arrived, he was ushered into the main briefing room where a long mahogany table and fourteen matching chairs and two easels with butcher's paper were assembled.

There was also a large aerial map of the Fromelles area.

There was only one other person in the room, a Lieutenant Colonel attached to General Haking's staff. He introduced himself as Lieutenant Colonel Groves and suggested General McCay be seated, as the other attendees would be arriving shortly.

McCay had to wait only five minutes before General Haig and General Haking and an assortment of officers came into the room and took their seats.

General Haig began the meeting with a briefing of where they were regarding the Somme. He was quite encouraged with the progress and wanted to press home the advantage by diverting the Germans' attention away from that battle by launching an attack on Fromelles. He felt it could be an "artillery demonstration" that would really ruffle the feathers of the Germans.

'By launching this attack using both British and Australian troops, we can form a useful diversion and help the Somme operations,' he declared.

Some of the officers were nodding in approval while others were just sitting in silence.

General Haig then passed the baton over to General Haking.

'Gentlemen, we have a great opportunity to teach the Germans a bloody good lesson and, as General Haig intimated, a lesson on effective artillery bombardment.'

'The plan is to utilise the Australian 5th Division comprising about six thousand troops who have just arrived fresh, along with approximately three thousand seasoned British troops.

We will begin the offensive with three days of artillery bombardment, firing many thousands of shells into the German trenches. My belief is there will be very few Germans left to greet our troops.

We then attack the German trenches with rifle and bayonet and, as I said earlier, we expect very little resistance. I firmly believe we will achieve all our objectives by lunchtime. Our boys should be enjoying their lunch in the comfort of the German dugouts. Are there any questions?'

'Yes, I have one,' said Pompey Elliott, the commander of the 15th Brigade of the Australian Imperial Force.

'What is it, Pompey?' Haking asked gruffly.

'Well, Sir, with the utmost respect, this operation seems inadvisable for a host of reasons:

'How so?'

'I feel we are rushing into this conflict without proper time for planning and the preparations could well be inadequate. I also fear the artillery do not have the experience to achieve their objectives. Finally we have been given the task of taking "Sugarloaf" which is the German strongpoint and is bristling with machine guns that can fire from each side as well as ahead. On top of all that, No-Man's Land is about four hundred metres without any cover at all. This operation could be a bloodbath!'

Pompey was obviously very concerned.

Sugar Loaf

Pompey knew he was going out on a limb but his men's lives were worth it.

'Maybe you should not take part in this, Pompey. Maybe it is all a bit too much for your sensitive skin,' remarked Haking in a very sarcastic tone.

Pompey ignored the comment.

'Sir, I took the liberty of doing some reconnaissance yesterday so I could be prepared for this meeting.'

'Did you now? Well what did you find out?' asked General Haking.

'I asked Major Howard to accompany me; he too has serious doubts about the offensive.'

General Haig looked at his officer with a questioning stare. Major Howard acknowledged him with a nod.

Pompey described Major Howard's and his own experience.

'I saw Major Howard and told him of my concerns. I asked him if he was willing to crawl out into No-Man's land and see for himself. We were both aghast at the terrain and the tremendous risks facing the Australian and British troops.

We were horrified at the four hundred metres of totally exposed land that needed to be covered before we reached the German front line. That is why I am against this offensive or should I say, at the moment, until we are better prepared.'

General McCay interceded.

'I can assure you all that the Australian 5th Division will participate with enthusiasm and great bravery. I support General Haking's plan completely.

'With due respect, General, our troops have not yet settled into this environment,' Pompey emphasised.

'Of our assaulting battalions, the 60th has not yet been in the front line on the Western Front; the 32nd and 54th have been here for part of a day, and the 59th a little longer; the 31st and 53rd have been here all of two days. The Germans have been here eighteen months and used their time very effectively. Their fortifications are well planned and constructed and they have the high ground. We plan to send nine thousand troops across a barren and unprotected No-Man's Land with the German machine guns just waiting for them.'

'You underestimate the tenacity of our soldiers, Brigadier General. Our boys are busting for a fight and if we delay this offensive they will be devastated. I ask the Australians to show some fortitude and defeat this motley German army. Anyway I don't understand why you are so concerned by the width of No-Man's land; by the time the artillery does its deadly job there won't be too many Germans left to fire at your troops. If you like we can appoint a British officer to lead the colonials if you don't have the heart for it,' said General Haking in a condescending voice

'That's enough!' shouted General Haig.

'Pompey and any other officer present has a right to be heard without fear of ridicule,'said General Haig.' In fact, General Haking, I, too, have doubts about your plan.'

'What doubts, Sir?'

'Similar to Pompey's, having listened to his concerns.'

'How can I allay your fears, Sir? I know my plan will work and the Germans will be defeated.'

'You are absolutely sure you will succeed?'

'I am, Sir.'

General Plumer asked for the floor.

'Gentlemen, I believe this should not be regarded as simply a show of artillery strength, nor as a diversionary tactic. This action should be seen as a glorious victory for the Allies over the German army. We should be driving them back to where they once came from. I for one, support General Haking's plan.'

'Thank you, General. For whatever reason, we have to decide whether we launch this offensive. Ultimately it is my decision but I would like to see a show of hands for those in favour of the action.'

General Haig surveyed the room and it was abundantly clear that the majority were in favour.

'All right. I will approve this plan, but if it fails I will be holding you, and only you, General Haking, accountable. Is that clear?'

'Absolutely, Sir' said Haking in a strong and confident tone.

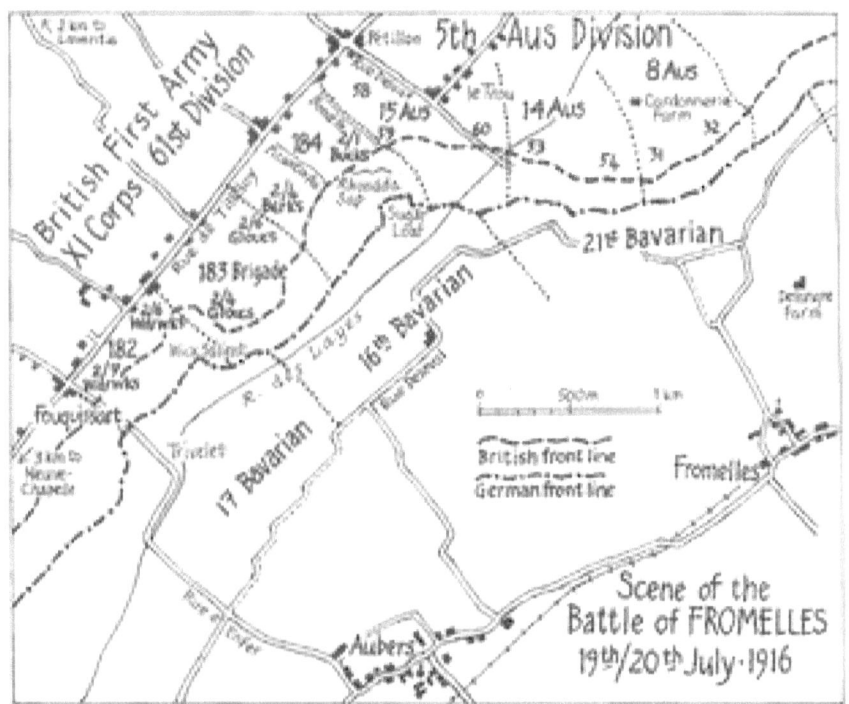

Waiting to Attack at Fromelles

Due to wet weather and other limitations, the artillery bombardment, originally scheduled for three days, was reduced to seven hours, and while intended to commence at 4 a.m. it finally began when the mist cleared at 11 o'clock in the morning of Wednesday, 19th July, with the infantry attack rescheduled to 6 p.m. instead of as originally planned for 11 a.m.

Pompey's fear of a blood bath was about to be vindicated.

The troops were not itching for a fight as Haking intimated. They knew the cards were well and truly stacked against them. They also knew many of them would lose their lives.

The allied bombardment was ineffectual. The Germans were able to begin shelling the Australian trenches by 2pm. They mercilessly shelled the communication trenches, reserve and support lines of both the British and Australian Divisions.

# We Will Fight Them in the Trenches

## Chapter 14

David Abbott

**Fromelles, Northern France 1916**

David Abbott was an Australian Digger. He was a bloody good soldier and quite fearless. When the Germans knocked out the communications, he volunteered to run back to the General

Headquarters with a message from Pompey informing Hacking that the bombardment was proving to be ineffective and that mounting a ground attack could mean a massacre of the Allied troops.

Pompey requested a delay on the assault.

'Who does he think he is? I knew we should have replaced him, the gutless bastard!' shouted Hacking to no one in particular.

He sent a hand written response to Pompey's request:

'Absolutely not, the assault will commence at the revised time of 6pm and we shall take the German line as planned.'

Haking gave the reply scribbled on a piece of paper to David Abbott to take back to the Australian commander.

Dave ran as fast as he could and arrived at Pompey's HQ one hour later. Pompey read the message screwed it up and threw it in the bin.

'He is a bloody madman – he'll kill us all,' thought Pompey.

General Haking distributed a letter to his officers who, in turn distributed the letter to the Platoon Commanders to be read to the troops just before the battle began.

*"Whilst our guns along the front of our real attack will be getting the exact range of the enemy's trenches without attracting undue notice When everything is ready, our guns, consisting of some 350 pieces of all descriptions, and our trench mortars, will commence an intense bombardment of the enemy's front system of trenches. After about half-an-hour's bombardment the guns will suddenly lengthen range, our infantry will show their bayonets over the parapet, and the enemy, thinking we are about to assault, will come out of his shelters and man his parapets. The guns will then shorten their range, and drive the enemy back into his shelters again. This will be repeated several times. Finally, when we have cut all the wire, destroyed all the enemy's machine-gun emplacements, knocked down most of his parapets, killed a large proportion of the enemy, and thoroughly frightened the remainder, our infantry will assault, capture, and hold the enemy's support line along the whole front. The objective will be strictly limited to the enemy's support trenches and no more."*

Pompey, as a senior officer, could show no cynicism in front of his troops but he knew Haking's plan was doomed and that he would lose many good men that day.

General Haking's Operations Centre

Diggers Operations Centre

It was 5 pm; the men had an hour before they were to go over the top, Pompey moved amongst them in the trenches, encouraging them and hoping to calm their nerves. They had a pretty good idea of what was to come.

Many of them were using this time to write letters home, others were smoking and chatting amongst themselves trying to steel themselves for the coming battle.

Dave went back to join his cobbers in the trench; he was in the 59th Battalion located very close to Sugar Loaf, their main objective.

'How did you go Davey? Enjoy your little stroll in the park?' joked his good mate, Sam Williams.

'Hardly a bloody stroll, Sam, I had to run flat out all the way to old man Haking's HQ and all the way back here. Mind you it was nice getting away from this fucking trench. Nice countryside too. I was tempted to stay.'

'You were not, you silly bastard. They shoot you for doing things like that.'

'Well, chances are Jerry is going to shoot me in the arse anyway,' joked Dave.

Just then they saw Pompey walking through their trench. He looked at Dave and thanked him for his speed and diligence in running the message to GHQ.

'Are you boys ready to give these Krauts a damn good flogging?' he asked.

'Yes, Sir,' they all responded.

'Well the shelling will cease very soon, so make sure you are well prepared. Check your rifles and fix your bayonets. Make sure you pull the pin on your hand grenades before you throw them.

'We will, Sir. Looking forward to giving the Germans a bloody good slap, Sir,' said the Major in charge of the platoon.

They heard the five-minute whistle and all wished each other luck.

Dave thought about his home in Sydney and his family, his mother and father and his younger brother, Jack. He wondered what they were doing now as he waited to go over the top, maybe for the last time. He had no idea what time it was in Sydney

He asked the bloke next to him, Dan Smith, but he didn't have a clue either.

'Never mind, I will find out when this tussle is over.'

He thought of Bondi beach and pictured the surf and the clear blue sea.

First Attack Wave, Fromelles 19th July 1916

The whistle sounded to go over the top. An officer was yelling encouragement to them all as he climbed the ladder with only a sabre in his hand.

He led from the front but only got as far as the top of the trench when he was shot through the eye and slumped back onto the ladder.

David climbed over the fallen officer and looked out across No-Man's Land; he knew that his chances were slim to make the four hundred metres to the German trenches but he was going to give it a bloody good try.

The smoke haze was thick from the artillery and the noise of shells exploding and machine guns firing was deafening. He could see his comrades being ripped apart by the relentless German machine guns. The air was thick with bullets hitting their targets and the smell of gunpowder was overwhelming.

Dave half crawled, half ran, towards the German line. He jumped in a shell hole for some protection.

He continued to hear the sounds of the battle; the screams of his mates as they were being hit were chilling.

The Germans were firing flares to illuminate their targets but with the heavy haze, it just made the battlefield even more surreal. Ghostly figures, some moving slowly, some running, some lying still no longer taking part in the battle, all this could be seen through the acrid mist.

He continued on over the endless hell they called No-Man's Land until he could see the German trenches. He lay there terrified but determined to succeed. Dave was flat out on the ground trying to avoid the barrage from the German machine guns. He raised himself up carrying his forty-pound backpack and ran.

Firing his rifle as he ran, he made it to the German trench. He jumped in and faced a German soldier. He thrust his bayonet into the German's stomach. He watched the German's eyes glaze over with a look of shock and pain; blood oozed from his mouth and he slumped to the bottom of the trench. This soldier – with a different uniform, a different language – possibly at another time and place, where they may have been friends, now lay dead on the bottom of the trench.

Dave turned to see another German with bayonet ready to thrust it into his chest. Dave reacted quickly thrusting his bayonet into the German; the enemy soldier reciprocated. They both stared at each, other and with a look of horror on their faces, both dropped to the floor of the trench, still connected by their weapons of war. This was how the two young men were discovered.

The Germans separated Dave from their own comrade and threw him on a wagon; he was then carried by light rail to a large burial pit at Pheasant Wood near the village of Fromelles. He was thrown in the pit along with another two hundred and forty nine Australian and British warriors, only to be recovered more than ninety years later. David Abbott is buried at the Fromelles cemetery with a headstone reading "Known only to God"

The German Soldier was Felix Rosenthal; he was taken behind the lines and eventually buried in the Fricourt German Military Cemetery with a headstone and a beautifully maintained grave.

Jack Abbey

Further down the line, crouched Jack Abbey, a Geordie from Northern Yorkshire who had emigrated to Australia a few years before and thought it would be an adventure to enlist and come over to France.

He had never been to France before and he was billeted to a French Family on a small farm not far from Fromelles where he had the opportunity to see a little of the country.

He had been looking forward to taking on the "bloody Germans" since he joined and this was his great chance to demonstrate his true worth.

Jack looked at his watch; it was 5.50pm. They had been told that the order to attack would be at 6pm. He was not a particularly religious man although he had been confirmed into the Church of England when he was a boy back home. Nevertheless he felt a desire to pray, asking that he would survive the battle but, if he did not, he felt a little better that his prayers may have been heard.

He also prayed for his family back in Yorkshire.

He heard the five-minute whistle and made sure everything was OK and that he had a bullet in the 303's chamber and a full magazine.

He turned to his good mate, Jim, and gave him a wink.

'We'll be right, Jimmie, you just stick with me.'

The whistle blew and they went over the top. He Jack ran as fast as he could straight for the German trenches. He could see Diggers falling all around him but maybe his prayer had been answered.

The noise was frightening and the German machineguns didn't stop spewing their deadly lead all over No-Man's Land. Blokes were being killed like flies.

His breath was short and rapid and he could feel his heart thumping in his chest, he had a cold sweat running down his back but he kept running.

Jack didn't see the German trenches until he was on them, as the haze from the battle made it near impossible to see two feet in front.

Jack made it into one of the German trenches along with some of his mates. Most of his cobbers were lying where they dropped in No-Man's Land.

The Troops Ready to go Over the Top

The Germans who had wreaked such death and despair had retreated back leaving their trenches to be occupied by the Australian and British fighters.

'Hey Jim can you believe these digs? Fritz had it bloody easy. I can't fucking believe it. He has been relaxing in these bloody concrete-reinforced bunkers; no wonder we couldn't kill the bastards with our bombardment. They were just having a nice cup of tea until we ran out of shells. They had lounge rooms better than most people at home, bloody sofas and gas stoves and a gramophone for God's sake!'

'Compare that to the squalor we had to put up with. Mud, water, rats and the constant stench of the overflowing bogs and on top of all of that, we could smell our mates as they were decomposing. Fuck that! I'm staying put, this is my new home.' said Jack stubbornly

'They reckon we have to move out soon,' said Jim in a forlorn voice.

'What the bloody hell for?' said Jack defiantly.

'I heard one of the Officers say we have to move on to the next German trench and take that bastard too.'

Just about then, a Corporal was moving among the men giving them the order to move out, but not to charge, just to take it slowly and stay alive.

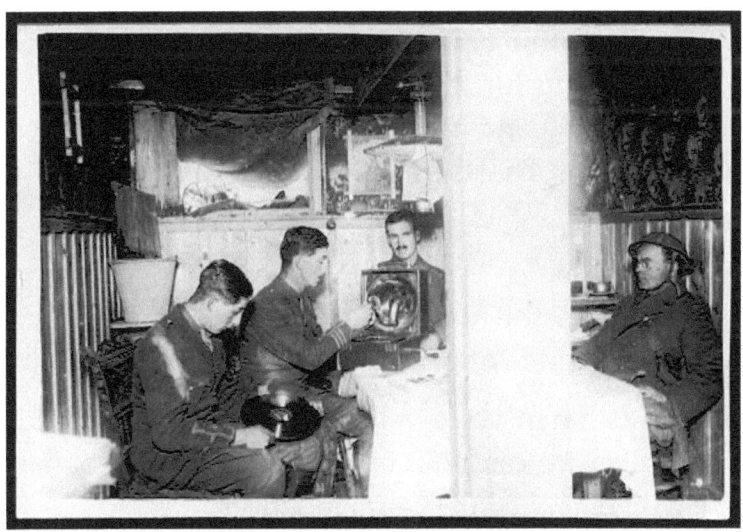

Captured German Dugout
Checking out Jerry's Record Collection

General Haking believed that the rear-most trench of the enemy's front system would probably be found at from 100 to 150 yards beyond the German front line and that the two allocated battalions of each brigade would suffice for an advance so limited.

The order was given and Jack and Jim went over the parapet reluctantly. When the remains of the division made it to the so-called German Trench, they found a ditch full of water, certainly not a second line of defence.

The Germans had worked out what had happed and opened fire, killing or taking prisoner all the Australian Diggers and British Tommies. They then moved back into their comfortable trenches and dugouts and waited for the next attack.

The attack never happened.

The allied troops, or what was left of them, withdrew to fight another day.

Jack and Jim were both slaughtered and buried at Pheasant Wood. They were both recovered and buried at Fromelles Cemetery but in unmarked graves.


It was now early morning. The men who had made it back to their own line were waiting for the call to attack again. They could hear their brothers moaning and calling for help but it would be suicide to try to retrieve them. The German machine guns would cut them down.

Major Thompson, an Australian officer who had led his men valiantly and had penetrated very close to the German Line, was lying on the wet cold ground taking advantage of a lull in the fighting.

He heard a German voice yell in good English, 'Do you want a one hour's truce so we can both bring our wounded soldiers back to safety?' 'We would!' yelled the German officer.

'Yes we would but I have to get approval from our high command,' Thompson yelled back.

'Can you allow me half an hour to get back safely and get the approval?'

'Yes, but be as quick as you can.'

Major Thompson ran across No-Man's Land on all fours to keep low. He made it back without incident and went straight to the communications officer only to find the lines had been knocked out of action by the German shelling.

McCay had moved his command post closer to their lines when the communications were disabled. McCay was now only seven hundred metres away from where Thompson stood. Thompson ran as fast as he could to Command and asked urgently to speak to McCay.

'Sir, the Germans have offered a one hour truce so that both sides can rescue their wounded. They are expecting an answer back within the next fifteen minutes.'

'Under no circumstances!' yelled McCay. 'They only want time to bring in more ammunition and reinforcements. We have Jerry on the back foot now and we will press on until they are defeated. We can gather our men when we take the ground, which should be by mid-morning tomorrow,' said a confident McCay.

'Yes Sir.'

Thompson knew he could not argue the point so he left and ran back to the front line.

He made his way back carefully to where he had spoken to his German counterpart.

'I am sorry but our Command has refused the truce.'

'I am very sorry to hear that,' exclaimed the German officer. 'Many more of our men and yours will die as a result. So be it. Go back to your position; we will not fire upon you,' said the German.

Major Thompson retreated back but did not go back to his trench. He heard a wounded soldier crying for help; he stopped and tried to ascertain how badly the soldier was hurt.

'Listen, soldier, I am going to put you on my back and we're going to get you back to the trench.'

'My God, this kid must be only sixteen,' Thomson thought, he can't be allowed to die so young.'

Thompson lifted him up and started to make his way back, when a shell burst ripped through both of them. They both departed this world, a world where this boy soldier without a name was too young to drink and had never known a woman. He was taught not to swear because to say 'fuck' was obscene yet what was truly obscene was this place of death where he was sinking into a putrid and vile pool of mud and despair. A world where those who did return home would not speak of it, as they knew their loved ones would not be able to comprehend the horrors they had endured. The cacophony of shell blasts and machine gun fire were at last silenced by this young boy's death.

A Shell Burst Killed Major Thompson and the Wounded Boy Soldier

# The Aftermath

## Chapter 15

More than 5,500 Australians became casualties in the single night of 19th–20th July. Almost 2,000 of them were killed in action or died of wounds and 470 were captured. This was perhaps the greatest loss by a single division in a 24-hour period during the entire war. Many consider Fromelles the most tragic event in Australia's history.

To the soldiers, the battle of Fromelles was an unmitigated military disaster, the dismal culmination of muddled planning and reckless decision-making by both Haig and Haking on the British side and McCay on the Australian side.

Haig went on to be promoted to Commander- in-Chief and conducted similar campaigns at Passchendaele and other battles.

Haking also continued on with the same tactics as at Fromelles. Both Haig and Haking commanded until the end of the war. When they returned to England, they were both branded with the term "butcher" and Haig was named as Britain's worst General ever.

'The nation must be taught to bear losses. No amount of skill on the part of the higher commanders, no training, however good, on the part of the officers and men, no superiority of arms and ammunition, however great, will enable victories to be won without the sacrifice of men's lives. The nation must be prepared to see heavy casualty lists.'

Written by Haig in June 1916 before the Battle of the Somme began.

# A Farmer's Dilemma

## Chapter 16

**Pozières, France 2012**

Jean-Claude Bouchard and his wife of twenty-five years, Sophie, have been farming since they were married. Jean-Claude, the first born son, inherited the farm from his parents, as had been the tradition in their family for the past three hundred years.

The farm is located just outside Pozières, in northern France, one of the most productive regions in the country; its main crop is wheat, which is 60% of the total farm production. The other 40% comprises potatoes and corn.

It is not easy being a farmer in modern France; there are enormous pressures for the farmers to secure their futures. Jean-Claude needed to find a way out of the tightening trap of falling prices and what the markets were willing to pay for his produce. He was also concerned about the EU's funding for French agriculture. The EU supports French farming at a greater level than any other European country. This funding was soon due to change quite dramatically and the emphasis would be on greener, more sustainable farming practices rather than traditional production volumes.

Jean-Claude and Sophie no longer had their two sons to help them on the farm. They both resided in Paris pursuing their careers in engineering and information technology respectively.

It was always a fear of Jean-Claude and Sophie that the 300-year farming tradition would end under their stewardship. They now knew that the farm had to be profitable and efficient because they would be forced to sell when they retired.

Jean-Claude was very concerned that this year had been a particularly wet spring and the ground was too moist to start ploughing at the normal time. It was the middle of September and if he didn't start ploughing soon his crop would be a poor one.

At last Jean-Claude felt he could start ploughing. It was the 20th of September and it was going to be tight. He had the tractor serviced some weeks ago and the ploughing equipment sharpened, so it was a matter of hooking up the plough and driving to the far field. The farm was very close to the infamous Mouquet Farm.

Mouquet Farm 1916

Over the years of working the farm, he had uncovered many battle artifacts including live shells, which he had to move to the edge of the paddock for collection. This was known as the "iron harvest".

Jean-Claude was ploughing at a rapid rate. He came to the end of the row and swung the tractor around for the next row when he saw something sticking out of the earth in the row he had just completed. He stopped the tractor and went over to investigate; it was a rifle. On further examination, he saw a human skull face up as though it was looking at the sun. He then saw many bones scattered over a small area. He could see bits of cloth, one with a badge of The Rising Sun: an Australian Digger.

Everybody in the village knew of the horrendous battle at "Moo Cow" farm as the Diggers called it. The Australians suffered over 11,000 casualties in trying to capture the farm: they were unsuccessful.

Jean-Claude had, in the past, unearthed remains of soldiers and had always contacted the Gendarmes. The last time this happened, the Gendarmes eventually came to inspect the remains and ensured they were not recent and therefore possibly a homicide. Then, once the Gendarmes were satisfied, he had to wait for the Commonwealth War Graves Commission to show up, which was not until the end of the following day. Because it was so late the CWGC had to come back the next day. They finally arrived at 12 noon and by the time remains were taken, it was 6 pm.

This effectively cost Jean-Claude three days' work.

He and Sophie and all the other people who lived in the area were more than appreciative of the sacrifices the Australian Diggers had made for France and their town in particular. In the village of Pozières there are many references to Australia and a large memorial had been erected.

But Jean-Claude knew he could not afford to lose any more time as his crops had to be sown by no later than the middle of November or he would be in real trouble. He had to make a difficult decision but he knew he could not delay. He climbed back onto the tractor did a circle and ploughed this brave soldier back into the ground. He felt guilty and sad, but there was no other way.

The soldier was David Abbott, Christine Abbott's great uncle.

His spirit started to gravitate towards a very bright light; he felt serene and at peace. He had been found at last after all this time. Then came the shock of being hurled back into the cold, hard earth.

Peace was not to be.

Dave would have to wait for the next time, if there ever was to be a next time.


When Jean-Claude returned to the farmhouse, Sophie could tell he was not himself, and asked what was wrong.

'I found the remains of a soldier today.'

'Where?'

'When I was ploughing in the far paddock.'

'Did you report it to the Gendarmes?'

'No, I feel very bad about it but, Sophie, we cannot afford any more delays or we will not have a harvest ready for market. I had no choice, I ploughed him back'.

'Oh, Jean-Claude, you didn't'!

'Sophie, I had no other choice.'

# Ours in not to Question Why, Ours is but to do or Die

## Chapter 17

**Fromelles, France 1916**

David Abbott

Dave Abbott was back in the trench, which was wet, muddy and stank of bodies starting to decompose. His Sergeant was going amongst his men ascertaining who was injured and who was OK. He came up and approached Dave who was trying to bite through some beef jerky.

'How are you now, mate?'

'I am OK, Sergeant, just a bit exhausted,' replied Dave with as much enthusiasm as he could muster.

'I'm looking for volunteers to go out there and bring back the injured. Are you up to it?'

'Bloody oath! I've got mates out there and I want them back here,' said Dave.

'Fair enough cobber, I will let you know when it is time to go over the top again.'

The sergeant moved on, looking for more volunteers.

He came back about an hour later.

'Cobber, it is time; it's quiet over there.'

Dave made sure he took off everything he could, including his weapon belt. He knew he wouldn't need his rifle or grenades. The idea was to slink across the ground keeping an ear out for any wounded Diggers. Dave slowly went over the top, not as he had done the previous day when it was a full-on charge.

He kept low.

'Can anybody hear me? Are there any Diggers there?' he whispered.

His comrades from his company were doing the same. Once he found a wounded Digger, depending on how big he was, he put him on his back and then ducked and weaved through German bullets until he reached the trench. Once the medics took the wounded soldier, Dave and his mates went out again. If he was a big bastard or his wounds were too bad, he called for a stretcher.

Dave and his fellow Diggers retrieved over two hundred wounded comrades over the following two days.

Jerry wasn't too bad and didn't give them too hard a time unless they got a bit bold and got too close to the German trenches.

Dave was on his last mission for the night to retrieve another wounded Digger, when he heard a call in front of him and edged slowly closer. Dave found a soldier in a shell crater.

'You alright if I put you over me back, cobber?' whispered Dave. 'Don't think the stretcher-bearers can get this close to The Huns.'

'Yeah, mate, I'll be right.'

Dave clambered down into the crater, got the Digger on his back and climbed out.

'Right now, here we go, mate, hold on.'

Dave started to hurry across No-Man's land; he had about three hundred metres to cover. He heard that horrible sound of a shell coming their way and thought 'Please let it be a dud.'

It wasn't. It exploded only metres from him and his young wounded comrade. The shredded parts of Dave and the young soldier were scattered all around the blast's epicentre. No longer recognizable as human, these bits were never recovered at least not by human hand. He and his mate were amongst 5,533 Australian casualties that day.

These men were not the cause of the war: they merely heeded the call to fight for King and Country. Others of much higher rank both social and military made that call. The Diggers who did the fighting and the dying were mostly simple folk who knew nothing of the politics or of the grand design for expanding an empire. Their job was not to die: their task was to do or die.

# The Agony and the Passion

## Chapter 18

**22nd April 2012**

Ed gathered the group together and they made their way to the bus. They were going to Ypres, the scene of three major battles and two smaller ones. The battle of particular interest was the Battle of Passchendaele.

Ed spoke into the microphone:

'Firstly, I would like you all to meet my nephew, Harry. He has been living in Ypres for the past twelve months, and has been studying the history and tactics used on The Western Front during the First World War. He begins studying at Duntroon Military Academy, in Canberra, next year. Harry will be joining us for the rest of the tour, and probably knows more about the war than me by now. Please feel free to ask him any questions.

OK, your first day has certainly been a big one and very emotional from what I observed. Our trip to Ypres is approximately thirty miles, which should take forty minutes so why don't you just relax and take in the beautiful scenery?'

Adam moved from his seat to sit next to Harry.

'Hi my name is Adam.'

'Hi.'

'What's it been like living in Belgium?'

'Really good, the people have been fantastic, particularly when they discovered why I was here. Australians are very highly regarded in this part of the world.'

'Did you learn to speak Flemish?'

'Yeah, pretty well, although it's not as fluent as my French.'

'Wow so you can speak two languages on top of English?'

'Three actually... my German is pretty good as well.'

'Did you pick them up while you have been staying here?'

'I could speak schoolboy French before I arrived, but the others I learned while I have lived over here. Are you travelling with your parents, Adam?'

'Yeah and my big brother.'

'How old is your brother?'

'Seventeen.'

'Same age as me.'

'Really? What a contrast.'

'What do you mean'?

'Well, here's you studying the war and everything and Ben couldn't give a damn about any of it; he just sits in the bus with his headphones on and has to be pushed to get out of the bus to see the memorials and battlefields. No interest whatsoever.'

'So he has no understanding that lads his age were fighting an horrific war and living in shocking conditions, fighting for their country, his country.'

'Nup, couldn't give a toss.'

'What about you, mate? How do you feel about it?'

'The more I see, and hear, about the war, the more I appreciate what our Diggers went through and the sacrifices they made. Unbelievable.'

'Well let's hope by the end of the tour, your brother starts to get an appreciation of what happened here all those years ago.'

'Doubt it,' muttered Adam.

It was six o'clock when the bus pulled up outside a very impressive building called "The Albion Hotel".

Ed announced that this was where they were to stay.

'I suggest we go up to our rooms and rest a while and freshen up before meeting in the lobby at say 7pm. Dinner is booked for 8pm, so we can have a drink in the lobby lounge and talk about the day.'

The group alighted from the Mercedes and entered the lobby. They checked in and did as Ed had suggested, went straight to their rooms for a rest before dinner.

George took the opportunity to telephone his wife, Anna, who had elected to stay in Paris while George took the tour.

'Hello, darling, how are you?

'Good thanks, hon. How's the tour going?'

'It's good, very good in fact.'

'Well, you have a few days left, so I hope it continues well for you, sweetheart.'

'How about you? Do we have any credit left on the card? George was half-joking.

' I'll have you know that I haven't spent much at all.'

'So, what have you been doing with your time?'

'I went to the Louvre yesterday; I spent pretty much the whole day there. It was fantastic and of course I saw the Mona Lisa but there is so much more to see. I'm planning to visit Marseilles tomorrow on a full day bus tour.'

'Don't see it all on your own. Remember I have three days there after the tour.'

'Don't worry. There's lots to see and do in Paris, my dear, I assure you.'

'Goodnight, darling.'

'Goodnight, honey.'

'Love you.'

'Love you too.'


Stewart and Philippe were looking forward to this part of the tour; both had lost their ancestors in the battle of Passchendaele. This battle was an integral component of "The Third Battle of Ypres".

Both men made sure they sat together at dinner so they could talk about what they knew of the battle.

As it turned out, neither really knew much at all about how their ancestors had died, other than it was in The Battle of Passchendaele.


Harry made sure he sat down next to Ben at the table. After small chat about school and rugby, and who would win the Bledisloe Cup (they both agreed it would probably be New Zealand), their conversation gradually turned to the Western Front.

'So how are you enjoying the tour so far, Ben?'

'To be perfectly honest, Harry, I am not really into all this war stuff.'

'But don't you appreciate the history and the sacrifices that were made? Did you know that over 45,000 Aussies lost their lives on The Western Front fighting for what they believed was right?'

'Harry, don't get me wrong, I know it was a horrific war but as far as I am concerned, all wars are horrific whether they be World War One or Afghanistan. What I can't get my head around is why we glorify such bloodshed.'

'Ben, nobody is glorifying war, what we are doing is remembering and hopefully learning for the future.'

'Well, we haven't learnt too much, twenty years later and there has been an even more horrific war and plenty more smaller conflicts since.'

'I understand your point, but the most important thing is to remember that guys the same age as us were sent away to a foreign land to fight because they were told by their country it was the right thing to do. We should remember them and admire them for their bravery.'

'I think we differ on that.'

Harry and Ben ate their dinner pretty much in silence after that discussion.

After what was a very pleasant dinner for the remainder of the tour party, they all retired to their rooms; it had been a big day with another big one to follow tomorrow.

Stewart went to bed and starting reading *Passchendaele* by Peter Barton He was horrified at the images and what he read. He could only try to imagine what the character, Archie, endured.

Stewart put down the book and turned off the light. He was just starting to doze off when he heard a loud clap of thunder followed by distant rumblings. He sat up, startled. He jumped out of bed and looked out the window. He saw lightning in the distance which looked quiet surreal;  clouds were shading a full moon, creating an eerie light show.

For thirty minutes he stood at the window listening to the thunder and watching the flashes of lightning behind the large grey clouds.

He went back to bed but within a minute or so he heard multiple claps of thunder and what sounded like machine gun-fire. He again got up, deciding to get dressed and go downstairs and walk around. Being a barrister, he had an inquiring mind. The hotel was set in two thousand acres of park-like grounds and he decided to wander around to see if somebody was igniting firecrackers or something more sinister.

He was not aware that the parklands behind the hotel were the scene of very heavy fighting during the war and that many allied and German soldiers lost their lives in this very place.

As he walked, he heard the noises again and a haze of smoke drifted across the park; it had a celestial look about it with the full moon shining through. He swore he saw soldiers running across the park with bayonets attached to their rifles, in a full battle charge.

He couldn't believe what he had seen or thought he had seen; he tried to dismiss it from his head. Stewart was a very pragmatic person who was often labelled a cynic, certainly not a person known to believe in the paranormal.

He returned to his hotel room and tried to get some sleep.

# Ghosts

## Chapter 19

**April 24th 2012**

Next morning, the usual bunch was at the breakfast table. The remainder had breakfast in their rooms. Ed had decided to have breakfast in the dining room and joined Stewart, Philippe, Lois and Terry and, wandering in last, Steve.

They all started enjoying their breakfast and talking about what lay ahead in the day.

'Wow, wasn't it a great storm last night? I've never heard thunder so loud,' said Stewart.

Everybody looked at him with vacant expressions.

'What do you mean, Stewart?' replied Steve.

'The thunder and the lightning. What a show! You must have heard it. It was like a cannon going off.'

They went around the table but no one had heard or seen the storm.

'You must be all very heavy sleepers,' proclaimed Stewart.

He didn't mention it again for the remainder of the day.

Going back to his room, he readied himself for departure at 9am.

Looking at himself in the mirror, he declared:

'Well, Stew, it could have been that hit on the head that has made you start seeing and hearing things that are not there'. He reflected silently.


The group boarded the Mercedes, which had acquired the name of "Murray", a name Steve and Ian came up with.

'These bloody Aussies have to name everything,' said Stewart, smirking.

They were heading back for their second night at the Albion Hotel in Ypres as their next battlefield was nearby. They were going to visit Messines. Ed explained that they would be visiting the battlefield of Pozières when they visited Villers-Bretonneux on ANZAC day.

Ed took the microphone

'Tonight we are going back to the hotel for a rest and then the bus, oops, I am sorry, I mean "Murray" will be out the front at 7pm. We are going to my favourite restaurant, De Ruyffelaer, in Ypres itself.'

Everybody felt they really needed the rest, as it had been a very full day. Adam and Ben, particularly, were exhausted and had no intention of going out to dinner with their parents. The hamburgers on the room service menu sounded excellent.

Terry and Stewart decided they would have a drink in the Lobby Bar at around 6pm. They had both indicated that there was something they needed to discuss without the rest of the group being present.

Terry arrived first and ordered a Johnnie Walker on ice; Stewart followed soon after and ordered a gin and tonic. When they had their first sip, they exchanged glances and Stewart started the conversation.

'Can I ask you, Terry, if you have seen or felt anything out of the ordinary while you have been on this tour?'

'Could you define 'out of the ordinary?' asked Terry

'Well, let me explain.'

Stewart recounted his experience the previous night with the sounds of cannon and seeing the ghostly battle in the park behind the hotel.

'I had a similar experience after the day at Fromelles in Lille.'

Terry listened intently.

'No shell fire, but I saw Germans marching in the streets and I saw and spoke to my Great Uncle Harry. Weird, really weird.'

'I am a paid up member of the cynics society… well, not really, but I could be. I deal in cold hard facts, evidence; I'm a bloody lawyer, for God's sake. This does not mix with my belief system, not at all. However, I know what I heard and I know what I saw.' Stewart was becoming agitated.

Terry agreed but could not explain what he saw and heard either. They both agreed to tell each other of any other experiences they may encounter in the future.

The rest of the group started to wander down and at 7pm they were all in the Lobby Bar ready for a beautiful meal. "Murray" the Mercedes was waiting for them; Ed was the last to arrive and they boarded the bus. They made their way to the restaurant and filtered in to take their places at a large table at the back of the restaurant. The menu looked mouth-watering and they made their selections. Ed ordered several bottles of wine. The group had developed a real sense of purpose and the dynamics worked very well; even though they came from different parts of the world, they all got on extremely well.

Grant was telling Mike about New Zealand and how beautiful and different the two islands were and how Mike should make a visit sometime in the future. Ian agreed with Grant but suggested that if he was going to come all that way, he should visit Australia and in particular, Tasmania, where he lived. Mike agreed with them both and promised he would discuss it with his wife and suggest it be the next trip they made out of Boston.

Ben and Adam enjoyed their hamburgers and coke followed by a banana split; both were full at the end of that meal and decided to get an early night.

They had a conjoined room with their parents, so they would not be disturbed when they got home from the restaurant. At about 9pm, Adam woke suddenly He had heard a huge explosion; he thought he had been dreaming, but then another and another. They just kept exploding until, at last, silence. He looked at his brother but Ben was in a deep sleep, oblivious to what Adam had heard.

Adam woke his brother.'

'Ben did you hear that?'

'Hear what?'

'The explosions.You must have heard them.'

'No, I bloody didn't. You must have been dreaming... now go back to sleep for God's sake.'

After some time, Adam, looked over at Ben but he was snoring.

He got out of bed and went over to the window. He couldn't believe his eyes; in the distance he saw huge mushroom clouds of smoke. Adam got dressed and went down to the lobby, where all seemed normal, nobody running around in panic. He went up to the reception desk and asked the receptionist what was happening. The man behind the desk looked puzzled.

'What do you mean, sir?'

'The explosions! What were they?'

'There have been no explosions reported by other guests.' The man's tone was dismissive.

'But you must have heard them, surely?' Adam raised his voice.

'I am afraid not, sir, but I will make some inquiries.'

He decided that the smoke was too far away to investigate at this time of night so he returned to his room.

He didn't get much sleep, but gradually dozed off; Ben was still snoring.


The group finished dinner, paid the bill and stood outside the restaurant waiting for "Murray", which duly arrived within a few minutes. On the way home Stewart was rather quiet, looking out the window until they reached the hotel. He had been thinking about the previous night and was wondering if something similar was going to happen tonight. Everybody went straight to their rooms as they knew the following day would be another big one: Messines.

Stewart lay in his bed wondering if he was going to hear the thunder of the howitzers tonight or was that a one-off experience? He lay there for about an hour but could not get to sleep. In the end he decided to get up and dress and go for a wander to the park at the back of the hotel where he had seen the ghost battle the night before. He circled the park for forty-five minutes but didn't hear or see anything. He decided to return to the hotel to try to get some sleep. As he was strolling back, he saw Terry.

'Couldn't sleep either, mate?'

'No. I thought I would come out here and see if I could see anything.'

'Did you?'

'Nothing.'

'Let's go back to the hotel and try to get some shut-eye. It's going to be a big day tomorrow.'

They walked back together.


Next morning, everybody came down for breakfast; nobody ate in his or her rooms. Adam decided not to talk about what he had experienced the previous night. Nobody would believe him anyway.

# They Heard the Blasts in London

## Chapter 20

Ed reiterated that they were visiting Messines; this was a very successful battle for the British, Australians, New Zealanders and the Canadians who all took part. The Allied success at Messines would become a template for the Battle of Passchendaele. The British High Command soon became aware of the expression "Horses for Courses."

Ed handed out the information pack, as was the norm at the start of each day. He drew the group's attention to a chart which itemised each of the mines and what Company had dug them. Adam just ignored it, as was his usual practice.

## June 1917

| Name of Mine | Charge (lbs) | Crater Diameter | Dug By |
|---|---|---|---|
| Hill 60 A | 53 500 | 191 feet | 1st Australian Tunnelling Company |
| Hill 60 B | 70 000 | 260 feet | 1st Australian Tunnelling Company |
| St Eloi | 95 600 | 176 feet | 1st Canadian Tunnelling Company |
| Hollandscheschour 1 | 34 200 | 183 feet | 250th Tunnelling Company |
| Hollandscheschour 2 | 14 900 | 105 feet | 250th Tunnelling Company |
| Hollandscheschour 3 | 17 500 | 141 feet | 250th Tunnelling Company |
| Petit Bois 1 | 30 000 | 175 feet | 250th Tunnelling Company |
| Petit Bois 2 | 30 000 | 217 feet | 250th Tunnelling Company |
| Maedelstede Farm | 94 000 | 217 feet | 250th Tunnelling Company |
| Peckham | 87 000 | 240 feet | 250th Tunnelling Company |

| | | | |
|---|---|---|---|
| Spanbroekmolen | 91 000 | 250 feet | 171st Tunnelling Company |
| Kruisstraat 1 } | 30 000 | 235 feet | 171st Tunnelling Company |
| Kruisstraat 4 } | 19 500 | (linked explosions) | 171st Tunnelling Company |
| Kruisstraat 2 | 30 000 | 217 feet | 171st Tunnelling Company |
| Kruisstraat 3 | 30 000 | 202 feet | 171st Tunnelling Company |
| Ontario Farm | 60 000 | 200 feet | 171st Tunnelling Company |
| Trench 127 Left | 36 000 | 182 feet | 3rd Canadian Tunnelling Company |
| Trench 127 Right | 50 000 | 210 feet | 3rd Canadian Tunnelling Company |
| Trench 122 Left | 20 000 | 195 feet | 3rd Canadian Tunnelling Company |
| Trench 122 Right | 40 000 | 228 feet | 3rd Canadian Tunnelling |

Ed briefed the group on the Battle of Messines.

'Some historians have said that this battle was the most successful of the entire war. If not, it certainly was on the Western Front. General Plumer was assigned to the task and it began on the 7th of June 1917 with the detonation of nineteen underground mines beneath the German lines. Those are the mines listed in the chart.'

## Flanders, Belgium 1916

General Haig was studying a report written by Major Norton-Griffiths, an engineer of high renown. Prior to the war, Norton-Griffiths had owned an engineering company that had built tunnels in Britain and also in South Africa and Australia. His company was given the task of blowing up oil wells in Romania to stop the Germans getting their hands on the precious commodity.

Major Norton-Griffiths

Major Norton-Griffiths had written a report to General Plumer recommending he and a team of engineers together with hand-picked sappers tunnel under the German lines and fill them with explosives with the objective of blowing the Germans to kingdom come. This, he ascertained, would allow the allied forces to attack and take the high ridge of Messines thus securing the Ypres salient.

General Plumer requested a meeting with General Haig to discuss the plan, while Norton-Griffiths accompanied him.

'So you think this plan will work do you, General Plumer?'

'Yes, Sir, I have gone over it thoroughly with Major Norton-Griffiths and I am sure it will work. The Major has extensive tunnelling experience and the methods devised by his company will mean the noise levels will be kept to a minimum so the Germans won't hear a damn thing, not until the explosions go off anyway.' They call it "clay kicking."

'Major Norton-Griffiths, I take it that you will be the officer in charge of the digging operation?' asked General Haig.

'Yes, Sir, I will report directly to General Plumer.'

'How are you going to recruit experienced diggers from the ranks, Major?'

'Sir, I have hired many men in my engineering company before the war. I know what to look for.'

'General Plumer I will approve this plan. Make sure it works.'

151

'It will, Sir, I assure you.'

General Plumer and Norton-Griffiths left General Haig's office and hopped into the Major's black Rolls Royce. The car was pristine when Major Norton-Griffiths landed it in France but it was looking a little worse for wear now.

They were pleased that General Haig had approved their plan but were very conscious of the long hard road in front of them.

'So, Norton-Griffiths, how are you going to convince the various commanders to release their men to go and dig clay?'

'I think I know how to do it, Sir.'

They arrived back at General Plumer's Headquarters and agreed to meet the next day to finalise the location and size of the mines they were going to lay.

Once they agreed on the plan, it was up to Major Norton-Griffiths to recruit the men needed.

Norton-Griffiths (on the right) with his Rolls Royce

He loaded up the Rolls with several cases of Château Lafitte Rothschild wine, which he had collected since landing in France.

He then drove around to various units trying to convince the commanders to release any of their men who had engineering experience.

He pulled up at the command post of Major John Davies.

'Hello, Major, I was wondering if we could have a chat?'

'Why not, Major. Come on in to my luxurious dugout,' he said in jest.

'I have a proposition for you.'

'Yes and what would that be, Major?'

'I need men with good engineering experience for a very important mission. I believe you have two such men in your company.'

'Do I ? And who would they be?'

'Corporals Smyth and Goodyer.'

'I don't think so, Major, they are two of my best men. Out of the question.'

'Well, may I suggest six bottles of Château Lafitte may encourage you to release them into my care?

'You're joking. Where did you find those?'

'Well, you can find them in my Rolls. Never mind where I found them.'

'All right, Major, you have yourself a deal.'

'Done.'

Major Norton-Griffiths used this tactic to ensure he had all the experienced men he needed for the project.

At the completion of his recruitment drive, he had recruited many miners from Britain, Australia, Canada and New Zealand.

General Plumer kept a very close watch on the tunnelling and after eighteen months of digging, the twenty-two mines were ready to explode.

Ed explained the strategy of the battle of Messines to the group.

'The objective of the attack was Messines Ridge, southeast of Ypres, a town you all know, and the Germans had occupied since 1914. The British knew they had to capture the Ridge before they could mount a much larger attack on Passchendaele, The Third Battle of Ypres.

General Plumer and his officers had been planning this attack for over eighteen months, reflecting Plumer's nature, a meticulous planner, who left nothing to chance.

He commissioned the laying of twenty-two mineshafts underneath the German lines running along the ridge. The plan was to detonate all twenty-two at the same time, 3.10am on the 7th of June 1917. Prior to the bombs going off, they would hit the Germans with artillery. They would then attack the Germans with infantry attacks. Tanks and gas would support the infantry.

One of the mines was discovered by the Germans and destroyed, while two others were detonated by the British as they were outside the field of the attack.

The Germans were also tunnelling frantically and on more than one occasion each side would encounter each other and deadly hand-to-hand fighting would take place many metres below the surface.

The British started shelling the Germans on the 21st of May, using two thousand three hundred heavy guns and three hundred heavy mortars; the bombardment ceased at 2.50am on the 7th of June. The Germans knew the British modus operandi and sensing an imminent attack, rushed to their defensive positions, with machine guns manned and flares launched to see if there was any British movement.

There was complete silence for twenty minutes. The Germans were increasingly nervous, then at 3.10 am the order was given to detonate the mines, which totalled six hundred tons of explosive. Nineteen mines exploded

The mines blew the crest off Messines Ridge. People reported hearing the explosions in Dublin and the Prime Minister of the day,

Lloyd George, heard it at number 10 Downing Street. No greater explosion created by mankind had ever happened and didn't happen again until the atomic bomb was dropped on Hiroshima.

Mine Crater at Hill 60

The effect on the German defenders was devastating. It was estimated that the explosion alone killed 10,000 men. The objective was taken in three hours.

There were two unexploded mines on the day and they were due to be dismantled, but they were left behind as the British went on to Passchendaele without really worrying about them. The documents describing where they were laid got destroyed in later battles so they were never dismantled. Nobody knew exactly where they were and it wasn't until 1955, one exploded during a thunderstorm. There were no real casualties apart from a cow. The remaining mine still lies dormant and everybody in the general area hopes it stays that way.'

The Battle of Messines was a great morale booster for the Allies and for the first time, the defensive German casualties of 25,000 exceeded the 17,000 allied troops.'

Ed finished addressing his small audience.

Adam reflected on his weird experience at Ypres.

Fred Vardy

Fred Vardy, Steve's great uncle, had been posted to Messines in May 1917. Initially he was in the trench at Hill 60, but the conditions became so hellish that he and most of his unit were moved elsewhere; only a skeleton group manned it for support purposes.

### Fred Vardy's Final Account: Hill 60.

'Under Hill 60 on the Allied side we had a very elaborate system of sap trenches and dugouts, a settlement underground. We had wooden stairways leading to our sleeping quarters but it was never possible to sleep much with bloody Fritz constantly firing shells at us almost non- stop. Further down, there were passages lined with wooden planks which led to larger barracks and that's where the HQ was housed. We were so far underground that when The Boche threw one of his heaviest shells at us, we hardly noticed.

On the morning of June 5th the Sergeant woke me. I wasn't too bloody happy as I had been carrying bombs until about 2am and I was buggered.

'Vardy, I want you to join the detail that is going to help the Aussies with their tunnel. The poor buggers are exhausted.'

'Yes, Sergeant'

I made my way through the labyrinth of tunnels, all nicely lit, with pumps every now and then pumping out the water. Sergeant Collins led us down until we saw daylight; I hadn't seen it for a while. We stepped out and I looked around but I didn't recognize exactly where we were. From what I could see, there was total desolation, just a charred ugly landscape. A very high and considerable wall of sandbags zigzagged away to the right and beyond. This was how the sappers disposed of the earth from the tunnelling. We were ordered to create a human chain to move the sandbags back into the galleries where they were going to be used for building a barrier against the force of the explosion.

I said to my mate, Bob, 'this isn't too bad, mate… keeps us away from the shells and bloody bullets for a while, anyway.'

'Yeah I was sick of hauling those bombs. Anyway these bags are a bit lighter and they don't go boom if you drop one.' They both had a laugh.

Just then a battery began to fire and the shells exploded on the ridge about a hundred yards away; another lot passed over and exploded on the hill behind us.

'No need to worry, lads, they're not firing them at us,' yelled Sergeant Collins.

We were making great progress, so the Sergeant thought it would be a good idea to lengthen the chain. Three of us moved around the corner and we continued on.

I was quite happy chatting with Bob and another young fella when we heard another shell but by the scream of it, we knew this one was intended for us. I ducked as it exploded opposite the corner of the sandbag wall. We all ran like hell for the sap; as I was turning the last bend, the young bloke a few yards in front of me crashed to the ground. He would not have been over eighteen and had just arrived from England. He had taken my position on the chain not long before. I should have taken that hit.

Bob and I tried to lift him but we couldn't manage it. Another salve of shells shook the tunnel, we had to move, we made it to the sap opening and Bob and I stopped and tried to get our breath hanging onto the timber stays, panting and frightened.

It was safe there, and we waited while the sergeant went to Headquarters for instructions.

A young Corporal had heard what had happened and insisted Bob and I go back and retrieve the young Tommie's body; we found him but could not lift him. He was a dead weight and covered with earth. Then another salvo, the corporal, yelled run! and we did, as shells rained down behind us. When the stretcher-bearers retrieved the young soldier, he had shrapnel in his brain and heart, yet he managed to run a dozen yards before he dropped.

Things were really starting to happen. The big guns were being brought in with no attempt to hide them from the Germans They lined them up, wheel to wheel. In the dusk our soldiers were assembling, coming in long files stretching forever.

Then the field guns being pulled by the horses came galloping up the road with the ammunition trains following close behind. I had never seen such activity. 'How will these poor bastards ever survive this?' I thought.

At midnight the young Lieutenant gave us orders to start moving off and Bob and I followed the rest of our unit along the duckboard track to our old position at Hill 60. We passed two dark shapes covered by old sacks; it was obvious these two soldiers had been there for some time. War gives no respect for the fallen, no peace, even in death.

We took our positions in the shallow trench at Hill 60 and waited and waited for the enormous explosions we knew were about to be unleashed on the unsuspecting German soldiers. There was complete silence. Bob thought he heard a bird singing as the sun began to rise. 'How could a bird survive in this hell?' I wondered.

We were told to lie on top in front of the trench in case it collapsed in on all of us.

'Freddie, I am fucking scared, mate, fucking scared,' Bob whispered to me.

'Don't worry, Bob, we all are. Just breathe deeply and think of walking in the front door of your home and giving your mum a big hug and a kiss.' That seemed to settle him a bit. Then the ground started to rock and it felt like I was on a small boat on rough seas. We watched as the earth caved in and huge pillars of fire shot into the sky; it lit the sky and seemed to be suspended for some time.

In the swirling smoke and fire, it seemed there were figures of men with total anguish on their faces rising into the morning sky. I thought this couldn't be the enemy soldiers being hurled up; there would be nothing left of them after that inferno.

Bob and I looked at each other in awe.

'I expected a huge bang, mate. I don't understand,' whispered Bob.

Just then, a huge roar swept across the salient; we were all hurled back into the trench. Then the huge bombardment commenced, adding to the mayhem. The flashes of thousands of big guns behind us hurling their shells into the enemy's lines and the constant sound of the Vickers guns pouring their deadly stream of bullets made this assault a deadly terrifying storm of death.

There must have been a few Germans left, for as we left our trench, they started firing their machine guns at us. I was running across no-man's land when I felt a sharp pain in my left knee. I staggered and fell into a huge crater. I rolled down to the bottom with my pack making it impossible to break my roll; bloody thing weighs a ton. I hit the bottom of the crater with a huge splash; it was full of dirty foul-smelling water. I was face down and could not roll over due to my pack and my wound. I just couldn't get any leverage.

It was here I died. I am here with two other soldiers, an Australian and a New Zealander. We still have not been found.'

Looking for Fallen Comrades

# United We Stand, United We Fall

## Canada's Defining Moment

## Chapter 21

The tour group boarded the bus and settled into their usual seats, Ed was amused that in every tour he had hosted, the people on the tour always went to the seat they selected on the first day. There would be hell to pay if someone sat in the wrong seat.

They were making their way from Ypres to Vimy Ridge. This was a significant battlefield, not only strategically, but it was the first time all the Canadian Divisions fought as one united army.

Ed started to brief the group:

'If we are to understand the significance of Vimy Ridge, it is important to understand some key issues.

Vimy Ridge was the high ground. It commanded views over the entire Douai Plain therefore the Allies wanted the Ridge to create a powerful position in Northern France.

It was critical to the Germans not to lose Vimy Ridge; if they did, their position in the entire region would be jeopardised. The loss of Vimy Ridge would expose a vast amount of German-held positions to the Allied guns. It also protected the Hindenburg Line, the last German defence.'

Both sides were more than aware that the previous times they fought over the Ridge in 1914 and 1916, in excess of 150,000 French and British lost their lives

Looking at Hill 145 from the Douai Plain

The Germans had a clear and uninterrupted view over the Allied advances, while the Allies could only use aeroplanes to view the German-held territory. The Germans were very good at shooting these planes out of the sky.

The German defences were, as usual, formidable, with barbed wire, machine gun nests and artillery. They also had an extensive network of tunnels, including very comfortable living quarters.

The battle plan was for the British forces to flank the ridge traversing across No-Man's Land while the responsibility for taking the Ridge belonged to the Canadian Canucks.

Every soldier and officer knew just how critical this battle was and how it would affect the outcome of the war.

An essential part of any campaign is the quality of the leadership. In this case, unlike Fromelles and other battles, the leadership was magnificent.

The two commanders were Lieutenant General Sir Julian Byng and Major General Arthur Currie who would lead a united Canadian force to take the Ridge. Many thought this was an impossible task.

'The only way we are going to win this battle, Julian, is to change the tactics that our British comrades have been using since the start of this bloody war,' General Currie asserted.

'I quite agree Arthur, we can not continue throwing good men at the German machine guns hoping they will run out of bullets before we run out of troops.'

Both these leaders had an enormous amount of experience and had seen the slaughter at Ypres and Verdun. They were going to conduct this battle with a new and effective methodology.

| Byng | Currie |

'I believe we need to develop new strategies that will minimise the casualties while ensuring we advance at a rate that will ensure us victory,' said General Byng.

'I agree, but easier said than done.'

'Well, Arthur, I think we both agree that we need to spend the time planning and making sure our preparations are completed before we launch this attack.'

The Generals developed a system of placing machine-gun, grenade and rifle specialists within a single platoon. These platoons would strike at the enemy, not in a straight line but in a much more fluid action where German defenders had less chance of merely mowing down the attackers. This strategy would find the attackers able to cover their own advances.

'We need to ensure that our men are well informed of the battle strategy and the officers are able to communicate with their platoons,' stressed General Currie.

'Indeed that is critical,' agreed General Byng.

It was decided that instead of directing the battle from behind the lines, safe and sound in a chateau like that of Haig and Haking, the Canadian officers would be fighting with their men and keeping a close tab on what was happening on the battlefield.

Generals Byng and Currie instructed their officers to brief each man on their objectives and they all received detailed maps. This would ensure that the Canadian troops were clear on their mission and if an officer was killed, they could proceed, knowing what needed to be done.

The date was the 8th of April 1917. The attack was due to begin the following day. The Generals called an officers' meeting to ensure they all had a clear understanding of the battle plan and that all the preparations for the attack had been completed. They were better prepared than any other army had been to date. They asked Lieutenant Colonel Sinclair, who had coordinated the preparations, to give the leadership group a final briefing.

'Gentlemen we have laid twenty-one miles of signal cable and sixty-six miles of telephone wire which has been buried on the battlefront. The tunnelling corps had dug eleven underground tunnel-ways to aid in the movement and protection of our troops. These underground roads are equipped with electricity, medical stations, supplies and rest stations. We have erected portable bridges to assist us in the movement of artillery pieces over the more difficult terrain and trenches. 'We are totally prepared to take on and defeat the German army.'

'Thankyou, Lieutenant Colonel, and very well done,' said General Byng.

'As you are all aware, we are going to use our Vickers machine guns as an attack weapon. They are light enough and we believe will prove to be very effective in the battle. No one has done this before; these guns have always been used as a defensive weapon,' explained General Currie.

The machine-gun fire became a supplement to the artillery barrage. During the attack, the lighter Vickers guns would be set up along with the Canadian advances, providing both cover and a true attacking power designed to keep the German troops from attempting their usual defence and giving them the opportunity of repairing their barbed wire barriers.

'Brigadier General Morrison, can you explain our artillery plan please?' asked General Byng.

'Certainly, General.'

'We started our bombardment of the German lines on the 20th of March. We have varied the intensity of the shelling to confuse the enemy as to when the attack would actually commence. We have established an enormous strike capability with our artillery; we have almost two hundred and fifty heavy guns, and almost six hundred field guns all aimed at the German positions. The bombardment will cease tomorrow when we attack. We have averaged two thousand five hundred tons of shells blasting the German positions every day so far. Our objective is to destroy the German communications, which we hope will stop food, ammunition and replacement troops from getting to their lines. Our reconnaissance tells us we have achieved our goal.

Our plan also calls for our artillery to keep a precise pace in front of our troops moving across No-Man's Land. We have been rehearsing this movement for some time. Our troops and shells will be moving at a pace of about one hundred yards every three minutes. We are hoping this will give our boys the protection they need from the German machine-guns and keep them silent, as their gunners will stay protected within the tunnels and trenches. It should also afford an element of surprise. We may well be in their trenches before they know it.'

'Well, Gentlemen, I think our bombardment plan should knock the Germans about a bit before we launch the ground attack. Don't you think? asked General Byng. All the officers agreed enthusiastically.

'Thank you, Brigadier General Morrison, well done.'

Supplying the Canadian Troops was a network of rail lines built to bring the huge numbers of shells into position. Special fuses were developed for shells that would cause an almost instantaneous explosion, designed to take out enemy barbed wire. That was something the British could not do at the Battle of the Somme. During the week preceding the attack (the "week of suffering" as the Germans called it) over one million shells were fired at Vimy Ridge.

One of the faults with the British bombardment method was that the Germans hunkered down in their secure dugouts, drinking tea and playing cards. When the shelling ceased, they knew it was time to enter their trenches and start slaughtering the enemy.

The essential difference between Vimy and other battles was the collection of good and detailed intelligence. Microphones were placed throughout No-Man's Land, aircraft and balloons were used to determine where the German gun and artillery placements were located.

By having the information available, the Canadians were able to destroy eighty five percent of the German batteries prior to the attack.

The Canadian Attack on Vimy Ridge

On April the 9th, 1917, at 5:28 am, the battle began. The weather was atrocious; there was a combination of snow and sleet when the Canadians exploded their underground mines, then when gas shells fell onto German positions and transportation routes, the artillery began to blast the German positions. All hell broke loose.

Over eleven thousand Canadian and British guns opened up on the Ridge. The Canadians kept to their timetable and followed their detailed plans. By early afternoon seventy percent of their objectives were taken.

Thousands of Germans were taken prisoner and many thousands more had been killed. However, still to be taken were the high ground positions called "the Pimple" which was the responsibility of the British forces attached to the Canadians and Hill 145, which was also yet to be taken.

By the morning of April 10th, Hill 145 had been taken and by April 12th, the Canadians had reinforced the British, attacking "the Pimple" which was taken as well.

By the end of the battle, all objectives had been met. The Canucks had established themselves as an elite fighting force. The German line had been soundly breached and the Canadians had fended off any thoughts of a German counter-attack.

Unfortunately British High Command, through ineptness, did not organise British and French battalions to take advantage of the breach in the German lines.

Apparently they did not believe the Canadians would be successful, basing their predictions on their own track record. The offensives of the British and French failed in the following weeks.

Canada suffered 10,500 casualties including 3598 killed in a battle which gained much, but was squandered by the Generals back in their chateaux well behind the front line.'

Canadian Shells Exploding

One of those lives lost was a young soldier from Quebec called Jacques Boucherhe He had recently married Anne Bellepoire and was missing her terribly. They had discussed before he departed for France the desire to begin a family as soon as he returned. He never returned. He was mowed down by a German machine gun just as his battalion was approaching the enemy's trenches.

Jacques never knew he had fathered a child; he never had the pleasure of bouncing his little girl on his knee or taking her to school on her first day.

He lay in the cold hard dirt for ninety-five years, one of the 'missing', when an excavator digging a pipeline uncovered his remains. The operator decided to call the Gendarme from Avion to take the remains and any artefacts that were with the soldier.

The Department of National Defence organized a massive investigation involving forensic scientists, historians and genealogists.

Experts quickly identified the man as Canadian because of the style of uniform buttons and helmets found in the vicinity. Based on the location of the remains, it was decided that he had died in the battle of Vimy Ridge. An anthropological survey of the remains, including the bodies' height, weight and previous medical conditions were undertaken. The team then analysed the men's teeth for strontium-90, a radioactive isotope passed through breast milk that affixes itself in children's molars and offers clues as to where a person was raised. He came from Quebec, Canada.

Genealogists hunted down the soldier's descendants and they agreed to provide a DNA sample from swabbing the inside of their mouths and after a painstakingly thorough investigation, Jacques Boucher was identified.

Jean Boucher and his sister, Catherine Martin, were both delighted but also sad. They knew their Grandfather had been reported missing and that their mother never knew him.

They both decided they would fly to France where their Grandfather would be buried with full military honours at the Vimy Ridge Cemetery.

Jacques is now resting in peace.

# Passchendaele

## "I have a Cunning Plan"

## Chapter 22

Lloyd George, the British Prime Minister, sat in his office at number 10 Downing Street, the same office as Sir Robert Walpole who received the residence as a present from King George II in 1735 and Henry Pelham who put down the 1745 Jacobite Rebellion and Robert Banks Jenkinson who was Prime Minister in 1815 when the Battle of Waterloo took place, ending the Napoleonic Wars.

He felt the history of the office and the history of the position he held.

The year was 1917; he had been in power for a year and what a year it had been. He had taken over from Herbert Asquith who had mismanaged the first two years of the war or that's how Lloyd George saw it and a majority of other Ministers agreed with him.

David Lloyd George was not an aristocrat, unlike Hebert Asquith, and tended to "say it like it was" which had been his reputation when he practised law.

The first action he took was to create a "War Cabinet" to oversee everything concerning the war, including munitions supply, approval of battle plans and the logistics of moving men into battle.

He was reading a report from General Haig and he was not particularly happy with what he was reading. Haig and his entourage were due at number 10 in thirty minutes to propose to the war cabinet a plan for a new battle in Flanders. Lloyd George felt they were best to redeploy the troops from the Western Front to help the Italians defeat the Austrians.

'It will be in Italy where this war will be won or lost,' he thought.

The President of the War Council, Lord George Curzon, knocked and entered the Prime Minister's office.

'Good morning, Sir'

'Good morning, George'

'General Haig, General Robertson and General Gough, along with their support staff are waiting in the cabinet room, Sir.'

'Are they? Well they can wait a little longer. I want your opinion on Gough's plan for Ypres, George.'

'Well, Sir, having read the brief, I am doubtful it will succeed. I certainly don't want to see another Somme.'

'I bloody well agree. I think we should be diverting the resources we have at our disposal to fighting the Austrians in Italy.'

'Sir, I think you should be prepared for a fair amount of opposition to that proposal.'

'We'll see. Come on let's get it over with.'

Lloyd George and Lord Curzon entered the cabinet room.

'Sit down, gentlemen.'

'Well, General Haig, would you care to present your plan?' said Lloyd George gruffly.

It was obvious to all, that these two men had little regard for each other.

'Sir, I believe we have the Germans on the back foot. We have worn them down through attrition. Now is the time to strike the deathblow.'

'And how do you intend to do that, General?'

'Sir, we will bombard the German lines for ten days straight, with three thousand guns. They will be slaughtered. We will then launch our ground attack across an eighteen-kilometre front.'

'That sounds like a similar plan you used at the Somme with the loss of over 400,000 men.' Lloyd George could not resist this barb.

'Prime Minister, this plan will work. General Gough and I have spent many hours preparing it and I think you should give it due consideration.'

'Go on, General.'

'We will move through Flanders and capture the submarine pens on the coast. They are sinking too many of our supply ships and, if not stopped, will threaten our victory against the Germans.'

There was a lot of discussion and argument but in the end Lloyd George had no alternative but to approve Haig's plan.


**April 25th, 2012**

At 9am, the entire group had gathered in front of the hotel waiting for the Mercedes to arrive. At 9.05am it drew up to the hotel entrance and they all boarded.

Ed took the microphone:

'Good morning,everybody. Are you all looking forward to the day?'

They all nodded, except for Ben.

'OK, the first stop will be the Passchendaele Museum.'

'Let me brief you on The Third Battle of Ypres or, as it is commonly known, as Passchendaele and, in particular, Polygon Wood.'

'To begin, let's hear what my Grandfather reported at the Battle.'

Australian forces involved in the Polygon Wood battle were the Fourth and Fifth Divisions, which, as well as the infantry, included artillery, engineers, medical personnel and the hundreds of men involved in supply and transport. All essential war material had to be brought forward by wagons along roads and tracks exposed to heavy shelling. Horses and drivers suffered greatly. While a cratered road was repaired, drivers had to sit and wait, controlling their horses as the shells fell around them.

They belonged to the finest class their nation produced, unassuming, country-bred men. They waited steadily until the break was repaired or some shattered wagon or horses dragged from the road, and then continued their vital work. No shellfire could drive them from their horses. The unostentatious efficiency and self-discipline of these steadfast men was as fine as any achievement of Australians in the war. (Charles Bean)

'The name 'Polygon Wood' was a farce. Shelling had reduced the wood to little more than stumps and broken timber,' Ed said.

The British artillery barrage commenced at 5.50 a.m. on 26th September, just as the Polygon plateau became visible.

'By about July, 1917, things were looking pretty bad; French mutinies were increasing and it was decided that the British Forces would need to take control of the Western Front.

This provided General Haig with an opportunity to launch an offensive, which was what he wanted all along. He bombarded the German positions for ten days prior to the attack, using 3000 guns, which expended 4,250,000 shells. With that level of intensity, the Germans certainly knew an attack was imminent.

Thus when the attack was launched across an 18-kilometre front, the German Fourth Army was in place to hold off the main British advance around the Menin Road, and restricted the Allies to fairly small gains to the left of the line around Pilckem Ridge. Similarly the French were halted further north by the German Fifth Army.

Menin Road 1917

British attempts to renew the offensive over the course of the next few days were severely hampered by the onset of heavy rains, the heaviest in thirty years, which created a thick muddy swamp. Tanks found themselves immobile, stuck fast in the mud. Similarly the infantry found their mobility severely limited.

The massive bombardment had destroyed the drainage systems and the millions of shells had created a moonscape difficult for the allied forces to advance.

Finally, with the army stuck in the muddy fields, the bloody offensive came to an untidy close. Many would afterwards call this offensive, actually a series of battles, after the name of the village that had become the last objective – 'Passchendaele'

Menin Road

The Australian Diggers joined the battle and participated in the battle of Menin Road on 20th September 1917. The atrocious weather had finally ceased and the fighting conditions improved. The Australian 1st and 2nd divisions advanced to Polygon Wood. The 4th and 5th Divisions became involved on 26th September and also attacked Polygon Wood. The fighting was bloody and intense. Fortunately, heavy artillery supporting their advance allowed them to fight off the German counter-attack. In just over a week, there were 11,000 Australian casualties.

The Third Battle of Ypres was a bloodbath: 310,000 allied casualties and an estimated 400,000 Germans. These numbers represent fathers and sons who would not be returning to their families.

The Australians captured Broodseinde Ridge, 4th October 1917.

Then the rains came pouring out of the heavens for five straight days, turning the ground into a heavy slimy bog. The Australians struggled to make any headway. With their boots being stuck in the mud and their ragged uniforms caked in mud and twice as heavy as they should have been, they retreated back to their original lines.

Broodseinde Ridge 1917

Fresh Canadian troops took over'.

Ed had just completed the briefing when they arrived at Passchendaele Museum.

'Ok, everybody, this is one on the best and most important military museums in Belgium.'

They wandered around the Museum with Ed as their guide, when after about an hour, Ed asked the group to board the bus. Harry noted that Ben was already seated.

'What did you think of the Museum, mate?' asked Harry.

'I didn't go in. I had more important things to do, like listen to "Powderfinger".'

'You really are something else, Ben, unbelievable.'

The next stop was Tyne Cot Cemetery, the biggest war cemetery in the world.

Tyne Cot Cemetery

| United Kingdom: 8,907 | Canada: 966 |
|---|---|
| Newfoundland: 14 | Australia: 1,353 |
| NewZealand: 519 | South Africa: 90 |
| British West Indies: 2 | France: 1 |
| Germany: 4 | |

Philippe wandered through the Canadian section with a sense of sadness yet also pride. The Canadians, the Canucks, were reputed to be one of the best fighting forces in the war. He thought about his Great Uncle and the supreme sacrifice he had made and for what?

Philippe was particularly moved by the grave of Private Peter Robertson, a Canadian, awarded the Victoria Cross for bravery for rushing a machine-gun emplacement and rescuing two men under heavy fire. He was killed saving the second of these men on 6th November 1917. Philippe had read about him when doing some research before departing for the tour.

The rest of the group also moved amongst the headstones; Adam asked his father why the Jewish headstones had a rock placed on top of them.

'In times past, the initial placement of the stones would prevent wild animals from digging up the body of the deceased. When people

177

returned to visit the grave later on, they would also bring along a stone to help further secure the body from digging scavengers. This repetition ensured that the dead would not be disturbed, and the stone marked the presence of someone who cared for the deceased.'

'Well, Dad, there certainly wouldn't be any wild animals here to disturb them.'

'Well, Adam, no wild beasts now but this has become a tradition and will always be observed by the Jewish race.'

'OK, thanks Dad, very interesting'


Ben did actually wander around the cemetery, but failed to read any of the headstones. He was more interested in the number of vapour trails overhead, wishing he were on one of those planes taking him home to Sydney.


Ed waited until the group came back together:

'We are now going to visit the 5th Australian Division Memorial and the New British Cemetery at Polygon Wood. There is also a memorial to the New Zealand Missing where 1200 men are listed.

Grant, no doubt you will want visit this memorial?'

'I certainly will be,' responded Grant.

When they arrived, they found a beautiful cemetery with the tall trees of Polygon Wood as a backdrop.

'Now I know we have several nationalities between us so you will probably want to go off in different directions. Just make sure you are back at the bus by 1pm. We have lunch boxes prepared by the hotel waiting for you upon your return.'

The Australian contingent walked amongst the graves and contemplated the horrible fact that there were 5770 Australian casualties at Polygon Wood out of a total of 11,000 in the overall battle…

As Christine and her family were walking amongst the graves, young Adam started to get that feeling again, the presence of someone behind him. He slowly turned around, only to find an Australian soldier standing there: he had his left arm blown off and there was a large bloodstain on his chest. Adam was petrified.

'Who are you?' The soldier stood there and stared, then responded:

'Your Uncle Jack.'

'You can't be! It's not possible.'

Adam hurried over to his big brother.

'I think I just saw a ghost.'

'Don't be daft. Your imagination is getting the better of you.'

'I did, I really saw a soldier who had an arm blown off and he had blood everywhere. He said he was Uncle Jack.'

'Well, you'd better introduce me.'

'I can't. He disappeared. Ben, you have got to believe me.'

Ben looked at his young brother and could see that he genuinely believed he saw a ghost.

'OK, Adam, I believe you, mate, but don't tell Mum and Dad or anybody else, for that matter.'

'Promise.'

Adam started to feel better knowing his brother believed him.

Ben didn't believe him; he just wanted to placate his young brother.

'The kid's delusional,' he thought.

Philippe was very aware that the Canadian forces had fought a tremendous battle against the Germans at Passchendaele. The

Australian and British troops were totally exhausted with very heavy casualties; it was up to the Canadians to defeat the German Army at Passchendaele.

Philip Gibbs said of the battle of Passchendaele:

*"The Canadians have had more luck than the English, New Zealand and Australian troops who fought the way up with most heroic endeavor, and not a man in the army will begrudge them the honor, which they have gained, not easily, nor without the usual price of victory, which are some men's death and many men's pain"*

*After a heroic attack by the Canadians, they fought their way over the ruins of Passchendaele and into the ground beyond it."*

The Canadian forces lost over 4000 men and a total of 16,000 casualties.

## October 1917 Flanders, Belgium

Antoine Bellepoire

Antoine was feeling very nervous; actually, he was downright scared. The noise of the artillery could be heard miles away as they were approaching the front to relieve the Australian, New Zealand and British Forces who had been fighting the Huns for weeks and weeks. They had suffered heavy losses and were totally exhausted and were now being relieved by the Canadian forces. They had been passing

180

the Australians, Kiwis and the Brits heading back as the Canucks were marching forward. They looked grey and exhausted with strange expressions on their faces; every one of them had the same look, very strange. The Canadians knew they were in for a hard time and hoped they could succeed against the bloody Germans.

Antoine was in the 4th Canadian Division, which had been very successful in the Battle of Vimy Ridge and the Battle for Hill 70. Both battles were successful because the Canadians had a well thought out battle plan and they had very effective artillery as well as well trained soldiers.

Antoine fought in these two Battles and was recommended for the Military Medal, one of the highest medals for gallantry.

They reached their line, which had been previously used by the ANZACs and British and waited for their orders.

The first attack, on the 26th of October 1917, involved the 3rd and 4th Canadian Divisions. It had rained every day since the 19th of October, and the Canadian assault quickly bogged down. The 4th Division was eventually forced to retreat to within 100 yards of its starting point. Antoine and his buddies were not impressed; they had suffered heavy casualties only to retreat back to their lines.

The attack was renewed on the 30th of October, with similar results. Once again the two Canadian divisions made small advances at a heavy cost. The 78th Canadian Brigade lost half of its strength on that day. However, Canadian patrols did reach the village of Passchendaele where they found the Germans preparing to retreat. When Antoine looked at the little town of Passchendaele he was horrified. There were no buildings left, just charred remains of what was probably a pretty little village. Corporal Bryant asked Antoine and two other men, Geoffrey Groves and Ken Hughes, to go forward ahead of the patrol and ascertain if there were any Germans remaining. They moved cautiously through the streets of rubble. They turned a corner and a hail of bullets came flying at them. Quickly they ducked for cover. They found a semi-demolished stone wall, which they peered over; they could see an old church which was pretty much in ruins and there was a machine-gun nest in the church foyer.

'You start firing, along with Hughes, when I give you the signal,' Antoine whispered.

'Hughes won't be able to. He has been hit pretty bad,' whispered Groves.

'Shit, OK. You'll have to go it alone but take Hughes' rifle in case you run out of ammo. Are you happy with that?'

'I suppose so. Yeah.'

'I am going to try and get close enough to throw a grenade and blow the bastards up.'

Antoine gave Groves the signal. He started to fire; at the same time, Antoine ran and threw the grenade. He hit the target; after the explosion there was a deathly silence. He cautiously approached what was the machine-gun nest. He looked in and saw three German soldiers. Two were clearly dead; the other looked at Antoine and held out his hand. Antoine felt compassion, knowing this kid had no choice in fighting this horrible war. Antoine grabbed his hand to help him up and Antoine and the young German soldier were blown to bits by the hand grenade the German was holding with his other hand. Antoine was posthumously awarded the Military Medal, which was sent to his parents in Canada.

He is listed as 'missing with no known grave.'


## Quebec, Canada 1917

Antoine's father, Henri, was checking the fruit fermenting in the large vats at the family's juice distillery. He was standing on a ladder about twenty feet tall. A postal messenger came into the Vat room and yelled up to Henri:

'Are you Mr Bellepoire?'

'Who wants to know?'

'I am from Western Union. I have a telegram for you.'

Henri looked down at the boy.

'Just leave it on the fruit-sorting table.'

'OK,' said the boy as he left the shed. Mounting his bike, he set off to deliver many other similar telegrams.

Henri kept doing what he was doing before he was interrupted. Finally descending the ladder, he looked at the envelope for some time. He walked out and climbed the hill where he was growing the grapes used for the juice, checking their condition. He then went into the house to have his lunch with his wife, Antoinette. He did not mention the telegram to her; he just ate his lunch and talked about the orchard and other trivial things.

He then went about his daily business, passing the table with the envelope several times without stopping to open it.

He went to bed that night with the envelope still lying on the table unopened. Antoinette noticed his quiet mood, but thought nothing of it.

Henri rose at 5 am, as was his routine, and walked in the dark to the distillery; he looked at the envelope for some minutes before picking it up and opening it.

*'We regret to inform you'* He dropped to his knees sobbing. He looked up and Antoinette was standing at the entrance to the shed. She knew.


## Passchendaele, Belgium 1917

The 1st and 2nd Canadian Divisions finally captured the village on the 6th November. The final action of the battle came on the 10th of November with an attack designed to straighten out the line. Even after this final action, the Germans still held the northern end of the Passchendaele Ridge. Currie's Canadians had suffered 15,634 casualties.

The battles around Passchendaele critically weakened the British army. They had a similar impact on the German divisions present on the Western Front in 1917 but the German victory in Russia was about to free up a new German army. In the spring of 1918, these fresh divisions would come close to breaking the British lines.

## April 2012 Passchendaele, Belgium

Philippe had been looking forward to visiting the village of Passchendaele. He discovered that Antoine, his Great Uncle, had died there and had been awarded a Military Medal for 'Bravery in the Field.' He had seen old photos of Passchendaele and the total devastation of the village was frightening.

The village church had been rebuilt, as had the entire village but it was with some trepidation that he decided to enter the church and meditate on what horror had happened in this now serene place. He walked down the aisle and noticed someone sitting in the first row in front of the altar. The man was dressed in full military uniform; not only was it a uniform, it was a Canadian Army uniform from the First World War. He turned to face Philippe and beckoned him to join him.

'May I ask you why you are dressed in uniform?'

The soldier told him that he felt it was appropriate to dress in uniform in this church.

'What do you mean?' asked Philippe.

'This is the place where my life's course changed forever.'

'I do not understand.'

'This is where I died.'

Philippe went white.

'You're Antoine?

'Yes'

Philippe was dumbfounded, shocked.

'Tell me how did you die?' he asked, his voice quivering.

Antoine described how a German hand grenade in this very church had blown him apart and how he was destined to a warrior's existence for eternity.

Antoine turned to face Philippe:

'You will never be able to find me or bury me. I will never be buried. I lie beneath this church.'

He stood and started to walk to the back of the church. Philippe was still in shock as he turned to watch his Great Uncle leave but he had already disappeared.

After about fifteen minutes of prayer and contemplation, he arose and left the church to join the rest of the group. He didn't mention to anyone his encounter.

Passchendaele in Ruins

# The Innocents of War

## Chapter 23

The year was 1914. Charles and Marguerite Moreau lived in the beautiful city of Ypres in Flanders, Belgium. They were lace-makers as were their parents and their parents before them. Their small factory employed thirty workers, all from Ypres and the majority of them lived in small semi-detached cottages, which were usually as neat as a pin with small gardens at the front.

They had three children, Marie 13, Louise 15 and Nicholas 18. The two girls attended Kylemore Abbey School and Nicholas worked in the Moreau Lace factory. The rumour of a war with Germany worried the family but not Nicholas. His Great Grandfather was a Captain in Napoleon's great army and he dreamed of similar glory.

The factory was successful and had a reputation for producing the finest lace, which was sent to cities such as Paris, London and Berlin, to name a few. The city of Ypres had been established since the first century BC, when the Romans conquered the Belgae people; the Flanders region has been invaded by successive armies and had suffered from the ravages of war. In spite of this, Ypres managed to establish itself as a financially and culturally rich city in the 12th century. By the 13th century, Ypres had gained the status of an independent city-state.

Ypres was a beautiful city with a population of just over twenty thousand inhabitants who enjoyed the parks and restaurants within the city's old fortifications. The ancient ramparts, including the Lille Gate, which dates back to 1385, were used by the population as a recreation area with trees and grass areas where the Moreau family were regular visitors on a weekend. Taking a picnic basket and a bottle of wine, they would enjoy the warm summer days.

The children often visited the moat area where a new outdoor swimming pool had been constructed, the "Bassin de Natation", while

Charles and Nicholas would throw a line into the river with the faint hope of catching a fish or two.

The people of Ypres were very proud of their city and in particular the "Cloth Hall" and Saint Martin's Cathedral next to it. The Cloth Hall was one of the largest commercial buildings of the Middle Ages, when it served as the main market and warehouse for the Flemish city's prosperous cloth industry. Most of the original structure was erected in the 13th century and it was completed in 1304.

The Cloth Hall

Life was good for the Moreau family until the nineteenth October, 1914. That was the date when the first battle of Ypres began between the German army and the British and French armies

The Battle of Ypres (and the numerous other battles that surrounded this Flanders town) has become linked forever with World War One. Along with the Battle of the Somme, the battles at Ypres and Passchendaele have gone down in history. The town had been the centre of battles before, beginning in the early centuries, due to its strategic position, but the sheer devastation of the town and the surrounding countryside seems to perfectly summarise the futility of battles fought in The Great War.

The land surrounding Ypres to the north is flat and canals and rivers link it to the coast. Control of the town gave control of the surrounding countryside and all the major roads converged on the town. To the south, the land rises to about 500 feet (the Messines Ridge) which would give a strategic advantage to whichever side controlled this ridge of high land.

British troops entered Ypres in October 1914. They were unaware of the size of the German force advancing on the town. However, numbers did not make up for experience, as the Germans used what were effectively students to attack professional British soldiers based north of the town at a place named Langemark. Eyewitnesses claim to have seen the German troops, with just six weeks' training, with arms linked, singing patriotic songs as they advanced towards the British. Fifteen hundred Germans were killed and six hundred were taken prisoner. A German General labelled it "The Massacre of the Innocents".

Fierce fighting took place around the town and neither the British nor the Germans could claim to control the area. At a place called Wijtschate (about 10 miles south of Ypres) a German corporal called Adolf Hitler rescued a wounded comrade and won the Iron Cross. Despite fearsome losses on both sides, neither could dominate the other.

The first days of November directly affected the town. Each day, Ypres was shelled and civilian casualties were high. This tactic set the scene for what Ypres was to suffer for several more years. By the winter, the Germans had not taken Ypres and heavy rain meant that any movement was impossible as the roads turned to mud. The first battle at Ypres limped to a halt.

Australian Diggers Marching Past the Cloth Hall and Cathedral Ypres

Charles and Marguerite were closing up the factory on a Wednesday evening. Marguerite had just completed the payroll ready to pay their work force the following afternoon. Business was not great but they were holding their own, despite the war. They had just locked the office door when they heard an almighty explosion and then another. There had been rumours that the Germans would be attacking the city but of course nobody had told the civilians anything.

They raced towards their home, which was a kilometre away at Boezingepoortstraat 6, a very good middleclass area. They turned the corner to find their home still standing but four doors down, their good neighbours, the Dubois's house was completely demolished. They raced inside to see if their daughters were all right. They were, but terribly frightened by the bombardment. Charles decided that they should pack some things and drive to the nearby town of Poperinge, which was only twelve kilometres away. Nicholas was at soccer practice so they would have to leave without him; Marguerite left him a note saying they expected to be back in the morning.

They all got into the Renault and started driving down the street when another wave of shells began falling around them. One shell hit their car and went through the roof, exploding. Charles, Marguerite, Louise and Marie were all killed instantly. They joined the other twelve million civilians who were slaughtered in World War One, predominantly in France and Belgium.

Nicholas heard the blasts and hurried home to see if his family was safe; he entered the house and read the note on the kitchen table that Marguerite had left for him. He felt a sense of relief as he went outside to see the devastation the Germans had wreaked and to see if he could help any of his neighbours. As he walked along the street, he spotted a black car, although there was very little left of it. Approaching it, with flames still lapping at the wreck, he recognised the number plate and when he peered inside, he let out an agonised scream that could be heard blocks away.

Nicholas was the only family member remaining. He joined the Belgian army the next day with his prime objective to kill as many Germans as he could.

The Moreau Lace factory was bombed six months later and never reopened even after the war.

The city of Ypres was virtually destroyed over the four years of the war. It was rebuilt stone by stone in the 1920's and 1930's and is now regarded as one of the beautiful cities in Belgium.

The civilian casualty rate is not often mentioned when the Great War is discussed but the twelve million who lost their lives through war and famine and disease are truly "The Innocents of War."

Ypres n'est plus qu'un impressionnant panorama de ruines ; la neige rend plus poignant encore ce spectacle de désolation. — Une colonne anglaise de ravitaillement défile ici au milieu des ruines.

Ypres residents return to their city destroyed

# The Dogs of War

## Chapter 24

The tour was on the way from Villers-Bretonneux to Messines early on the sixth day of the trip.

'Ed, I knew horses were used extensively along the Western Front but I was unaware that dogs also played a significant role in the battles. Could you tell us all how they were used?' George asked.

'Certainly, George. Does everybody want to hear the answer over the microphone or do you all just want to shut your eyes and catch up on some sleep?'

They all showed interest, so Ed took the microphone:

'World War One saw the first large scale use of war dogs in military history, and it was no longer more or less haphazard but organized and specialized.

During the Great War, vast numbers of dogs were employed as: sentries; messengers; ammunition carriers, pigeon carriers  and food carriers; scouts; sled dogs; draught dogs; guard dogs; ambulance dogs; ratters; Red Cross casualty dogs and even cigarette dogs.

It's estimated that Germany employed over 30,000 dogs for such purposes and the Allies employed similar numbers.

Many different breeds saw active duty during the war, depending on the job at hand. Bulldogs, Bloodhounds, Farm Collies, Retrievers, Dobermans, Airedales, Jack Russell and Wired Fox Terriers, Sheep Dogs and German Shepherds were all used in a variety of roles. Purebreds did not have any advantage over mixed breeds; what was important was that they displayed the proper character.

Preferred were dogs of medium build and grey or black in colour for stealth purposes, with good eyesight and a keen sense of smell. But the temperament and disposition of the dog usually came first!

193

Countless Red Cross Casualty Dogs also known as Mercy Dogs took part in World War One, saving thousands of lives from both sides.

One particular dog called "Prusco" should have earned the Victoria Cross in my opinion. He was said to have located and found more than 100 wounded men after the Battle of the Somme.

Another famous ambulance dog was "Michael".

The ambulance dogs' training gave them specific skills but also encouraged them to think for themselves. The dogs were trained to bring the wounded man's cap or helmet back to the trench, and then lead medics to their fallen comrade. But often the soldier had lost his cap, or his helmet was fastened too tightly under his chin, for the dog to remove it. Then the dog would have to use his initiative and pick a different item, anything that could be used to make the point: 'Wounded man! Send help!'

Michael, a French Red Cross dog, made headlines with one decision he made. After a sweep of a battlefield, Michael returned carrying the glove of a wounded soldier, identified by the newspapers only as Henri. He could scarcely wait for the attendants to bring a stretcher before he started off again, his great intelligent eyes imploring them to hurry.

Michael led them to a remote part of the battlefield where they found Henri "lying still and cold." After a hasty check, they decided Henri was dead and hurried back to their trench without him.

The dog refused to accept the medic's decision and returned again and again for assistance. When he was ignored, Michael disappeared. Late that night, by the light of a full moon, a French soldier on guard duty noticed an odd movement. No more than twenty feet away, creeping slowly toward the trenches was a large dark object. The soldier had his rifle raised and was ready to shoot but then cried out! It was Michael! The dog had come back with a battlefield souvenir no one could ignore. Michael was dragging Henri with parts of his uniform literally torn away by the dog's teeth; Michael, the dog, had dragged Henri from the battlefield, inch by inch, back to the safety of the trench. Miracle of miracles, the young soldier was breathing. Henri was whisked to a hospital, and eventually recovered.

The Germans called their dogs Sanitatshunde (sanitary); equipped with their saddlebags of medical supplies, they sought out the wounded, and gave comfort to the dying. Thousands of soldiers, on both sides, owe their lives to these remarkable animals.'

Ed looked around the bus and could see everybody was very moved by Michael's bravery and dedication.

'Then there were the messenger dogs, considered by some as the real heroes of the war. These dogs were credited with indirectly saving thousands of lives by delivering vital dispatches when phone lines broke down in between units at the frontline and the headquarters behind. These brave dogs faced many obstacles, such as barbed wire, slit trenches, shell holes and chemical gases.

Two of the more unusual dogs that were used during the Great War, were the ratters, and the YMCA cigarette dogs. Ratters were the terriers, whose natural instincts helped to keep the rat-infested muddy trenches clear; and the small Cigarette Dogs, sponsored by the YMCA, had the task of delivering cartons of cigarettes to the troops, stationed on the front lines. You certainly would not get that today: the anti-smoking lobby would be up in arms!

Then there's one other type of dog that I have not mentioned: the mascot dog.

Soldiers of both sides adopted many dogs as mascots while fighting during World War I. Mascots, by their happy demeanour and the keen interest they showed in everything and by their readiness to respond to every kind word and to every friendly act, helped to relieve the feverish strains of war, and to keep up the morale of the men in the trenches as it seemed nothing else on earth could do. Most of the dogs we own today would fall into the category of Mascot Dogs.

Some of you would remember Rin Tin Tin. He was actually a German messenger dog that was captured by the Americans. At war's end, his handler shipped him back to the USA and he became a film and television star.

Unfortunately there were close to 10,000 dogs killed in action.'

A Messenger Dog

Ambulance Dog

# War Horse

## Chapter 25

Grant was a very keen horseman throughout his life. New Zealand had a reputation for breeding beautiful horses, particularly racehorses, which they sent over to Australia and they won all the premium races, including the Melbourne Cup, twenty eight times.

Grant was keen to discover how horses were used in the war and what contribution they had made to the war effort, particularly a horse called "Warrior" of whom he had heard, but knew very little about.

Ed was also a horse lover and had done quite a bit of research.

'Initially the British thought that the Great War would be like other wars, where the cavalry would lead the charge and open up the gaps in the enemy's lines for the infantry, who would penetrate and annihilate the enemy.

Trench warfare put an end to that tactic although one of the last great cavalry charges took place at Moreuil Wood on 30th March 1918.

At 8.30 am on 30th of March, General Seely, a Canadian, and his aides travelled towards the Moreuil woods from where his forces were stationed on the other side of the River Avre with orders to cross the river and delay the enemy advance as much as possible. At 9.30am, upon reaching the wood, they received fire from German forces who were occupying it. Seely ordered The Royal Canadian to send sections to protect the village of Moreuil, while other sections were to seize the northeast corner of the wood itself. While this was being undertaken, Lord Strathcona's Horse, an elite Canadian horse regiment, was ordered to occupy the southeast face of the wood and disperse any German units found there.

General Seely's horse ,'Warrior', was a much beloved horse of both General Seely and his devoted handler, Jack Thompson.

Warrior was champing at the bit; it was a miracle he had survived this far. He would charge the advancing German army, unfazed by bullets, bombs and shells, even as his fellow horses were falling on either side. He survived major battles at Ypres, the Somme and Passchendaele.

Warrior and General Seely painted by Sir Alfred Munnings in 1918

Warrior was about to lead one of the last great cavalry charges in history at Moreuil Wood. This would be a battle that was critical. To win victory here would contribute greatly to stemming the German Spring Offensive.

One thousand magnificent horses stood proudly behind Seely and Warrior.

The Troops looked to General Seely for leadership. He was very popular with his men but not as popular as his horse. Warrior was a symbol of strength for the battle-weary soldiers. The troops thought of Warrior as invincible and for good reason. In 1915, an exploding German shell cut the horse next to Warrior clean in half and Warrior did not even get a scratch. In another instance, a stable was completely destroyed by a shell just after Warrior had left it. He had to be dug out of the mud, which was up to his back at Passchendaele. He survived many close encounters but the Krauts just couldn't kill him. Up until now; would he survive Moreuil Wood?

Cavalry had been made all but redundant by trench warfare. The Germans had disbanded theirs at the end of 1917.

Horses were easy targets but at full gallop, they could move hundreds of men half a mile in a couple of minutes.

Seely took the brave decision to charge. Warrior could not be held back; he was ready to lead the charge and had no fear as he raced ahead, ignoring enemy bullets.

In fact, Seely could not hold Warrior. "He was determined to go forward," after they had crossed the bridge and come up out of the hollow and with a great leap, he started off.

All sensation of fear had vanished from him as he galloped on at racing speed. There was a hail of bullets; of the original twelve who led the charge, five fell, along with their horses.

On the eastern side, Lieutenant Flowerdew led his cavalry, seventy-five in all, at full gallop out of a hollow to be confronted with two rows of machine-guns, which were positioned to halt a tank attack they suspected was being mounted. One soldier survived, albeit badly wounded; he crawled his way back to the Canadian lines to tell his Captain that all the boys and their horses had been slaughtered.

Warrior and Seely were now well and truly in the Wood and what they saw was hand-to-hand fighting at its most fierce with bayonets being thrust into flesh, both human and horse.

After the battle, many riderless horses were wandering around with blood streaming from their wounds and many were put down then and there.

Seely was summoned to the command centre six miles north at Gentelles early the next morning to help plan for another attack later in the day. Warrior became lame in the dark and could not be ridden. Seely was gassed in the battle and both his replacement horses were killed in the fighting. Warrior had escaped again.

Warrior and Seely were able to join the victory parade in Hyde Park, London, and Warrior lived a leisurely life until 1941.'

Ed went on to explain the main purpose of the horses and mules that were enlisted to help with the war effort.

'The War Horses were with the British and Commonwealth forces from the very beginning, and they were with them until the very end. They served on the front lines and in the rear and were instrumental in supporting the supply lines. In the very hell of the trenches and across the hell of No-Man's Land, supporting the Allied attacks. They were there and they died in great numbers. They persevered in the torrential rain and the sticky mud, ignoring the shells and bullets raining down, to supply their comrades with ammunition and food and water.

The beast that contributed more to the success of the allies was not the cavalry horse carrying the elite warriors into war, it was the light draught horse and the pack mule. Without them, the allies would not have been able to defeat the German war machine. They were conscripted from the farms, cities, factories and coal- mines, from Britain, Australia, New Zealand, America and Canada and then shipped to the killing fields of France and Belgium.

The light draughts were used to pull light artillery and ambulances and to carry supplies and munitions: they were the army's logistical support team.

The heavy draught horses were the heavy weights, much larger and sturdier and they were teamed to pull the larger artillery pieces. As the guns got bigger and bigger, they were replaced by tractors and even trains to transport them.

The true stayers were the light draught and the mule; they proved their worth again and again. From the beginning of the conflict when there were 25,000, their numbers rose to nearly 500,000 by the autumn of 1918. In total, the number of horses and mules listed at the end of the war was an incredible one million.

The German army had a similar number in their service.

The sad fact is nearly 8,000,000 horses died in The Great War.

That figure could have been considerably more if it were not for the Veterinary Corps and their dedication.

The Remount Service was the organisation given responsibility to acquire mules and horses for what they and High Command thought would be a short war. They were criticised for purchasing too many: one hundred and sixty thousand.

The horses and mules were thrown into the front very early on when there were retreats and rear guard actions, which made it very difficult for them.

"We could see ammunition wagons trying to replenish and getting about half-way to the gun, then a couple of shells would burst, blowing the drivers and horses to smithereens; it was a terrible sight but the last two days had made us used to it."

Gunner, J W Palmer remembered the difficulties they faced in keeping their horses fed and watered during the painful retreat:

*"The position over the rations for both men and horses was rather precarious. These were the days when we went without rations of any kind, or water. The horses were more or less starved of water. On the retreat we went to various streams with our buckets, but no sooner had we got the water halfway back to them, than we moved again."*

Eventually the retreats of 1914 ceased and the day of the trenches began but the workload for the horses and mules continued. The transport of equipment and munitions was brought up to the front lines and the horses could go where trucks could not.

The key to the horse and mule's health was feeding them adequately; the average ration for a horse was twelve pounds of oats, ten pounds of hay and some bran mash at least once a week.

There were no stable facilities, which was fine in summer but winter proved to be a major problem; the order came through to clip their winter coats so that parasites and skin disorders would be minimised. Many horses froze to death in the first winter of the war. The order was rescinded and they survived with their warm winter coat intact.

The war horses were proving their worth but the supply from the United Kingdom was drying up.

The Remount Service cast its eyes over the Atlantic to America and discovered they had an abundance of horses and mules, as did Canada.

They were purchased in their thousands and transported to the East Coast where they were loaded onto transports and sent to England. There they were assessed and rested back to peak condition and then transported to France to serve the Commonwealth Forces.

As the war progressed, many city slickers found themselves caring for the warhorses. They soon learned how to get the best from their animals. One particular young soldier approached his captain about the oats he was given for his horses. 'What seems to be the matter with the oats, soldier?' 'Well, Sir, they are so small they get stuck in the horse's teeth' was his reply. 'Well, that's bad, very bad. Maybe you could requisition for some tooth picks."

The love for the horses and mules was not just restricted to their handlers, the fighting soldiers would lament in their diaries about the mutilated horses and mules scattered over the killing fields. It would seem that they could accept the death of a comrade or mate but had difficulty accepting the death and mutilation from human hands of defenceless and innocent animals. It was terribly wrong.

It was not an unusual scene to see a handler kneeling beside his fallen horse, crying over the loss of his best mate, with the ammunition cart still attached having been hit by German shellfire or machine gun fire. The Germans targeted horses and mules to disrupt the distribution of supplies to the front.

The offensives were always dangerous for the horses as they would often get entangled in artillery fire or mown down by the deadly machine gun fire. Even German aeroplanes would target the horses and mules, which were a pretty easy target for the Red Baron and his mates.

The sheer workload could bring a horse or mule to the point of total exhaustion and sometimes death and the cold winters could result in an animal freezing to death.

Many animals died from the gas attacks, despite having gas masks fitted.

The War Horses and Mules were highly regarded and an essential element in the Allies success and therefore the animal's health was a top priority. Disease and fatigue were the horse's biggest enemy and to combat them, the Army established Convalescent Horse Depots where they would be taken for treatment and cure. The fatigued horses were rested in fields way behind the front lines, a world away from the shells, mud and bullets.

Only the best and fittest horses and mules were retained by the army after the war. The vast majority were either sold off at rock bottom prices or sold to French butchers, not a particularly fitting end for animals that were regarded as heroes.

There were a few exceptions: a number of officers passed the hat around to purchase their favourite horse called "David", who, apart from convalescing when wounded, was with them every day of the war.

There was also a gun team of magnificent black horses who. after the war, were given the honour of transporting the coffin of the Unknown Soldier to Westminster Abbey. The team was finally retired in 1926 and the "Old Blacks" spent the remainder of their lives grazing in Devon.

Mules on the Frontline

We should never forget the magnificent contribution these wonderful animals made to the war effort and how many thousand were sent to the slaughterhouses at war's end.'

The Handlers Loved Their Horses

Warhorses struggling With Their Load

# Blood Sweat and Tears

## Chapter 26

**1915**

Archie had been waiting to see some real action for some time. He had been stuck in the trenches since he arrived in France but now with this massive bombardment going on, it was obvious that they were about to advance on the German lines. He was also sick of the continual shelling from the Huns. He was sick of the drenching rain and the bloody mud. It was hard to get some sleep when shells kept exploding all around him; his clothes were wet and he hadn't had his uniform off for a month. He could feel the lice biting him, without letting up. He said to his best mate, Bob:

'Do you think we should move?'

'Where are we going to bloody move to?

'Oh I don't know, down the trench a bit. See if we can find Sam.'

'I don't think that's going to help; anyway, I'm snug here if one can be snug in this fucking rat-hole.

'Okay, it was just a thought.'

Bob brought out his notepad and pen and started writing a letter.

'Who are you writing to, mate?'

'Who do you think I am writing to? Lorraine, of course.'

'Fair enough,' chuckled Archie.

'In some ways, I'm glad I don't have a wife.'

'Why not?' asked Bob.

'Well, if I had a wife and I'm over here and she is back there, I'd be worried about her and she'd be worried about me.'

'Yeah, you do worry but there is nothing like having a woman who loves you and misses you and will be there when we get home from this bloody war.'

'Yeah, I suppose not.'

'I'm going try and close my eyes for a while. I think I'm going to need all the energy I can get for tomorrow,' said Archie.

'Good luck,' said Bob.

Archie didn't get much sleep due to the incessant shellfire and troops moving through the muddy trenches, getting ready for the battle.

At 4 am, they got word from the officers that the bombardment was due to stop at 5am; they would then launch gas canisters into the German trenches. Once the gas settled, they would advance with very little German resistance, as most of them would be dead, either from the artillery or the gas. That was the plan anyway.

Their good cobber, Sam Williams, was further along the trench about two hundred metres; they made a pact that they would all have a smoke in Fritz's trench after the battle.

Sam was waiting for the whistle. He had his full battle pack on, which was bloody heavy. He thought about his family in Bristol and looked forward to seeing them soon, when this bloody war was over. He had a little brother who would be seventeen by now, he thought. He was terrible with birthdays and ages. He hoped like hell that this fucking thing would end soon so his little brother, Jack, would not join him in this hell on earth.

Little did he know Jack had enlisted, lying about his age and was on his way to the front to join his big brother.

Sam waited for the artillery to cease. It stopped. Right, now gas the bastards and let's get on with it! He could see  the gas being expelled from their trenches and start to drift towards the German line, but then the strange yellow greenish gas started to drift back towards their own trench

Sam started to feel a burning pain in his throat and eyes.  The pain was unbearable in his chest; it felt like he had been stabbed in the sternum. Sam was having trouble breathing.

He started to cough uncontrollably and his eyes were stinging like he had never felt before. He began vomiting and tried to swallow his own spittle but his mouth was dry as and his tongue felt terrible. He knew he had to lie down; the bottom of the trench is where the gas was accumulating. Sam breathed in the gas and as he lay there in shocking pain, he drifted into unconsciousness and then died. He had just been killed by so-called 'friendly fire'.

Bob and Archie got themselves prepared for battle. At 5am exactly, the incessant noise of the big guns ceased; they waited, they saw the gas drift, they looked at each other and nodded.

The whistle blew; they both scrambled over the parapet and started to run as best they could in the slimy mud, trying to avoid the craters everywhere. The noise was deafening and soldiers were dropping like nine pins all around them but they just kept running.

Archie received a blast of machine gun fire, which almost cut him in half. Bob looked over and saw his mate slowly crumble into the mud. He put his head down and started to advance slowly. The haze from the smoke, and the sun beginning to rise, made it difficult to see anything clearly.

He lifted his head and could not believe what he saw; Archie seemed to be alive and walking straight towards the machine-gun nest that cut him down. Bob yelled out to him but Archie was walking as if in a trance. When he reached the German position, he looked back at Bob and just kept walking out of view. Bob dismissed it as an illusion or something created by the haze from the gas and shellfire.

Bob survived Passchendaele and survived the war. He went back to Edinburgh and his wife, Lorraine, and started a family two years later. They had two boys. Twenty years later, both boys were killed in the Second World War, in France. Bob knew it was a fallacy, 'the war to ends all wars', for wars would go on forever, taking the lives of the very finest young men and women but no politicians.

Menin Gate, Ypres

Ed gathered up the group and they boarded the bus. When they were on their way, Ed announced their final stop for the day would be Menin Gate, Memorial to the Missing.

'The Menin Gate is one of the most visited war memorials in Western Europe, if not the world. During World War One, there was no gate such as the one we will see today. Instead the men who marched to the front to fight in the Battles of Ypres passed through a gap in the town's old ramparts and crossed a small stretch of water.

Many thousands of men passed over this bridge, many to their deaths. It was felt appropriate that after the war, an imposing monument should be built to commemorate those who died in battle but had no final resting place. Sir Reginald Blomfield designed the Menin Gate and the Imperial War Graves Commission approved his design. Work began in June 1921 with a grant of £150,000 from the British government. It was finished in July 1927.

The land around Ypres is dotted with many cemeteries but these are invariably for those who were killed, identified and then buried with a headstone named accordingly. These cemeteries also have headstones marked 'Known unto God' or 'A Soldier of the Great War' for soldiers whose bodies were found but could not be identified. There are about 40,000 of these unnamed headstones around the Ypres Salient.

The Menin Gate is for those men whose bodies were never found. There are 54,896 names of men who died between 1914 and August 15th 1917 and who have no known grave. We can only hope that they rest in peace and are not disturbed by ploughing, excavating ditches for pipelines or for building sites. We hope that if they are discovered, they are given a full military funeral and attempts are made to identify each soldier. One soldier covered over again is one too many.'

When they stopped at The Menin Gate, they were all impressed with its grandeur, well, all except Ben. The architecture was impressive but what really was significant were the 53,000 names etched on the stone, including the ancestors of Philippe, Stewart and Steve.

Ed said 'Before you get off the bus, I just wanted to tell you there are 40,244 names from Britain inscribed on the gate, 6198 Australians and 6983 Canadians.'

Grant asked Ed about the New Zealanders.

'The New Zealand memorial is at the New British Cemetery and Messines.'

Steve was keen to find his Great Uncle's name etched in the memorial wall that surrounds the cemetery. He found it: "Frederick Vardy died on the seventh of June 1917". It was an emotional moment.

After spending forty-five minutes at the monument, they boarded the bus and headed back to their hotel where they would spend another night.

The next day the group would be exploring the Somme.

Ed gave them a briefing as they headed back to their hotel.

Menin Gate 1917

# French Blood Flowed Like a River

## Chapter 27

**2012 France**

'Before I talk about The Somme it is important to learn about the Battle of Verdun,' said Ed.

'It was this ferocious battle between the French and German armies that predicated the Battle of the Somme.

One of the costliest battles of World War One, both in casualties and time, Verdun exemplified the 'war of attrition' pursued by both sides and which cost so many lives.

By the winter of 1915-16, German General Erich von Falkenhayn was convinced that the war could only be won in the west. He decided on a massive attack on a French position 'for the retention of which the French Command would be compelled to throw in every man they have'. Once the French army had, in his terms, 'bled to death,' Britain would be fighting alone on the Western Front and would be brought down by Germany's superior strength.

Falkenhayn targeted the town of Verdun and its surrounding forts. They threatened German lines of communication and lay within a French salient (a bulge in the line), restricting their defenders. Verdun was a Gallic fortress before Roman times and later, a key asset in wars against Prussia. Falkenhayn knew the French would throw in as many men as necessary to secure its defence. He realised that this would enable him to inflict the maximum possible casualties.

He massed artillery to the north and east of Verdun to pre-empt the infantry advance with an intensive artillery bombardment. French intelligence had been warning the French High Command for some time, however they chose to ignore the advice. Consequently, Verdun was utterly unprepared for the initial bombardment on the morning of 21 February 1916. German infantry attacks began that afternoon and met little resistance for the first four days, taking a heavy toll on the French forces.

On 25th February, the Germans occupied Fort Douaumont. French reinforcements arrived and, under the leadership of General Pétain, they managed to slow the German advance with a series of counter-attacks. Over March and April, the hills and ridges north of Verdun exchanged hands, always under heavy bombardment. Meanwhile, Pétain organised repeated counter-attacks to slow the German advance. He also ensured that the Bar-le-Duc road into Verdun – the only one to survive German shelling – remained open. It became known as La Voie Sacrée ('the Sacred Way') because it continued to carry vital supplies and reinforcements into the Verdun front despite constant artillery attack.

German gains continued in June, but slowly. They attacked the heights along the Meuse and took Fort Vaux on 7th June. On 23rd June they almost reached the Belleville heights, the last stronghold before Verdun itself. Pétain was preparing to evacuate the east bank of the Meuse when the Allies' offensive on the Somme River was launched on 1st July, partly to relieve the French.

The Germans could no longer afford to commit new troops to Verdun and at a cost of some four hundred thousand French casualties and a similar number of Germans, the attack was called off. Germany had failed to 'bleed France to death' and from October to the end of the year, French offensives regained the forts and territory they had lost earlier. Hindenburg replaced Falkenhayn as Chief of General Staff and Pétain became a hero, eventually replacing General Nivelle as French commander-in-chief.

So the British felt compelled to relieve the French who were utterly exhausted and their troops so depleted that if the Somme offensive had not been initiated when it was, the German army could have swept into the Champagne Valley and to Paris.'

Ed continued with a description of the infamous Battle of the Somme.

'To most people, the Somme signifies the carnage on one day-July 1st 1916. It was the day that the British Army suffered its greatest ever losses in a single day with nearly 60,000 casualties. But the actual battle for the Somme raged until November of that year, and saw massive fighting again in 1918. The Somme really was the killing fields.

What remains is truly incredible. There are sites seen today that you will never forget. We tour the Somme battlefield covering major sites from the disastrous first day and through the whole five months of the battle, and then look at some of the events of 1918. We will visit Delville Wood, the Welsh memorial at Mametz Wood, the sunken road where the Accrington Pals were virtually wiped out, Sausage Valley, the Pozières battlefield and Windmill Hill. The Australians in our group will be interested in these two sites. We will also visit the Courcellette, the site of the first major use of tanks supporting Canadian troops, and the nearby tank memorial. We include Albert, the Thiepval Memorial to the Missing and the Ulster Tower. An undoubted highlight for me and I am sure for all of you, will be our guided walk around the incredible preserved Beaumont Hamel battlefield site.'

'Ed, who were the Accrington Pals?' asked Mike.

'The Accrington Pals are probably the best remembered of the battalions raised in the early months of the First World War in response to Kitchener's call for a volunteer army. Groups of friends from all walks of life in Accrington and its neighbouring towns enlisted together to form a battalion with a distinctively local identity. The Battle of the Somme was the battalion's first major action; they suffered heavy losses in the attack on the 1st of July 1916, the opening day of the Battle. The losses were devastating on a community where nearly everyone had a relative or friend who had been killed or wounded. The story becomes no less tragic with the passing of the years.'

ACCRINGTON. BATT" E.L.R. B C° N° 1 PLATOON.

The group of tourists could not comprehend what that would have been like and put it down to another horrific war story.

'So, it's going to be another big day; use your time at the hotel wisely, no night clubbing!'

They all laughed and proceeded to go to their rooms.

Harry looked over at Ben and saw that he had been dozing throughout Ed's briefing.

'Waste of space,' he thought.


Terry knocked on his Mother's door.

'Mum, we still have not had our chat about some of the mysterious things that have been happening,' said Terry.

'What do you mean, Son? I am not aware of anything 'mysterious', as you call it.'

Terry recounted his experiences in Lille

'I can't believe it, Terry. Are you sure you didn't dream all of this?'

'Mum, I was in the street. I saw and spoke to Great Uncle Harry. I saw the German troops marching; I have no doubt in my mind. I have been doing some research on the Internet and you would be surprised just how many ghost stories there are revolving around the battlefields of World War One.'

'So, tell me one of these ghost stories you have researched. I am interested to know.'

'Ok, Mum, how about this one?'

Terry showed Lois the story he had bookmarked on his laptop.

'Bob Baker was from Hobart, Tasmania. He had enlisted in June of 1916, and he had fought in the Battle of Pozières and The Battle of Hamel and Villers-Brettoneux under General Monash. They were now moving on Germany herself, past the Hindenburg Line and beyond. The date was 15th September 1918 and the days of trench warfare were over. Jerry was on the run and the warfare was fast- moving. Bob was trying to get some sleep in a foxhole, which they used for cover and rest. As he was dozing he heard a voice call his name, not his usual name, but his nick name of "Butch". He looked up but there was no one around, so he closed his eyes again ,when he heard the voice again, but louder:"Butch"; this time, Bob sat up but still did not leave the foxhole. Finally a scream in his ear: "Butch! Get out!" Bob leapt up and ran; he was more scared of the voice than anything the Huns could throw at him. Bob ran up the hill behind him, totally confused, when he heard the familiar whine of a German shell coming. He hit the ground and heard it explode. He lifted his head to see his foxhole totally demolished: it was a direct hit on where he had been dozing. He sat down and wept; only one person ever in his life had called him "Butch" and that was his brother who had been killed in the Battle of Fromelles.'

'So I take it this Bob Baker lived through the war to tell this story?'

'He did and came home with a Distinguished Service Medal and a piece of German shrapnel in his thigh.'

'Another one I discovered was even more astounding: an Officer called William M. Speight had seen a phantom figure in his dugout one night. The next evening he invited another officer to witness the strange spectre; sure enough, the two of them witnessed the spirit of a

British Officer walking around in the dugout, then he stopped pacing and pointed to the floor. Speight gathered a party of engineers to take apart the floor boards, then sent for miners to dig down a few feet to see if something was underneath the soil, thinking perhaps this dead officer had buried something valuable and maybe wanted it sent home, but what the miners uncovered was something of far greater importance: it was a mine, a German one filled with High Explosives and a timer timed to go off in 13 hours' time. The engineers came back and defused the explosives and took them away, no doubt to be used in a British mine somewhere else.'

'There are many more stories, Mum, and I can understand why: there are more ghost stories emanating from the Western Front and other battlefields from the Great War than anywhere else in time.'

Lois, being a good Catholic, would not normally entertain such stories but it was her son who was recounting them and speaking of his own experiences. She assured Terry that she believed him but would prefer not to discuss the topic again, not in the near future anyway. Terry bade her goodnight. Lois lay in her bed for quite some time thinking about it, before drifting off to sleep.

Ed got the group together in front of the bus and started to brief them on what happened on the first day of the Battle of the Somme.

'The plan was that the Battle of The Somme would be a significant break-through for the British. It wasn't; it was a complete bloodbath. It was like leading lambs to the slaughter. General Haig was severely criticised then and still is today.

The plan was to attack on a twenty-four-kilometre front between Serre and Curlu, north of the Somme. The French would use five divisions to attack a thirteen-kilometre front south of the Somme. Allied artillery pounded the German lines for seven days prior to the attack, using one million six hundred thousand shells. The British commanders were so sure they had destroyed the German defences that they ordered their troops to walk slowly towards the enemy lines. The idea was that once the trenches had been secured, the cavalry units would then round up the fleeing Germans.

The Germans had had plenty of time to prepare and fortify their bunkers; they intended to stay in France for a while, and they also had a week's notice that there would be an assault by the British and French. The other thing the Germans had going in their favour was the fact that many of the British shells failed to explode. When the bombardment started, the Germans simply moved below out of harm's way and waited for it to cease, then climbed back to their positions and let the bastards have it. That's what they did; at 7.30am, 1st July, the whistles were blown to start the attack.

The British started to walk towards the German lines, all eleven Division; the German machine guns started firing en masse. The slaughter had begun. A few units did manage to infiltrate the enemy trenches but unfortunately they had no back up so they had to retreat. When this horrific day came to a close, nearly 60,000 British casualties were counted, with over twenty thousand dead, the largest loss in their history. Sixty per cent of the officers were killed on that first day.

When General Kitchener called for volunteers, many towns and counties heeded the call and created 'Pals' Battalions, such as the renowned Accrington Pals. These Pals Battalions suffered catastrophic casualties. Whole units fought and died together, with dire effect on their towns and communities.

The French Army enjoyed better success. They were better armed and faced a weaker defence, but unfortunately they were unable to capitalise and had to retreat to their earlier positions.

Haig's magnificent breakthrough plans were to be relegated to the scrap heap; he decided that future advances would be limited and they would concentrate on the southern sector. On 14th July, the British were able to take the German positions, but once again could not take advantage. The following two months became a nasty stalemate with the Allies not progressing much at all. Haig introduced tanks for the first time but they proved to be all but useless; they were too small, lightly armed and tended to break down with monotonous regularity.

October was extremely wet, turning the battlefields into a muddy quagmire so finally in mid-November the battle ended. The allied troops advanced a miserly eight kilometres into enemy territory.

The Battle of the Somme created four hundred and twenty thousand British casualties; the French suffered one hundred and ninety five thousand and the Germans around six hundred and fifty thousand.'

## The Somme, France 1916

Albert Shearer hadn't seen his brother, Archie, since they had left their training camp in Scotland. They had been assigned to different units: Archie was with the 15th division and Albert had been assigned to the 9th. He knew quite a few of the lads in his unit as they were from Leith where he grew up so it wasn't that he lacked mates. However he did miss his big brother, Archie, and hoped he was all right.

Albert had been billeted with a French family for the past few weeks. They were very nice but seeing he didn't speak French and they didn't speak English, communication was a bit of a problem. The wife, Edith was an excellent cook, so life was pretty good... that is, until he received word that he was to report to command. He was looking forward to seeing some action and giving Jerry a lesson or two so he went off with enthusiasm and a sense of purpose.

He met his good mate, Jackie McDonald, when he arrived, and soon after, Jimmie White joined them. As they sat on some ammo boxes, they talked about their respective billets.

'Hey, Alby, what was your place like, mate?' asked Jackie.

'It was really a nice house just out of town and the family was really friendly but it was a bit hard communicating, not speaking the lingo and all.'

'What about the children?'

'They had two, about ten and twelve I would guess.'

'Ah, so you didn't have an eighteen year-old daughter that was just dying for some British meat, then?'

'No, mate, no such luck! You're not going to tell me that you cracked it lucky, are you?'

'Well, as a matter of fact, I did.'

'What was she like, you bastard?'

'Very nice indeed, couldn't get enough of me. She used to sneak up to the loft where I was sleeping every night and "How's your father?" if you know what I mean.'

'Well, mate, those memories will keep you going throughout this fight.'

'So what about you, Jimmie? How did you go?' asked Jackie.

'Nothing like you, mate, very quiet. I stayed with an elderly couple on a farm too far out to visit the village, so I ended up helping them around the farm. They were a nice old couple but I would have preferred your billet.'

A young officer started doing the rounds, alerting the men they were due to move forward to their trenches in the next thirty minutes or so.

The time came and they started marching towards the British lines. They were told that there would be a bombardment before the attack to soften up the Germans before they beat them up.

Once positioned, they could hear the shells being fired from the 15 inch Howitzers that fired a shell weighing 1450 pounds over 12 kilometres. They were throwing everything at the Germans.

The bombardment went for an entire week. Jackie was starting to get pretty pissed off with the constant noise and the cramped space in the trench.

'Fuck this, I haven't slept since the bloody shells started raining down on the bloody Germans.'

'Don't be too annoyed, mate,' said Albert.

'These shells are going to make this attack into a walk in the park. There's no bloody way that they can survive this. They'll be all dead by the time we reach their lines.'

'Well, I hope they're not all dead, because I want to shoot a few of the buggers,' said Jimmie.

Just then they heard a huge explosion, then another and, in fact, they heard ten in all.

'Fuck me,' said Jackie, they were our mines. The Germans will be mince-meat by now.'

Then complete silence. It was 7.30am; they heard the whistle to go over the top. Their officers ordered them not to run, just walk.

Why run? Most of the Germans would be dead.

Mine Explosion, The Somme 1916

Albert, Jackie and Jimmie all started to walk towards the German Lines and then they heard the sound of machine-gun fire. Soldiers were being torn apart by a massive onslaught of bullets. They all hit the ground together and stared at each other.

'So, all the fucking Germans will be dead, will they?' yelled Jimmie.

Albert got to his knees and was about to say to his two mates, 'come on, let's go.' A stream of machine-gunfire tore through his head and neck almost decapitating him. He slumped to the ground. Jimmie and Jackie crawled on their bellies but to no avail. The Germans, thanks to Haig's grandiose plans, butchered them also.

# School Days

## Chapter 28

**July 1916**

Jane Shearer had just turned fourteen. She was a boarder at St Georges School for Girls in Edinburgh, Scotland, one of the best schools available for young women, both in the academic sense and for personal development. Jane was in her final year, during which she excelled in English, History and Geography. Her Mathematics and Science were acceptable however, even though she passed Latin, she detested it.

Life in the boarding school was good, with lots of companionship but also it was very strict, with harsh discipline if a girl was caught smoking or wearing make-up.

Jane was considered a model student and had been elected School Captain in her final year; she was also the champion archer of the school for the past three years and a member of the hockey team.

Her best friend was Mary Turner who came from Glasgow and shared the same love for archery and hockey as Jane; Mary always came runner-up to Jane in the competitions and would have loved to beat her best friend, even if only once; it was not to be.

Jane, first row, second on left, Mary, back row, last on right.

Jane was very proud of her two older brothers, Archie and Albert, who had both enlisted to fight in the war, Archie in 1915 and Albert just eight months later in 1916. Jane was also very concerned for them; she had read the newspaper reports about various battles and the number of lives lost and she prayed each night that God would protect them both and bring them home safely.

About twice a month, her parents would visit her and they would go out in her father's new Ford Model T, the most popular car in Britain at the time. They would drive north and visit places such as North Berwick, which can be spotted for miles, even from Edinburgh; this is due to the extinct volcano, named North Berwick Law, which sits at the southern edge of town. The volcano can be climbed for amazing views across both sea and land.

The beaches and shoreline in this area are relatively unspoilt and peaceful, with plenty of bird life and seals off shore.

Her House Mistress, Mrs Black, came to Jane to inform her that her parents would be arriving that morning to take her on a day trip. Jane was puzzled, as they had visited her the previous Sunday. She got herself ready in her best outfit as was the norm for these outings and waited for them in the school reading lounge where she could keep an eye out for them coming up the drive way. She only had to wait fifteen minutes, when her parents, Moira and John, arrived. She greeted them and got in the back seat of the Model T.

'It is always wonderful to see you both, but I don't understand why you are visiting two weeks in a row. You must really miss me.'

John looked at Moira, hoping for the right thing to say to their beloved daughter.

'We do miss you, darling, but we need to talk to you about something important. We are going home to Leith. You haven't been home for a while.'

Jane started to worry. ' What could be so important? Were they going to tell her she had to leave school in her final year?'

It only took forty-five minutes to arrive at their pretty sandstone house with the beautiful rose gardens her mother tended so carefully.

They went into the front sitting room and Jane's mother went to make some tea, and she returned fifteen minutes later with the good Royal Doulton set.

'My goodness, I don't normally get this treatment. We usually drink from the kitchen set. Now what is the occasion? What do you have to tell me?'

John turned to his beautiful daughter they both loved so much

'Jane, my dear, we have some very sad news.'

Before he could go on, Jane dropped her tea on the table, breaking the cup.

'No, don't tell me! NO!' she ran outside into the garden sobbing uncontrollably. Her parents followed her out and guided her back inside and sat her down.

'Which one?' she asked through her tears.

'It was Archie,' said her father through teary eyes, 'he died in a place called Loos in France. We don't know how he died but we know he died with honour fighting for his country. We have been told he will be buried with full military honours; we will visit his grave, I promise, when this terrible war is over.'

Jane stayed with her parents for a week. They talked a lot, they cried a lot but now it was time to go back to St Georges and finish her schooling. All the teachers were sympathetic, as they were with the other fifteen girls who had lost relatives in the war so far.

Jane started to get back into the swing of things and her results from her mid-year exams were good. The housemistress was pleased with the way she continued to excel at archery and her friends all treated her the same as they had before.

One night in the dormitory at the start of July, at about 2am, she was woken from a deep sleep by a sensation that felt like someone had sat on the side of her bed. She looked in the dim light but could not see anybody, then another sensation on the other side. Jane thought she was going mad, and then an image appeared. It was, she thought, her brother, Archie; then her brother, Albert, appeared.

Archie spoke to her 'Janie' (only her brothers called her 'Janie'). 'We wanted to come back to let you know we are fine and will be watching over you for the rest of your life. We are both very proud of you and now you are the only child left, it is important to look after our Mother and Father.'

Jane looked at Albert and cried 'I didn't know you were dead, too; why didn't they tell me?'

'Sorry, Janie, but even Mother and Father don't know yet. I only went over to the other side yesterday.'

'Oh my God, this is all too much. It was hard enough learning about Archie, but now you, too.' Jane could not be consoled.

'Janie, we have a very special message for you: listen carefully.'

'We want you to enrol in the Edinburgh School of Medicine for Women. We want you to become a Doctor and help others, do you understand?'

'Yes, but I don't know if I am smart enough.'

'You are, believe me, we know you are.'

'I will try my hardest,' said Jane, weeping into a handkerchief. 'How will I know you are watching over me?'

'Don't worry, Janie, you will know, I promise you. You will feel our presence.'

'Janie, we have to go now but just know that we are always here for you.'

Jane closed her eyes .When she opened them, both her brothers were gone.

The next morning, the House Mistress pulled Jane out of her Latin class and informed her that her parents were here to see her. Jane knew why.

Jane went on to become one of the pre-eminent doctors in Scotland and lived until 1985. Three children, two sons and a daughter and ten grandchildren survived her.

# Snakes and Ladders

## Chapter 29

**1918**

Athol McKenzie was now a seasoned warrior having fought at the Somme and Passchendaele. He had arrived on the Western Front in May 1917; it was now 4th November 1918. Athol was not aware that The Great War, "the war to end all wars" was only seven days away from ending, although he knew Fritz was on the run back home, tail between his legs and the Allies looked like they would win this war... that's if there ever is a winner in such conflicts.

Athol was in the 3rd Division of the New Zealand infantry. They were marching on Le Quesnoy which was an old fortress town occupying a strategic position in north-eastern France. It had been in German hands since 1914, and there were several thousand German troops still in the town. The walls of Le Quesnoy could have been quickly destroyed by heavy artillery, but Command decided not to mount such an assault on the town. Instead, several battalions of the 3rd New Zealand Rifle Brigade were given the task of scaling the walls and capturing the fortress town.

There was a competition between the 2nd and 4th Battalions as to who would enter the town first; the former advanced on the town in the direction of the Valenciennes Gate, and the latter pressed forward from the west. The German defenders were demoralised, but their officers were not prepared to surrender without a fight.

This set the stage for one of the New Zealand Division's most spectacular successes of the war. When a section of the 4th Battalion reached the inner walls about midday on the 4th of November, they had already scaled several of the outer ramparts with ladders, supplied by the engineers. The riflemen could only use a narrow ledge to mount their ladders to reach the top of the inner wall. Led by Lieutenant Averil, the battalion's intelligence officer, they quickly scaled the walls. After exchanging shots with fleeing Germans, the New Zealanders entered the town. The garrison quickly surrendered.

Just over ninety New Zealanders lost their lives in the battle, however they captured a thousand German soldiers. This was the last battle New Zealand took part in before the end of the war.

During the First World War, New Zealand lost 18,052 of its finest young men and 69,214 were wounded; this equated to 1.64% of its entire population and was the second highest percentage after Serbia.

Athol McKenzie had risen through the ranks from Private to Second Lieutenant. This was because he showed real leadership and valour at The Somme and Passchendaele. The other reason was the infantry had lost so many of its officers in battle. He was planning the assault with Lieutenant Averil.

'Command have ordered us to take the town without killing too many Frenchies, mate' said Les Averil.

'How do they plan for us to take this bloody big fortress without blasting the bastards first?'

'We have got to keep Fritz busy on those ramparts with rifle fire and we split up the 2nd and 4th and surround the buggers. We meet up and force the Germans to surrender.'

'Sounds good in theory, Les, but we still have to get over those ramparts which look about sixty feet tall, then we still have the fortress wall to get over. Holy hell!'

'Well, Lieutenant, they're our bloody orders so we better get on and follow them.'

Athol went back to his unit and briefed his men.

'So we go over tomorrow, lads. By all accounts, the Germans are at the end of their run, we could all be home for Christmas, so let's not make a mess of it.'

The attack was launched next day, 5th November 1918. Lieutenant Averil led the attack, supported by second Lieutenant McKenzie. McKenzie's initial doubts were proving to be justified.

'Bloody hell, these German machine gun nests are giving us real grief, Lieutenant McKenzie,' shouted Private Baker.

'Just keep going, Baker, we will get the bastards eventually.'

Things did start to improve and McKenzie and his men did advance to about one mile east from Le Quesnoy. They captured about five hundred German Prisoners who looked pretty relieved to be out of the fighting for good.

The Germans were not about to surrender the town they had held for the past four years so Les and Athol knew they would have to mount an all-out assault. The Germans had all that time to organize their defences and, in true German style, they did it very well, defending the moat and causeways of outer positions. The ramparts, they estimated, were over sixty feet high.

So it became obvious that the small town had to be assaulted. Reconnaissance patrols supplied information that the German positions were cleverly organised and the ramparts were also high.

Eventually the Kiwis got to the outer ramparts. Lieutenant McKenzie led a patrol to try to capture a German machine-gun nest.

'You blokes, come with me!' shouted Athol. 'We need to take that machine gun position if we're to get any closer.'

His patrol consisted of fourteen of New Zealand's finest.

'Right, men, we need to get close enough to hurl some grenades at the bastards, then we need to advance and shoot any survivors if there are any. I want you seven to take the left flank and I will lead the right. Does everybody understand what we need to do? Right let's go.'

Athol got in a position near the moat to throw his first grenade; the others in his group followed. They could see the second group doing the same from the other side. Athol gave the signal and fourteen grenades were hurled at the same time, exploding in unison.

'Nobody could survive that, Baker, but we need to proceed with maximum caution, just in case'.

They made their way slowly until Athol popped his head over the mound.

'They all look dead to me, men.'

He was right. There wasn't much left of them.

Now that they had the cover of the moat and the smoke, they dragged up the ladders and started to scale the ramparts.

'Don't bloody fall off the ladder, fellas, or you will be dead and you don't want that on your epitaph. *He fell off a ladder*. Better: *He died in battle killing twenty five Germans.'*

They all started up the forty-foot ladders with a couple of blokes holding them steady from below.

Athol was the first one up and was greeted by a German Captain who shot him through the forehead; Athol died instantly and fell to the moat below. One week from war's end, he had served over two years on the Western Front. Athol didn't make it home for Christmas.

The Kiwis, with great bravery and determination, captured the fortress and town of Le Quesnoy, liberating the five thousand French villagers and capturing a thousand German soldiers, as well as many guns and artillery.

There were great celebrations in the town. Strange thing was, Private Baker could have sworn he saw Lieutenant McKenzie laughing and celebrating with the French townspeople in the village square.

THE INNER RAMPART (LE QUESNOY)

# Monash's Blitzkrieg

## Chapter 30

**1918**

General Sir John Monash

Ed was an admirer of General John Monash; he was Australia's most revered soldier.

Ed explained to the group why he admired the man so much.

'General Monash was born in Melbourne on 27th of June 1865. He attended Scotch College where he was Dux in his final year; he then went on to Melbourne University where he studied engineering and arts. He obviously used both sides of his brain,' Ed commented.

'He was also a keen debater and an amateur actor. He really was a well-rounded individual. In 1884 he joined the university company of the 4th Battalion, Victorian Rifles.

Monash was quite the "driven" young man, ambitious and intelligent. He worked on the construction of the Princes Bridge in Melbourne and in 1888 was placed in charge of constructing a new railway even though he had not yet qualified. A keen womaniser throughout his life, Monash married Hannah Moss in April 1891 after having had several other relationships, some quite scandalous by contemporary standards. He could almost be described as the Errol Flynn of his day.'

'That's the first interesting piece of news I've heard, since this bloody tour started,' thought Ben.

Ed continued

'Let us examine his tactics at the Battle of Hamel.

Things were starting to go the Allies' way after the Australian force's success under Major General John Monash at the Battle of Hamel, which took place on the 4th of July 1918. The date was ironic as it was not only one of the first times the Americans had fought in the war but also the first time they had served under a foreign commander.

The battle was decisively different under Monash's plan, compared to the bombardment prior to attack that the British had adopted throughout the war. This tactic, of course, gave the Germans plenty of notice that an attack was coming and time to prepare themselves for the attack. Monash had been appalled at the horrific casualty rate from the British methods and their concept of "save our equipment but sacrifice the infantry". In his own words, the aim was *'not to expend itself upon heroic physical effort'* but *'to advance under maximum possible array of mechanical resources, in the form of guns, machine guns, tanks, mortars and aeroplanes to the appointed goal'*

Using tanks to help protect the infantry and using the element of surprise with creeping artillery from behind, war historians attribute to him the invention of the "Blitzkrieg".

Monash went on to say *'A perfected modern battle plan is like a score for an orchestral composition, where the various arms and units are the*

236

*instruments, and the tasks they perform are their respective musical phrases. Every individual unit must make its entry precisely at the proper moment, and play its phrase in the general harmony.'*

Monash and the five Australian divisions, achieved success at Hamel only three minutes past the planned battle time of ninety minutes. If the British model had been adopted, it would have taken weeks, with many more men lost.

There were 1062 Australian casualties and 176 American casualties. The Germans lost 2000 men, with 1600 captured; most of the German equipment was seized.'

British Mark IV Tanks 1918

Harry Daniel senior was pleased to be under the Australian commander. Up until now, he had fought under British commanders who seemed to use the troops as cannon fodder.

At first he didn't know any better and just followed orders but after three years in battle, he had developed some understanding of the tactics being used. He had been badly wounded in the Battle of Passchendaele and spent two months in England recuperating in hospital. He now felt fine, although his leg ached every now and then. The cobbers he fought with from home had all died in various battles but he made new ones along the way. One of those mates was Curley Simmonds, who came from Sydney, but that didn't worry Harry, a Melbourne boy through and through. The word was out that they were going to launch another attack on the Germans defensive lines, this time with only Australian troops.

Harry told Curley 'I like the idea that we run behind the tanks which might give us a chance, instead of being mowed down like flies, as we were at Passchendaele.'

At first light they were ordered out with no bombardment before, which was a total surprise to the Germans. The first thing Fritz knew was the sight of hundreds of tanks and thousands of diggers heading for them. Harry was trotting beside a tank and, when appropriate, firing at the Germans in their trenches. Planes were overhead dropping bombs into the German defences while the artillery was blasting them, as Harry and the Australian army approached. It was all over in ninety minutes and Harry and Curley captured more than twenty German soldiers. 'A bloody good day's work!' they both thought.

They headed back to their positions and looked forward to a break but not for long: the Battle of Amiens was due to begin just four days later, using the same tactics that had been so successful in the Battle of Hamel.'

Ed continued to address the group with a description of the Battle of Amiens.

'The battle of Amiens was fought between the 8th of August and the 11th of August 1918. The battle started the "one hundred day offensive", which ultimately led to the end of the war. Using Monash's Blitzkrieg tactics, the Allied forces advanced over fifteen miles on the first day. This battle lifted the morale of the Allied forces and demoralised the German forces, which encouraged a large number of German surrenders.

The days of the infamous trench warfare ended with this battle. Monash's plan, accepted by the British and French High Command, used tanks and other machinery extensively, as they did in the Battle of Hamel. The fighting became mobile and fast-moving and finally drew to a close when the armistice was signed on the 11th of November 1918.

The plan entailed the need for utmost secrecy to ensure the element of surprise. The French under General Foch had no tanks but insisted on participating in the battle, along with the British, Australian and Canadian troops. The Allies were adamant that no bombardment would precede the attack, as they were insistent on maintaining the element of surprise. The French therefore agreed not to use their heavy guns until forty-five minutes after the attack had begun.

The level of security for this attack was unprecedented so as to ensure they achieved the level of surprise that the plan demanded. In the early hours of August 8th, the British, Australian and Canadian infantry moved into position as a dense fog enveloped the battlefield. Aeroplanes above the fog drowned out the noise of the tanks which were there to support the infantry. In this eerie misty atmosphere, the artillery, as agreed, began their bombardment forty -five minutes after the assault had begun.

In the thick fog the tanks were moving in what they hoped was the right direction.They were, with the first objective taken by 7.30am; most of the German field artillery was overrun and captured.

The fog started to lift by 8.30 am, giving the German guns a clear view. They opened fire on the Allied tanks, taking many of them out. The Australian Diggers maintained their incredible pace and soon captured most of the German guns. A major objective, the German "Amiens Defence System", had been captured. Equally successful were the Canadian and French attacks; fifteen miles of the German front, south of the Somme, had been captured. Never before had the Allies been so successful in a single day. Thirteen thousand German soldiers were captured, with the French taking three thousand five hundred alone.

The following day was not as spectacular as the previous one and did not achieve the same results; there was no supporting artillery as the infantry had moved too quickly and the tank force, which numbered five hundred on the first day, had been reduced to six. The Germans were shelling the advancing troops, slowing down the Australian Diggers. The Australians managed to slip across the Somme and capture the village of Chipilly, despite the Germans holding the ridge above the town.

By August 10th the Battle of Amiens was over, a decisive win for the Allies and the beginning of the end for the German Army.

A few days after the battle had ended, King George V knighted John Monash for his success in the field.'

Tanks being employed in the Battle of Amiens

# Letters From the Front

## Chapter 31

Harry had just turned thirty-six; he had survived the battle of Hamel and the Battle of Amiens. He and the Australian troops were delighted that the Germans were surrendering and retreating back to their fatherland. He was hopeful that this bloody war would end soon and he could go back home and marry his darling Emma and start the family he always wanted.

He had received letters from Emma on a regular basis; despite the mayhem, the postman always seemed to track him down He had written only a few letters to his parents and he felt now was the time to write and give them a true account of what life on the Western Front was really like.

Harry M.M

July 2 1918

Dear Mum and Dad,

A few lines to try and tell you what it's like out here. I am giving no state secrets away, only telling bare facts, so I think I can sign my name at the end of this letter, I did intend to write to you a few days ago, but there was an awful din going on. We were staying in a cellar in the day and working in the trenches or in front of the trenches at night. It was impossible to sleep on account of the noise and the shells kept striking the house and pieces of it kept falling off, I nearly copped it on the head a couple of times.

There has been some very heavy fighting round this way for the last two weeks, I have been living in the Trenches since July without much of a break we are all wondering if they will ever relieve us, and wonder when in the hell are our relief boys will get here. Gas hit us a few days ago, I had my mask on but I still got a bloody horrible headache out of it and my eyes won't stop itching. Still it will pass and it really is nothing compared to the conditions we have to endure in the trenches. They are constantly wet with muddy clay coating everything a lot of my cobbers have got trench feet and one had his left foot amputated; it really is a horrible thing to get. I did have it but mine was treatable and I only had a week off in the hospital.

I am sick of these trenches though, we constantly have lice in our uniforms and you just can't get rid of them. We never have enough to eat and pretty well survive on tea and biscuits with a little bit of jam. I sound like I am complaining a lot but truly it is hell on earth and I can't wait to get back home.

There was some real action the other day. We were in our trenches as per bloody usual (sorry Mum) and my officer, Lieutenant Jack Brady and I crawled out into No-Man's Land with another ten Diggers as it was quiet. We wanted to check if Fritz was up to anything that we should know about. Well the Germans spotted us and all hell broke loose, they were strafing us with their machine guns and all I could do was lie flat and keep my head down. About six of my mates got killed that day but thank God I survived and made it back to the trench. Just as I crawled back in, Jerry had worked out his range and shells were raining down all around us. Quite a few of our boys got killed and about twenty horses went down. It is always sad when horses get killed strange it affects you more than when our Diggers get killed, I suppose we are so used to it now. Mind you a sad thing happened the other night we were out doing barbed wire in front of the trenches, All our blokes had been warned that we were out there, we had almost finished when two of our men were shot right through the head by our own, you never read things like that in the papers.


August 12

Sorry I got a bit busy Mum and Dad so this letter is taking a little while to write.

I got my wish. We are now out of the trenches and on the move, chasing Fritz back to where he bloody belongs. I don't miss the trenches at all. I think I mentioned how sick of them I was.

I was in Amiens recently. I expect you don't know where that is, it was a mass of ruins, and two or three streets were on fire in fact it has been burning for eight days, and the sights were horrible, dead horses in the streets and the stench was vile, wounded horses wandering about leaving a trail of blood in their wake in fact it was a city of the dead, one part of a horse in one place and the other in another. I caught one the other night while out running a message and the poor thing was frightened to death, I gave it a feed and tried to get it to come with me to shelter from Jerry's shell fire but it was too frightened to move, thought I would have to leave him there as I needed to seek cover and the shells were getting a bit too near for my liking but he decided to come with me. One of the Officers was good enough to bring him back to our dugouts.

I am giving it to you as it really is, Mum and Dad but I think it is important for you to know what this war is really like. Before I left Melbourne, I thought I was heading off for a great adventure, that we would be fighting a war full of gallantry like the Knights of old England.

I didn't reckon being in a uniform that has not been washed for over six months and still covered in lice and my mate's blood and brains.

I didn't think I would see Diggers on the side of the road that had been dead for two or three days with no one to bury them.

I have been living in Hell.

Mum and Dad, the signs are that Fritz is under the hammer and retreating back to where he came from. I hope that I will be home soon and see you and my darling Emma and start living a normal life.

Much Love

Harry

Harry placed a photo of Emma on a stone and wrote his last letter to his sweetheart.

August 1918

My Darling Emma,

I am sitting on a stone-wall in a place called Chipilly, a tiny little village that we just took from Jerry after a very hard and furious fight. I really think that we are getting close to the end of this war and we should all be coming home soon. I am not sure when of course but from what I hear it will be before June next year. Maybe you should start planning our wedding for September, as that is a nice time of year in Melbourne.

We are starting to move through some pretty countryside instead of the desolation and burnt out towns that we have got used to over the past couple *of years. I had a week's leave a few months ago and went to Paris, it really is a beautiful city but boy they know how to charge. I think since the Yanks arrived everything has gone up.*

*I have lost a few good mates in the fighting and I do miss them, I have met some other blokes though and we have all been lucky so far and kept out of harm's way as it were. My leg still aches from the wounds I received but other than that, I am in good health.*

*As you well know, my love, I am a man of few words so I will sign off now as the Lieutenant has told us our platoon has to move out.*

*I love you very much.*

*Harry*


Harry and his platoon of twelve were asked to go outside the town and skirt around the back of the ridge and see if they could take out the machine gun nests that were giving the boys some curry. The Lieutenant in charge was James Osborne. He was only twenty-four and came from Ballarat, not far from where Harry was born. He split the platoon into two with six, including himself, taking the left flank and Harry as the senior soldier, leading the other six up the right flank. As they approached through some thick forest, they could hear the machine guns firing off their rounds at the village below, although as yet they had no visual contact.

Harry heard a sound in the trees ahead but before he or any of the others could respond, grenades were being hurled at them. They exploded before they hit the ground and Harry and two other soldiers in the group were ripped apart. Harry's body was separated from his limbs and his head was twenty metres away. They never collected and buried his body.

Harry Daniel MM died at age 39 on the 10th of August 1918.

He is still listed as Missing.

Both Annie and James Daniel were home at five o'clock on the 12<sup>th</sup> of September when the minister brought the dreaded yellow envelope. Nothing could pacify their utter grief; their youngest son, a war hero who had won a Military Medal at Passchendaele, was gone. No wedding, no grandchildren, nothing. Jim looked at his distraught wife

'Annie, we know Harry made the ultimate sacrifice for his country and we must never forget his bravery and dedication; he has made us very proud.'

'I don't care about  making us very proud. All I know is my youngest boy is dead and lying in a field in a place I have never heard of. I just hope they find him and give him a proper burial.' Annie's sobs were uncontrollable.

The next day Jim was melancholy but knew it was up to him to tell Emma, Harry's fiancée. He walked to Emma's house and knocked on the door.

When Emma opened it, and looked at Jim, she screamed.

'No, don't tell me! Go away. You are playing a trick, you must be,' and slammed the door in Jim's face.

Emma just sobbed and sobbed for what seemed an eternity: finally she opened the door and Jim was still standing there, tears running down his face.

'I am sorry, Mr Daniel, please come in.'

Jim stumbled in and Emma hugged him; she had never hugged Jim before but they just held each other tight and cried together. Finally they separated and Emma invited Jim into the kitchen. Emma offered him a cup of tea, which he accepted. Through sobs, she made the tea and they sat at the kitchen table.

'Do you know what happened, Mr. Daniel?'

'No, Emma, we only just received the telegram. We do know he was listed as Missing in Action, Presumed Dead. We can only pray that they recover his body so he can receive a proper military burial. They did say that Harry's medals, including the Military Medal for

Bravery in the Field, would be sent to us. I promise one of those medals will go to you.'

They both consoled each other and Emma promised that she would not be a stranger to the Daniel family; then Jim left. As he was walking home, he knew that he would never again have to undergo something so traumatic.

# How Are You Going to Keep Them Down On Mouquet Farm?

## (After they've Seen Paris)

## Chapter 32

**23rd April, 2012**

'Pozières was a place that became legendary amongst the Diggers: "if you survived Pozières, you could survive anything" was the catch cry.

The group were looking forward to their visit to the town but also to visiting Mouquet Farm where much of the fighting took place.

They met down in the lobby and the bus pulled up precisely at 9am. Once boarded, Ed started to brief them on the carnage that occurred at Mouquet Farm.

'Success on the Somme came at a cost, which at times seemed to surpass the cost of failure, and for the Australians, Pozières was such a case. In the fighting at Pozières , around the Windmill and northwards along the ridge towards Mouquet Farm (The Diggers called it either Moo Cow or Mucky Farm). Here the AIF suffered more than 23,000 casualties in little more than six weeks, between 23rd of July and 5th September 1916. Of these casualties, nearly 7000 were either killed, had died of wounds, or were "missing". That is slightly less than Gallipoli, however the Gallipoli Campaign took place over eight months. Australia has never lost as many soldiers, killed or wounded, in any other battle we have fought in, since Australia was founded in 1901. Today, the sacrifices of these men are still commemorated every year by the people of the town of Pozières, France.'

Mouquet Farm 1916

Marching into Battle, Mouquet Farm

The first stop in the village of Pozières was to have morning tea at the famous Le Café Tommie, run by Dominique Zanardi and his wife. As they entered the cafe they were amazed at all the war memorabilia covering the walls: there was even a trench system behind the café. Ed had booked a table and everybody took a seat.

Ed passed around an article that had been published in a number of newspapers and magazines.

'Read this article and then I will introduce you all to Dominique.'

During the war it is thought that a local French photographer, almost certainly an amateur, possibly a farmer, has offered to take pictures for a few francs. Soldiers have queued to have a photograph taken to send back to their anxious but proud families in Britain or Australia or New Zealand.

More than 90 years later, at least 400 glass photographic plates preserving the images were found in the loft of a barn at Warloy-Baillon and cast out as rubbish.

The survival of the images is owed to two local men: Bernard Gardin, aged 60, a photography enthusiast; and Dominique Zanardi, 49, proprietor of the "Tommy" café at Pozières, a village in the heart of the Somme battlefields.

M. Gardin was given a batch of about 270 glass plates by someone who knew of his hobby. He approached M. Zanardi, who has a collection of Great War memorabilia, including a football dug up 12 years ago inside a British soldier's rucksack. M. Zanardi, it turned out, already had 130 similar plates which he had gathered from other local people.

"About three years ago, someone bought a barn near Warloy-Baillon," M. Zanardi said. "They found the glass plates in the loft and just threw them out as rubbish. Many of them were picked up and taken away by passers-by. I started collecting them and had reached over 100 when M. Gardin turned up with this great batch of 270. They must also, originally, have come from the same source. There may be many more out there which we have not yet found."

M. Gardin and M. Zanardi have had prints made, at their own expense, from the original plates. M. Gardin describes these as "9 x 12 centimetre glass plates, of the kind used at the time by amateur photographers. A professional would have used a camera with bigger plates, 18 centimetres x 24."

Ed showed them all an album containing about one hundred photos, some, a portrait of a single soldier, others, group photos. This was only a quarter of the collection that Dominique and Bernard had acquired.

Dominique approached their table and introduced himself; strangely, he did not acknowledge Ed or Harry's presence.

He explained the reason he established "Le Café Tommie" was because of the respect he had for the British, Australian, Kiwi and Canadian soldiers who fought in the Pozières region and saved their village from German domination.

He also told the group that he regularly went walking in the fields surrounding Pozières and Mouquet Farm, looking for war artefacts, and had found the remains of soldiers who had either been dug up and were about to be covered over again by the excavator or simply left on a pile of dirt and clay. He had also found remains in the ploughed fields of farmers who could not afford the time to report their finds to the authorities. He estimated about fifteen sets of remains had been saved by him, after reporting the find to the Gendarme and the Commonwealth War Graves Commission. All fifteen now had graves in a war cemetery: only three had been identified.

They drank their morning tea and coffee and explored around the café's grounds before returning to the main street of the village where they met up with the bus.

# Uncle Sam Joins the Fray

## Chapter 33

### 1917 France

The United States President, Woodrow Wilson, was very reluctant to enter World War One. He declared the U.S neutrality and insisted that both sides respect America's rights as a neutral country.

Americans were deeply divided about the war in Europe, and how involvement could disrupt progressive reforms. "Top of the Pops" at the time was "I Didn't Raise My Boy to be a Soldier".

In 1916 Wilson narrowly won re-election with a slogan: "He kept us out of the war."

Although claiming neutrality, it became clear that America began to lean towards Britain and France.

Wilson knew that wartime trade with the belligerents was important to the American economy; trade boomed with the Allies.

The cash reserves of the Allies and the Germans were being eaten up by the war effort; they asked the USA for a line of credit and so in October 1915, President Wilson approved loans to both sides, although the Allies were the biggest benefactors. Loans to the Allies totalled $2.25 billion by 1917; on the other hand, Germany had loans outstanding of $27 million.

Germany announced a resumption of unrestricted submarine warfare in January 1917, which was an extremely provocative move, particularly after Germany sank the "Lusitania" in 1915, killing almost 2,000 people, many of them Americans.

Germany was bullish about winning the war within five months and therefore even if America entered the war, it could not mobilise quickly enough to change the course of the war, or so Germany thought.

What really pushed Wilson to the limit of his patience was the "Zimmerman Telegram", a telegram containing an offer to Mexico that if it declared war on the United States, Germany would commit to Mexico to assist her to recover the territory it had lost during the 1840s, including Texas, New Mexico, California, and Arizona.

The telegram and the fact that Germany had attacked three US ships during March led Wilson to ask Congress for a "Declaration of War".

In 1917, a High German official scoffed at American might: "America from a military point-of-view means nothing, and again nothing, and for a third time, nothing." The U.S. Army at the time had only 107,641men.

Within a year, however, the United States raised a five million-man army. By the war's end, the American armed forces were a decisive factor in blunting a German offensive and ending the bloody stalemate.

To raise troops, President Wilson insisted on a military draft. More than twenty three million men registered during World War I, and 2,800,000 draftees served in the armed forces. To select officers, the army launched an ambitious program of psychological testing.

# "Retreat! We Just Got Here"

## Chapter 34

In March 1918, the Germans launched a massive offensive on the Western Front in France's Somme River valley. With German troops barely fifty miles from Paris, Marshal Ferdinand Foch, the leader of the French army, assumed command of the allied forces. Foch's troops, aided by eighty-five thousand American soldiers, launched a furious counter-offensive. By the end of October, the counterattack pushed the German army back to the Belgian border.

American entry into the war quickly overcame the German military's numerical advantage. In June 1918, some two hundred and seventy nine thousand American soldiers crossed the Atlantic; in July, over three hundred thousand; in August, two hundred and eighty-six thousand more. All told, one and a half million American troops arrived in Europe during the last six months of the war. By the end of the conflict, the allies could field six hundred thousand more men than the Germans at any one time.

On the eleventh hour of the eleventh month 1918, came peace at last.

The United States suffered 323,000 casualties, The British Empire three million, two hundred and thirty four thousand and Russia, a devastating nine million, one hundred and fifty thousand.

William Hansen, Mike's Great Uncle, was one of the Americans killed in action at Belleau Wood.

Ed described the American actions.

'These comprised two related actions, firstly at Chateau-Thierry from the 3rd to the 4th of June and then at Belleau Wood itself from the 6th to the 26th of June. The Battle of Belleau Wood saw the wood re-captured by U.S. forces.

Chateau-Thierry formed the tip of the German advance towards Paris, some 50 miles southwest. Defended by U.S. Second and Third Divisions, dispatched at the behest of the French by AEF Commander-in-Chief, Jack Pershing, the Americans launched a counter-attack on the 3rd and 4th of June with the assistance of the French Tenth Colonial Division; in a spirited action, together they succeeded in pushing the Germans back across the Marne to Jaulgonne.

Rejuvenated by success, first at Cantigny at the end of May, and now at Chateau-Thierry, General Bundy's Second Division forces followed up Chateau-Thierry two days later with the difficult exercise of capturing Belleau Wood.

Second Division's Marine Corps, under James Harbord, was tasked with the taking of the wood. This perilous venture involved a murderous trek across an open wheat field, swept from end to end by German machine gun fire, a fact that continues to generate controversy today among some historians.

As a consequence of the open nature of the advance on the wood, casualties on the first day, the 6th of June, were the highest in Marine Corps history (a dubious record which remained until the capture of Japanese-held Tarawa in November 1943).

Marine Inspecting German Gun Placement

Fiercely defended by the Germans, the wood was first taken by the Marines (and Third Infantry Brigade), then ceded back to the Germans -and again taken by the U.S. forces a total of six times before the Germans were finally expelled. Also captured were the nearby villages of Vaux and Bouresche

The battle ran from the 1st to the 26th of June and by its end, saw U.S. forces suffer 9,777 casualties, of which 1,811 were fatal. The number of German casualties is not known, although some 1,600 troops were taken prisoner. More critically, the combined Chateau-Thierry/Belleau Wood action brought to an end the last major German offensive of the war.

The French name for the wood, Bois Belleau, was subsequently officially renamed Bois de la Brigade de Marine, in honour of the Marine Corps' tenacity.'

U.S. Marines in Battle

# ANZAC Day 2012

## "N'oublions jamais l'Australie"
## (let us never forget Australia)

## Chapter 35

**April 25ᵗʰ 2012**

Ed began his briefing on the bus on their way to their hotel in Amiens, just a short distance from Villers-Bretonneux which was convenient as the Dawn Service began at 5.30am and they needed to be there well before. Ed was a proud Australian and he was about to brief the group on a very important Australian battle; he knew the non-Australians would also appreciate the sacrifices made by the Diggers. Ben, as usual, seemed indifferent.

'The Somme was not kind to the ANZACs. One out of every two that fought in the region became a casualty; all in all, 22,000 Diggers. Their courage and determination in terrible conditions ensured they had proven themselves very worthy of their reputation as brilliant fighters capable of doing the impossible. The British High Command would call upon their courage again at Villers-Bretonneux.

The villages in France and Belgium never forgot the Australians who liberated them from the Germans or saved them from being occupied, "N'oublions jamais l'Australie" "Let Us Never Forget Australia" is emblazoned on the Villers-Bretonneux School.

**1918, The Somme**

'The Hindenburg Line was the last line of defence the Germans built in 1917. It was a mass of barbed wire, block-houses and well-constructed trenches. The village of Bullecourt sat slap bang in the middle of the line and became a fortress town. This defence line had never been penetrated and no wonder, with barbed wire in some places one hundred metres thick.

On the night of April 17th, the Australian forces attacked the Germans stationed at Bullecourt; they had no artillery and the tanks that were meant to break through the barbed wire were either broken down or became bogged down in the snow.

Major Percy Black was one of the officers leading the attack.

He yelled out to his men ' Come on, boys, bugger the tanks!'

He charged full on, into the wire. His men leapt forward with him and fought their way into the German trenches. The Diggers were the first soldiers to break through the Hindenburg Line. Once they got through, they looked for Major Black to share their success. They found him dead on the wire, his pistol still in his hand.

So many ANZACs had been killed in the attack that there were only a few left to defend the trenches. Once the Germans realized this, they mounted a counter-attack and overwhelmed the Diggers who were forced to withdraw.

The only order given was 'fight it out like Australians.'

The Australians returned with fresh troops three weeks later and again captured Jerry's trenches. The Germans mounted counter-attack after counter-attack for the next two weeks but finally gave up and withdrew.

The reason the village of Bullecourt is so grateful to Australia is that 10,000 of Australia's finest young men were either killed or wounded liberating their village.'

Memorial to Australian and British Soldiers at Bullecourt

Plaque on Villers-Bretonneux School

## 24th April 2012

The tour group checked into the Mercure Amiens Cathedrale; the plan was to go to the allocated rooms, rest up a while and meet in the lobby bar to discuss the schedule for the day. At 6.30 pm they all assembled at the bar; Christine and Tony's boys were going to eat at

McDonalds -at last, a town big enough for a McDonalds and very close to the Hotel.

"Murray" was on time and the restaurant was only ten minutes away.

The restaurant Ed had selected, Le Bouchon, was an excellent traditional French eatery. They all arrived and Ed ordered some very good wine, including two Australian Cabernet Sauvignons to mark the occasion. Seven of the group of twelve were Australians so tomorrow would be a very moving occasion for them, particularly when they all had ancestors whose names were etched on the memorial they would be visiting the next day.

Ed passed a copy of the morning's proceedings to everyone at the table:

*Official Anzac Day commemorations, 2012*

*ANZAC Dawn Service*
*Wednesday 25th of April 2012*
*Time*
*Site Opens 3am*
*Ceremony Commences 5.30am*
*Venue The Australian National Memorial*
*Villers-Bretonneux*

Villers-Bretonneux Cemetery

The next morning as they stood in the cold darkness in front of the memorial, they all contemplated what had taken place not only in Villers-Bretonneux but also across the entire Western Front, Gallipoli and The Middle East. Soldiers who had left their homes for "the Great Adventure" were only to be confronted with horrible conditions and far too many were asked to throw their lives away in ill-conceived and badly executed battle plans. Yet despite the odds, the Diggers and all the Allied soldiers had achieved the ultimate prize: Peace.

They also contemplated just how long that peace had lasted before the next generations were sent away to the Second World War and then Korea, Malaya, Vietnam, Iraq and Afghanistan. All up, over 100,000 Diggers have lost their lives, all in their prime.

The total fatalities occurring in wars since 1900 is 265,000,000 and we're still counting.

Then in the darkness they heard the drums escorting the catafalque party to the cenotaph; they took their places at each corner facing outwards with their rifles reversed to show that the dead were now at peace; if only that were true.

The ceremony proceeded with the singing of hymns and the address given by the Australian Minister of Veteran Affairs. Wreaths were laid, but the most moving part of the ceremony was the lone bugler playing The Last Post followed by a minute's silence, then Reveille and the national anthems of Australia, New Zealand and France. Each member of the group placed a poppy at the base of the cenotaph. They all dedicated the poppy to their missing ancestor lying in a field somewhere in France or Belgium.

The Dawn Service moved almost every one of the five thousand attendees with its poignant reminder of the sacrifices made and the futility of war. Ed emphasised 'how important it was to remember the 300,000 soldiers from both sides, still missing with no known grave'.

'If we could find and bury every one of the missing, we would need a cemetery two hundred acres in size; that equates to over one hundred and thirty football fields. Can you imagine 300,000 white crosses as far as the eye could see? Of course we won't find many of them and that is why we must ensure when a soldier's remains are uncovered, they are treated with the respect we show our fallen from the current wars such as Afghanistan.

Our Governments refuse to accept that some of these missing soldiers are not reported when found and are covered over, simply because of the delays it would cause in earth-works or ploughing. They must instigate new methods to ensure this does not continue to happen.'

Ed commented that his own Government did not organise an ANZAC Day ceremony on the Western Front until 2008, despite the fact that over eighty percent of those Australians killed in the Great War were fighting on the Western Front.


After the ceremony, the group made their way to the traditional *"gunfire breakfast"* hosted by the people of Villers-Bretonneux. Each year, the villagers prepare a traditional ANZAC day breakfast of eggs and bacon with coffee and rum. Adam had never tasted rum before so he was first inline. Ben had had the occasional nip after a Rugby game.

Diggers' Gunfire Breakfast

After breakfast, Ed took the group to the Lochnagar Mine Crater. The mine was detonated beneath the German lines on the first infamous day of the Battle of the Somme. The crater, despite erosion, still measures one hundred metres across and is more than thirty metres deep.

'Just another bloody big hole, if you ask me,' thought Ben.

The next stop was the museum at Bullecourt.

Mr Jean Letaille, owner of the Bullecourt Museum,
holds the barrel of a German tank.

The group enjoyed the visit to this private museum where there was a collection of artefacts, including a German tank and various shovels for trench digging; there were also many types of guns, including the Lewis machine gun used so effectively against the Germans.

Ben had to admit to himself, he had enjoyed looking at the guns and ammunition and all the other machinery of war.

# Bring In The Storm Troopers

## Chapter 36

### 1918 France

The year was 1918 and the Germans knew they had to mount a massive offensive if they were going to win the war. Initially the Allied Forces were taken by surprise due to the lack of intelligence, which was meant to come from the British High Command; as a result, the Germans captured many towns and were moving on the city of Amiens. The British High Command was fearful that if the Germans captured Amiens, the war might well be lost.

'They quickly brought back the ANZACs from Belgium to be used as 'storm troops', (similar to our modern SAS), to be utilised where they were needed most. The first engagement for the Australians was at Dernancourt, which is located on the road to Amiens. There were 25,000 German troops against 4,000 Australian Diggers. The Diggers defended Dernancourt against all the odds and drove back the Germans.

The next village in the Germans' sights was Villers-Bretonneux; they used mustard gas, firing canisters into the village, and opened fire with large guns. At nightfall, the Australians stormed the German trenches and drove the Germans out.

Brigadier General G. W. St G. Grogan. VC, of the British High Command described this action as *"perhaps the greatest individual feat of the war"*.

The ANZACs then entered the village and fought house to house. The French and Australian flags were raised at last over Villers-Bretonneux at the cost of twelve hundred Australians killed in the action. They made some makeshift crosses to place on the newly dug graves and only then, they realised the significance of the date, the 25th of April 1918, ANZAC Day, the third anniversary of the Gallipoli landing. Two of the Diggers at the burial were Gallipoli veterans, Jack Brown and Harry Newland. They both had survived three years of death and brutality since they first stepped onto the coarse sands of Gallipoli, but only one would go home.'

Waiting For Treatment at Villers-Bretonneux

'When we enter the village of Villers-Bretonneux,' Ed continued ' you will see an Australian flag; it is on top of the Australian National Memorial where the names of 10,982 Australians are etched in stone; they were killed in France and Belgium. None of them has a grave. May they rest in peace and not be dug up to make way for a supermarket or a new road, then simply reinterred  without ceremony.'

Ed was obviously quite emotional about this.

'The main road leading to the village is Rue de Melbourne and you will find a restaurant called Le Kangourou and then there is the school built from donations by Australian school children in the 1920s.'

# The Beginning of the End

## Chapter 37

**1918**

Charles Wooley had proved to be a courageous fighter, along with his compatriot Australians in the 47th Battalion; he had been promoted to Corporal and then Sergeant. He had fought in The Battle of Pozières where he won a Military Medal for Bravery in the Field and at Passchendaele. It was at Pozieres that he took out a German machine gun nest, killing all the German soldiers, and then returned to his trench with the captured machine gun to be used against the Germans.

Sergeant Wooley was now moving stealthily in the moonlight approaching the village of Dernancourt; with him were sixteen Diggers of his battalion. It was their intention to take up a position along a railway embankment facing the village. The other platoons from the 47th had also taken up their positions and were waiting for the call to move on the village. The 9th Battalion Royal Scots Guards were being relieved. They too had an awesome reputation as fighting men.

An officer from the guards addressed Charles:

'Who the hell are you?'

'The 47th and 48th Australians,' responded Charles.

'Thank God for that. You will hold him'

Captain George Mitchell, 48th Battalion, quoted in Charles Bean's account: *"The Australian Imperial Force in France, 1918, Official History of Australia in the War of 1914–1918,* Volume V, Sydney, 1937, p.172"

'By 'him' was meant the German Army which on 21 March 1918 had begun a major offensive from positions on the Hindenburg line east of Péronne. The German aim was nothing less than the capture of the city of Amiens and the splitting of the French and British armies in northern France. It was a final grab for victory before the strength of the American forces arriving in France reached a point where the German Empire could not hope to win the war. By late March the Germans had pushed the British right back across the old Somme battlefields east of Albert and were poised for another push towards Amiens. The divisions of the AIF, now formed into the Australian Corps, were rushed south piecemeal, to shore up the crumbling British line immediately west of Albert and to relieve exhausted British units.'

With Charles was Stanley McDougal, a fellow Tasmanian from Recherche Bay at the southernmost tip of Australia; the French landed there in 1792 and for a short while, colonised the area, planting vegetable gardens and fraternising with the local aboriginal population. The reason McDougal and his father before him lived in such a remote location was that it was heavily wooded with exotic Australian native trees which were much sought after by furniture makers in Hobart and mainland Australia. Stanley was a saw miller; he was also a magnificent warrior.

Stanley McDougal V.C.

In the dusk light, on the 28th of March, Sergeant Stanley McDougal, "Steamer" to his mates, after the Stanley Steamer motor vehicle, was lying on the embankment with Charles and their men.

'Did you hear that?' Steamer asked Charlie.

'No, I didn't hear a thing.'

'Listen. There it is again. I reckon the pricks are creeping up on us. Fuck. They are! I can see the bastards. You wait here! I'm going to warn the others along the bank,' Steamer whispered.

Sergeant McDougal ran along the sunken road, yelling a warning but by this stage, German grenades were going off like firecrackers.

Charles caught up with him.

'Slow down, you silly bastard, you're going to get yourself killed,' he yelled.

'Thank God our gunners are opening up on them. That'll slow the bastards down a bit.'

Just at that moment Charles saw the Australian gunner slump: he either had been killed or wounded, but either way, the Lewis Gun was now dormant and the Germans were progressing.

'I'll grab it! Cover me, Charlie, I know how to operate these things.'

Steamer grabbed the Lewis gun and started to run towards the Germans, firing as he went. He took out two light machine gun teams who were trying to cross the embankment and many others fled back to where they came from.

'Right who's next?' he thought to himself. He saw Germans starting to occupy fox-holes on their side of the bank. He sprayed them with machine gun fire and those he didn't kill or wound fled back. By this stage Charlie had caught up with him.

'Right, Charlie, let's get a few more.'

He started to fire at the retreating Germans from the top of the bank and got quite a few.

'I think you got them, mate,' said Charlie.

'Yeah, reckon I did.'

Just then Steamer looked in the other direction to the south.

' Shit, they are crossing over the embankment down there! Quick, Charlie, let's get the bastards.'

He started to fire at them with great accuracy, while the Lewis was getting so hot that his right hand started to blister badly.

' I can hardly hang on to this thing anymore, Charlie.'

'I'll hold it for you ,mate, you just concentrate on your aim and shoot the bastards!'

Together, with Charlie holding the gun and Steamer using his good hand, they became a deadly team. They captured a group of German soldiers and as Charlie and another Sergeant were about to lead them off, a German officer levelled a pistol at their backs.

McDougal saw him.

'Look out behind you.'

Charlie shot the officer with his rifle.

Sergeant Stanley McDougal was awarded the highest military honour, the Victoria Cross, for his bravery and gallantry that day.

Charles Wooley was recommended for a Distinguished Service Medal. It was approved.

Charlie's wife, Sophie, received his DSO Medal in December 1918.

He had died from wounds received in Dernancourt two days later.

The village of Dernancourt also suffered badly that day; the British bombarded the village until they saw the Germans retreating. The British and Australian troops made their way down the hill to liberate the village but the Germans positioned themselves to fire on the troops with machine guns. It was in this action that Charles Wooley died.

'Bloody hell, I thought we had killed all the bastards,' said Charlie to his men.

Shells were landing and exploding all around them and soldiers were dropping like flies as they tried to make their way forward. Charlie and his platoon finally made it to the town when Charlie heard a loud crack and then nothing: his head exploded from a sniper's bullet.

His men made a make-shift grave outside the village but did not mark it, as they were soon engaged in another fire-fight.

Charles's grave was never found, never to be discovered. He still lies there.

# Spanish Flu

## Chapter 38

*I had a little bird,*
*Its name was Enza.*
*I opened the window,*
*And in-flu-enza.*

Captain Robert Hall of the American 3rd Division was sitting in a small wood with his troops dispersed amongst the tall trees. They had just been involved in the battle of Chateau-Thierry and despite heavy losses, they felt encouraged by their success. Captain Hall was giving his men a well-earned break before the next attack, which he knew was going to be a tough one. They had been instructed to take Belleau Wood.

He noticed a few of his men had come down with heavy colds in the last few days and they were not really coping well. He decided to call in the Medics from HQ, a few kilometres away.

The Doctor arrived early the next morning, looking exhausted.

'Are you all right, Doc? You look buggered,' said Hall.

'You don't know the half of it, Captain. We have a major pandemic on our hands and if we can't work out how to arrest it, you won't have many of your men left for the next fight.'

'What in the hell are you talking about, Doc?'

'Just as I said. There is a pandemic influenza infecting many of the troops, probably on both sides.'

'How can you tell who's got this thing?'

'It starts off as a cold, you know influenza, and within a few days, many are dead. More survive than die, but from what I have seen, thousands are dying and we can't seem to stop it.'

Captain Hall looked over at his boys and he could see that about a quarter of them had influenza.

'This could be a disaster.'

IT WAS.

Tent Hospital to Treat Soldiers With Spanish Flu

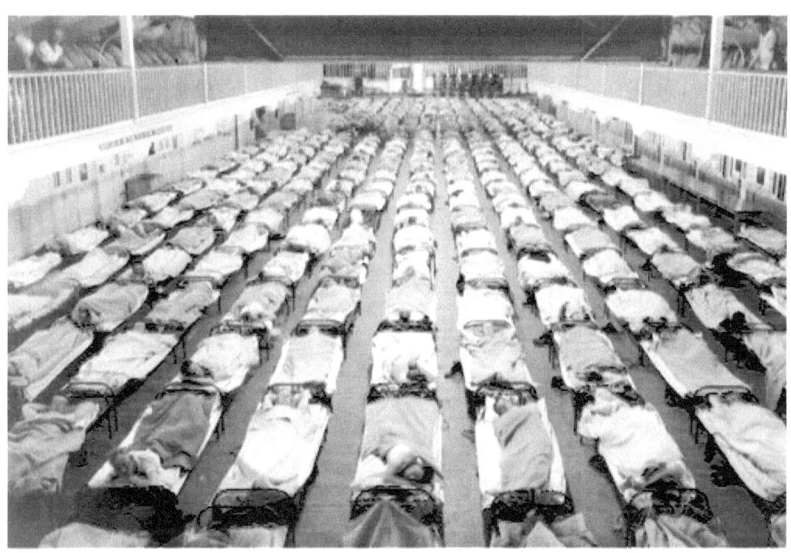

Makeshift Hospitals Were Established

Spanish Flu hit the world in the summer of 1918. The Great War was coming to an end with the death rate approaching twenty million people. By the time Spanish Flu disappeared in 1919, it had claimed between seventy and one hundred million people.

In today's terms that would equate to one hundred and sixty million killed, including civilians, through war, and four hundred and sixty six million dying from Spanish Flu.

No one really knows where Spanish Flu began, some say China, others claim the Middle East. There is also conjecture as to why it was called "Spanish Flu" again, some say because of the high mortality rate in Spain, others say it was because Spain was neutral and therefore had a free press, which could report what was really happening.

More current thinking places the beginning of the pandemic in the United States.

The pandemic eventually had a disastrous effect on the Germans and its allies, inflicting massive casualties through sickness which they could ill afford as the British and its allies were having significant success on the battlefield.

Military convoys became breeding grounds for the virus. Many died on the ships, as the symptoms were a brief fever rapidly followed by death. The virus caused uncontrollable haemorrhaging that filled the lungs and patients would drown in their own blood. It was near impossible to isolate the patients from the rest of the troops in such a confined space.

The reasons for the pandemic essentially remain unknown. The deprivations of a world war are held responsible by some scientists, although the virus similarly swept through non-war affected countries like the USA, India and much of Europe.

For example, four hundred and fifty thousand civilian deaths occurred in the United States. The majority of deaths were in the twenty to forty age groups. In Britain some two hundred and twenty eight thousand civilians died and four hundred thousand in Germany. Hardest hit, however, was India with a reported sixteen million casualties alone.

Each nation at war went to great lengths to conceal the extent of losses suffered through the virus, concerned that such reports would serve to encourage their enemies. In reality, each was suffering as badly as the other.

Curiously, in mid-1919, the pandemic withered and died abruptly without a treatment having been found. Scientists continue to believe that a repeat of the pandemic, albeit in a varying form, could find modern science equally as unprepared to meet a repeat of the flu challenge.

# The Spirit of War

## Chapter 39

**26th April 2012**

It was the last full day of the tour; the group had completed the full circle of the Western Front and were once again at Messines. They didn't quite understand why they were revisiting Messines instead of going somewhere they had not been to before.

Nor could they understand the need for such an early start: 6am on the bus seemed a little extreme.

'Ed, we all understand the significance of the Battle of Messines but why are we back here?' Philippe asked.

'That's a good question, Philippe; I have decided to include a very special experience for you all, something that will stay with you for the rest of your lives.'

This seized the group's attention,

'So what is it?' asked Steve.

'You won't have to wait long. We're nearly there.'

The group started to talk amongst themselves, trying to guess what Ed was up to. Finally, "Murray" turned into a green rolling field and there, in the middle of it, was the biggest hot air balloon any of them had seen.'

'Wow, that's incredible!' said Ben. This was the first positive reaction he had all tour.

'Awesome!' proclaimed Adam.

The rest of the group were also suitably impressed, although George did show some trepidation.

Ed explained what was going to happen:

'This balloon was manufactured by Ballonbau Warner, a German manufacturer they are regarded as the best in Europe. The pilot we have today is one of the most experienced in France. May I introduce you to Alain Beaumont?'

'Good morning, everybody. As Ed explained, my name is Alain and I will be your pilot today. May I say that this is my twenty first-year flying hot air balloons, so I have finally come of age in that respect. As you have no doubt noticed, I speak English reasonably well as I lived in the U.S.A. for nearly sixteen years. This will make it easier for you to ask me questions when we are flying.

The basic safety rules are: don't jump out of the basket once we are up there.' Everybody laughed.

'There is no smoking and no animals are allowed; apart from that, it is simply a matter of enjoying yourselves and taking in the sights.'

Steve asked 'Are we suitably dressed for the conditions up there, Alain? We didn't get any notice we were going to be hot air ballooning today.' He glanced at Ed with a slight grin.

'You can wear a T Shirt if you like because we travel on the wind. It is always calm in the basket.

Are there any other questions? You are all aware of the principle that hot air rises? OK, let's get going! If you could all climb the stairs into the basket, we will take off.'

Once everybody was in the basket, Alain fired up the gas burner and the balloon gently started to rise. George's nervousness started to dissipate as he felt the balloon rise in quietness, interrupted only by Alain firing more flames into the balloon. Christine could start to better understand the topography of the Messines Battlefield as Ed started to explain where they were.

Then something simply astonishing happened: they saw two World War One British Bristol F.2 fighters scream past them, pursued by two German Albatross D1s. The German fighters were firing their machine guns, as the Bristols tried hard to lose them. Then one of the Bristols was hit and smoke started to stream from its engine. The pilot fought to right the plane but to no avail; it started to corkscrew down until it plummeted into the ground and exploded.

The German planes then turned to the other Bristol however they lost it in the clouds until the Bristol came screaming out with the sun behind him, blinding him to the Germans. He fired his guns at the tails of both Albatrosses and badly damaged them both. First one, and then the other, plummeted into the battle-scarred earth.

The group in the balloon was horrified, looking to Ed or Alain for an explanation. Harry, looked at Ben, and was pleased to see Ben's reaction was total shock. No such explanation came. Ed simply pointed to the far horizon as a huge explosion rocked the balloon, then another and another; they all thought the balloon may go down. Huge plumes of smoke and fire towered into the far sky. Adam now knew that what he heard from the hotel room in Ypres was real, or as real as whatever was going on now. He turned to Ben and said.

'I told you I heard explosions.'

Ben just looked back blankly.

When there was silence at last, they saw huge guns firing their shells great distances into what looked like German trenches. This bombardment went on for some time.

'Come on, Ed, what's going on?' shouted Philippe.' How could you arrange such an incredibly realistic re-enactment?'

'Watch,' was Ed's simple answer.


Allied troops began to leave their trenches, firing as they progressed across No Man's Land. They made good progress until the German machineguns opened up on them. The group was shocked; soldiers from the Allies and the Germans were being slaughtered. All the carnage they imagined from the descriptions of the battles on the tour was there to see, men dropping with horrific wounds, and others running past them into the maelstrom.

Everybody, apart from Ed and Alain, was in total disbelief. They noticed that the balloon was starting to descend and, fearing for their lives, they dropped down and kept their heads low, not looking out until the basket gently rested on the ground.

'Everything is fine. You can all disembark now,' said Ed.

No one moved.

'I can assure you that you are all safe. Please leave the basket.'

Steve was the first to stand up. He couldn't believe his eyes. They had landed in a beautiful field ringed by poplars, with a picture book village in the background.

'Where have they all gone?' asked a bemused Steve.

When the others in the group heard Steve, they all stood up. Ben was the last to rise. They looked around. They were totally confused. They did as Ed had asked and climbed out of the basket. Alain bade them all farewell and fired up the balloon again and slowly ascended into the azure sky, drifting off to the north.

Again Ed spoke: 'I know what you have all experienced has been horrific and confusing. I have booked rooms in that little village over there for the night and, over dinner, I will explain what went on today. Don't ask me questions now. I won't answer them. The bus is here to pick you up. I will follow later and meet you at the Varlet Farm, which you will really like. The owners have made their large dining room available to us.'

The group boarded the bus for the short trip to Varlet Farm and were greeted by the owner, Charlotte, who showed them all to their suites.

They decided on the bus not to discuss what they saw from the balloon but to wait until Ed gave them an explanation.

Dinner was scheduled for 7 pm so they all just retired to their rooms and reflected on the most incredible day they had ever experienced in their lives.

At 7 pm exactly they were all seated and were looking at the menus; even Adam and Ben joined the dinner for once. Then Ed entered and sat at the table. Alain was with him and he sat next to Ed.

The group simply stared at Ed. No one uttered a word.

Ed began to speak: 'What you all saw and experienced today was the essence of war, the very spirit of the great conflict. I hand-picked you all to go on this tour not because of you, as individuals, but who your ancestors were and the ultimate sacrifices they made and are still making today.'

Christine was about to ask a question but Ed held up his hand.

'Christine, you can all ask questions when I have finished but not before. I am sorry, but that's the way it has to be.'

Ed continued. 'At this stage, I should confess to you all who I really am. I am Charles Edwin Bean. I was a war correspondent during the Great War, following the ANZAC troops into battle. I witnessed the true tragedy of war, an example being my description of Pozières.

Imagine a gigantic ash heap, a place where dust and rubbish have been cast for years outside some dry, derelict, God–forsaken up–country township. Imagine some broken–down creek bed in the driest of our dry central Australian districts, abandoned for a generation to the goats, in which the hens have been scratching as long as men can remember. Then take away the hens and the goats and all traces of any living or moving thing. You must not even leave a spider. Put here, in evidence of some old tumbled roof, a few roof beams and tiles sticking edgeways from the ground, and the low faded ochre stump of the windmill peeping over the top of the hill, and there you have Pozières.

At this stage, Terry could not help himself.

'You're telling us that you are Charles Bean? Well, I searched for Charles Edwin Bean when you first introduced yourself as his Grand Nephew. You look like you are in your middle to late thirties, yet Charles Bean was born in 1879. That would make you about a hundred years older than you look!'

'Yes, it would be impossible in your world but not in mine.'

'*Your* world ? What do you mean?' Terry looked perplexed.

'I thought you would have all worked it out by now. I am the spirit of Charles Bean. Now may I continue please?'

Terry started to interrupt again.

'Terry, I don't understand why you are so bemused. Didn't you have a conversation with your Great Uncle Harry in the street outside the hotel in Lille?'

'Well, yes, I think I did.'

'You did, I can assure you. Let me continue and you all may understand a little better.'

Ed continued, with the group dumbfounded and hanging on Charles's every word.

'If you remember, I told you I hand-picked you all. How could I do that? In the spiritual dimension, you can do things that mortals would deem impossible.

I can also inform you all that the story about Brad's mother was true. She did die; he cancelled the tour by sending you all an email.'

'Well I never received such an email,' said Mike.

'No, I intercepted them to ensure you would all join the tour.'

'How in the heck could you do that?' demanded Christine. 'Oh, don't bother… I forgot your spiritual status.'

'I have to ask you to keep your comments to yourself until the conclusion of my explanation, please!'

'What you all saw from Alain's balloon today… oh I apologise, I have not introduced Alain. Alain flew balloons during the Great War and was regarded as the best of his day. Without his aerial observations, the allies would have lost many more men.'

'Let me continue. What you saw today was not a re-enactment, it was real, or 'real' in the sense of the spiritual world. All those soldiers are spirit soldiers who had fallen in battle, but have never been recovered. They have no known grave and are destined to fight their battles for eternity. There is only one reprieve: if they are discovered, identified and buried or buried *known only to God'*, they no longer take part in the battles. They then finally Rest in Peace.

All the battles I described are being played out over and over. What you saw and heard at Messines continues for eternity.

You may have heard reports of soldiers' remains being uncovered along the front and reinterred due to the red tape involved in reporting the find.

Can you imagine a 'spirit soldier' being unearthed, knowing he has been released from the torment of war and then thrown back into the mayhem?'

Ed then opened the forum to questions.

Terry was the first: 'Ed… sorry, Charles '

'I will answer to both names, Terry, go on.'

'As you mentioned when we were in Lille on the first night, I thought I saw German soldiers marching POWs through the streets. From what we saw and have learned today, I did actually see spirit soldiers didn't I?'

'That's right, Terry. What you saw was real in another dimension.'

'Can I also tell you that when I saw and spoke to my Great Uncle Harry, he said, "Find me" and now I understand what he was alluding to.'

'Terry, Harry just wants to rest in peace. They all do.'

Adam spoke up: 'Mine is not really a question, Ed, it is more an affirmation that I heard and saw the nineteen mines explode at Messines.'

'You certainly did, not only from your hotel room, but also today from the balloon.'

Christine and Tony both looked over to Adam and acknowledged him.

Ed looked at Stewart, 'Well, Stewart, you're the great cynic. What are your thoughts?'

'Ed, I really don't know what to think. I deal in cold hard facts. Lawyers don't, or shouldn't, fantasise, however, I know what I saw today and everybody else saw it at the same time. It can't be a mass delusion. I also acknowledge I saw a battle in the parklands at the rear of the hotel in Ypres. I believe everything you have told us and I am devastated that I can't help these lost souls.'

'Maybe you can, Stewart, maybe you can,' said Charles/Ed.

Ben was unusually quiet, although he did look for Harry, to ask a question but could not see him.

'I would ask you all to move into the private saloon bar next door. Alain and I have a surprise for you all.'

They did as Charles asked and saw standing at the bar several soldiers in uniform, drinking beer and deep in conversation.

'May I have your attention please?' said Charles in a voice that all could hear.

'I would like each of you standing at the bar to step forward and introduce yourself please.'

The first soldier stepped forward: 'My name is Harry Daniel. I died at the Battle of Fromelles. I have not been found.'

Lois and Terry looked on in amazement.

Ben was dumbfounded; this young warrior was the Harry from the tour. He had been conversing with a ghost for days.

Charles announced to the group to let the soldiers introduce themselves and then there would be plenty of time to acquaint themselves with their ancestors.

The next soldier to introduce himself was also Harry Daniel.

'I am young Harry's uncle. I died at The Battle of Amiens.'

All the soldiers stepped forward and introduced themselves, their families looking on in awe.

What they all noticed was that the fallen soldiers were wearing their medals. Three of them stood out: Harry Daniel had a King George Military Medal as did Antoine, while Charles Wooley had both the Military Medal and the Distinguished Service Medal. All of them had various other service medals, including the Victory Medal, the 1914-1915 Star and the Army Medal.

Finally Charles announced that it was time for the families to reunite and discuss whatever they deemed appropriate.

It was a very emotional scene with the ghosts of the fallen soldiers hugging their descendants and laughing and crying as the night wore on.

Ben asked Harry what it was really like, fighting in the war.

'Ben, it was hell on earth, yet the comradeship and closeness we all felt, in diabolical conditions, was wonderful. I spoke to you about fighting for one's country, and everything I told you on the tour was true. I experienced most of it.'

'Harry, may I shake your hand?'

'No, Ben. But you can give me a hug. At last, I can see you understand the meaning of the 'Spirit of War'.'

Ben joined his brother, his mother, and father, who were talking to David Abbott. He felt a sense of euphoria; this experience had been the most important in his life.


At about 11pm, Charles announced that it was time for the evening to come to its natural conclusion.

'Today you have witnessed and experienced what others would only dream of. I hope you feel privileged and blessed. I am convinced that I chose the right group to work with me on this project.' The project I refer to is to ensure our brave soldiers who fell in The Great War and are listed as missing are either found and given a proper burial, or at least left in peace and not disturbed.

I will ensure you all have the information you need, to go back home and champion this very noble cause. All the soldiers here tonight, your relatives, belong to the missing. They are still fighting their battles and they are relying on you all to help them.

I would now ask you all to say your farewells and move back into the dining room.'

There were some very emotional scenes as they all bade their brave soldiers farewell.

As they were leaving, Philippe looked back. There was no one in the bar.

# The End

# Epilogue

I wrote the following article at the request of the online News Ltd magazine, "The Punch" who were aware of my efforts through LetThemRIP.com to ensure all soldiers, not just Australian, are either left in peace or, if discovered, buried with full military honors.

So far, the Governments of Australia and New Zealand have dismissed my claims and are perfectly happy to carry on as usual.

Readers of this book can visit the Face Book Page Let Them RIP to acquaint yourselves with this unacceptable situation.

Let them
R.J.P.

"As we approach the Centenary of the First World War we start to think about the tremendous sacrifice so many of our Diggers made. It is unimaginable to think that over 60,000 young men died at Gallipoli and the Western Front. When you visit the battlefields of France and Belgium and the cemeteries and memorials, you see countless numbers of white crosses honoring the fallen. Many of those crosses are for soldiers who are "Known Unto God".

At the various memorials such as VC Corner and Menin Gate, the names of those who were missing in action are engraved in stone. The Australian Government's official estimation is that there are approximately 18,000 Diggers lying under the fields of France and Belgium, Diggers such as Harry Daniel who died at the age of 17. He lied about his age so he could join the Great War in 1916. He was sent to Gallipoli and survived and was then sent to France and died in the unnecessary slaughter in the Battle of Fromelles. He was in the 59th Battalion and was one of the first to "Go Over the Top"; he was probably killed in the first five minutes of the battle. His body has never been found. We owe Harry and the other 18000 Diggers and many thousands more of other nationalities buried beneath the fields of France and Belgium the dignity and honor they deserve. Harry was my Uncle.

That is why I started Let them RIP (www.letthemrip.com)

In April last year I read an article by Ian McPhedran. The article was based on the experiences of his friend and fellow author, Paul Daley, and well known photographer Mike Bowers, while on a research trip to the Western front for their new book.

Their French guide, Dominique, discovered a Digger in an excavation trench:

*'Now, on Saturday, we find ourselves standing in the bitter wind, the mud sucking at our boots, beside a one-meter newly excavated drainage ditch outside Mouquet Farm near Pozières – the scene of a bitter three-week battle in August 1916 that claimed 11,000 Australian casualties – as Mr Zanardi gingerly passes us bones that we, in turn, place in a hessian sack.*

*He uncovers the soldier's boots, still holding the bones of his feet, and places them on the side of the ditch. As we carefully carry the rest of the man's remains from the ditch to the bag containing his skull and his jawbone, his arms and his legs, one thought dominates: dignity and glory do not belong to the battlefield.*

*As with the many thousands of others who lost their lives in the terrible fighting on the Somme during World War I, the battlefield has claimed this soldier's identity. And were it not for Mr. Zanardi he would probably have stayed anonymously beneath the sticky mud of the Somme for an eternity.'*

This story really moved me. Paul and Mike tried to notify the Commonwealth War Graves Commission but, being a weekend, they were closed. The Mayor of Pozières , Bernard Delattre, was planning to remove the body from the site on the day to prevent it from being reinterred by the bulldozer on the site. He called the Australian Embassy in Paris to inform them an Australian Digger had been uncovered but received no response.

To ensure the soldier was not covered over with the mud and clay until the next excavation, Paul and Mike retrieved the Digger themselves. They delivered the bag of bones to the CWGC on the Monday.

Is this what we picture when we stand with our heads bowed, as the Bugler plays "The Last Post" on ANZAC day? Is this what President Barak Obama was thinking when visiting The Unknown Soldier's grave at the War Memorial recently? We have, according to the Australian Government, 18,000 soldiers lying beneath the fields of France and Belgium; they deserve to be allowed to Rest in Peace.

I have been proposing to the Government since ANZAC day 2010 for a set of procedures to be established so that we can ensure our Diggers are protected.

At the very least, a regulation should be initiated to ensure if any excavation work in the battlefields is to take place in order to dig trenches or foundations for a new building, a permit is required and the Commonwealth War Graves Commission and the Police are notified. Then, if remains are found, there is no excuse for the authorities not to be present and remove the remains in an orderly fashion according to the regulations.

Some other options are:

1. Create an incentive program that entices the French farmers to report any finds rather than ignore remains and plough them back.

2. Speed up the process so that the farmers are not penalised by interrupting work on their farms.

3. Establish a facility in Northern France that can identify the remains by DNA and badges etc.

4. Create a publicity program to notify all relatives of Diggers MIA from WW1 battles to register and contribute DNA samples for identification purposes.

5. Once the remains are identified bury them in an appropriate war cemetery with full military honours.

If it proves to be too difficult to achieve the first option then I propose a second option: Non-Tillage Farming.

This farming practice has been adopted all over the world, including Australia, where 22,239,000 acres are farmed this way.

In essence, it would mean that the French farmers would not be continually and repeatedly ploughing up our Diggers.

This would require an investment from the Government, including equipment and training. It is also a very 'green' method of farming.

Third Option:

The Government leases farms along the trench lines of the major battlefields where the Australians fought.

The lease would be a year for each farm and would have to be very advantageous to the farmers to ensure their cooperation.

Then a controlled and properly monitored dig could take place.

Fromelles was a wonderful example of what can be achieved and having attended the ceremony, I got a true sense of the importance of honouring our fallen soldiers who gave their lives for their country.

I met Lambis Englezos in Melbourne on the 19th of July 2011 at the ceremony celebrating the one-year anniversary of the Fromelles cemetery. One thing I learned from him is persistence.

Questions have been asked in Parliament and I have written to many people. What comes across clearly is denial or just plain apathy.

The Prime Minister of Australia in early 2012 was Julia Gillard. She told Parliament that it was all 'media hype' and all remains are reported and buried.

The Leader of the Opposition at that time was Tony Abbott who did not even give me the courtesy of a reply, neither did the majority of Parliamentarians contacted.

I decided to write this book to try to bring the message of the missing to the notice of people around the world.

Many of us have been affected, despite nearly one hundred years passing.

My Grandfather, my father's father, enlisted in 1915 and joined The Australian Light Horse. He was sent to England where the authorities decided to transfer him to be trained as a Gunner. He was badly injured in training and was dispatched home.

If he had not been injured, he would have fought on the Western Front with a twenty percent chance of being killed.

If he had, my Father would not have been born and neither would I.

**Garry Willmott**

# BIBLIOGRAPHY

## Web Sites

http://www.anzacday.org.au

http://militaryhistory.about.com/od/worldwari/p/BelleauWood.htm

http://www.firstworldwar.com

http://virus.stanford.edu/uda/

http://canadaonline.about.com/od/ww1battles/ig/Pictures-Battle-of-Vimy-Ridge/Mule-Team-Drawing-Ammunition.htm

http://www.ww1battlefields.co.uk/others/vimy.html

http://doglawreporter.blogspot.com.au

http://www.wehrmacht-awards.com

http://myweb.tiscali.co.uk/philsnet/T%20Hampson%20WW1%20Diary%20100.htm

http://community-2.webtv.net/Hahn-50thAP-K9/K9History2/

http://www.historylearningsite.co.uk/ypres_world_war_one.htm

http://www.ww1-world-war-one.info/WWI-World-War-1-information-History-War-Casualties-Cost.htm

http://www.vimyfoundation.ca/newsletter_articles/courage-and-valour-at-vimy-ridge-canadians-earn-the-victoria.html

http://www.adoptadigger.org/blog/item/the-lost-diggers-as-seen-on

http://www.australiansatwar.gov.au/stories/stories_ID=181_war=W1.html

http://www.ww1westernfront.gov.au/battlefields/mouquet-farm-1916.html

http://www.worldwar1.com/pharc.htm

http://www.english.illinois.edu/maps/ww1/photoessay.htm

http://www.worldwar1.com/heritage/marnetaxis.htm

http://www.greatwardifferent.com/Great_War/Paris_at_War/Paris_at_War_01.htm

http://www.firstworldwar.com/battles/marne1.htm

http://www.mercurynie.com.au/anzac/victoriacross.html

http://www.historynet.com/world-war-i-battle-of-hamel.htm

http://www.firstworldwar.com/diaries/atmessinesridge.htm

http://www.wereldoorlog1418.nl/battleverdun/kortverdun/index.htm

http://www.nzhistory.net.nz/war/le-quesnoy/battle-accounts-lt-averill

http://www.vlib.us/medical/

http://www.firstworldwar.com/battles/ypres3.htm

http://www.kingandempire.com/cemetery_P.html

http://www.1914-1918.net/bat15E_Fromelles.html

http://www.awm.gov.au/units/event_159.asp

http://www.ozebook.com/ww1/westernfront/documents/45.html

http://www.ww1westernfront.gov.au/battlefields.html

http://en.wikipedia.org/wiki/Charles_Bean

## Books

| The Great War | Les Carlyon | Pan Macmillan | 2006 |
|---|---|---|---|
| The Western Front Diaries | Jonathon King | Simon & Schuster | 2010 |
| Fromelles | Patrick Lindsay | Hardie Grant Books | 2008 |
| ANZACS on the Western Front | Peter Pederson | Wiley | 2012 |
| 'Fighting France' | Edith Wharton | | 1915 |

## Photos

All the photos used in this book are public domain without any known copyright.

The soldiers' photos are all unknown, apart from Harry Daniel, Junior.

www.ingramcontent.com/pod-product-compliance
Lightning Source LLC
Chambersburg PA
CBHW021956010726
47494CB00003B/766